Through the Arc of
The Rain Forest

I have heard Brazilian children say that whatever passes through the arc of a rainbow becomes its opposite. But what is the opposite of a bird? Or for that matter, a human being? And what then, in the great rain forest, where, in its season, the rain never ceases and the rainbows are myriad?

A NOVEL BY KAREN TEI YAMASHITA

Through the Arc of The Rain Forest

COFFEE HOUSE PRESS :: MINNEAPOLIS :: 1990

TEXT COPYRIGHT © 1990 by Karen Tei Yamashita
COVER PAINTING by Renaldo Lopez de Oliveira.

Coffee House Press is a nonprofit literary publishing house. Support from private foundations, corporate giving programs, government programs, and generous individuals helps make the publication of our books possible.

The publisher thanks the following organizations whose support helped make this book possible: Dayton Hudson Foundation; Cowles Media/Star Tribune; Meyer, Scherer & Rockcastle; Minnesota State Arts Board; Northwest Area Foundation; and United Arts.

To you and our many readers around the world, we send our thanks for your continuing support.

COFFEE HOUSE PRESS books are available to the trade through our primary distributor, Consortium Book Sales & Distribution, www.cbsd.com or (800) 283-3572. For personal orders, catalogs, or other information, write to: info@coffeehousepress.org.

LIBRARY OF CONGRESS CIP INFORMATION

Yamashita, Karen Tei, 1951–
Through the arc of the rain forest : a novel / by Karen Tei Yamashita
p. cm.
ISBN 0-918273-82-X
1. Title
PS3575.A44TA   1990
813'.54—DC20   90-40471
CIP

PRINTED IN CANADA
9 8 7

CONTENTS

Part I: The Beginning

3   CHAPTER 1: KAZUMASA ISHIMARU

9   CHAPTER 2: BATISTA AND TANIA APARECIDA DJAPAN

16   CHAPTER 3: MANÉ DA COSTA PENA

19   CHAPTER 4: GGG

22   CHAPTER 5: CHICO PACO

28   CHAPTER 6: JONATHAN B. TWEEP

Part II: The Developing World

35   CHAPTER 7: THE PIGEON

45   CHAPTER 8: THE PILGRIM

52   CHAPTER 9: THREE HANDS

58   CHAPTER 10: FORTUNE

66   CHAPTER 11: SAVED

Part III: More Development

73   CHAPTER 12: THE FEATHER

80   CHAPTER 13: PILGRIM'S PROGRESS

86   CHAPTER 14: KARAOKE

90   CHAPTER 15: PRENDAS DOMESTICAS

94   CHAPTER 16: THE MATACÃO

Part IV: Loss of Innocence

105   CHAPTER 17: THE BALL

114   CHAPTER 18: FEATHEROLOGY

122   CHAPTER 19: MICHELLE MABELLE

128   CHAPTER 20: PROMISES

134   CHAPTER 21: HOMING

Part V: More Loss

141 CHAPTER 22: PLASTICS
150 CHAPTER 23: REMOTE CONTROL
158 CHAPTER 24: TRIALECTICS
162 CHAPTER 25: RADIO
170 CHAPTER 26 : PIGEON COMMUNICATIONS

Part VI: Return

179 CHAPTER 27: TYPHUS
186 CHAPTER 28: CARNIVAL
196 CHAPTER 29: RAIN OF FEATHERS
202 CHAPTER 30: BACTERIA
206 CHAPTER 31: THE MARKET
209 CHAPTER 32: THE TROPICAL TILT

Author's Note

The story that follows is perhaps a kind of *novela,* a Brazilian soap opera, of the sort which occupies the imagination and national psyche of the Brazilian people on prime-time TV nightly and for periods of two to four months, depending on its popularity and success. This is not an exaggeration. The prime-time *novela* in Brazilian life is pervasive, reaching every Brazilian in some form or manner regardless of class, status, education or profession, excepting perhaps the Indians and the very isolated of the frontiers and rural backlands. In traveling to the most remote towns, one finds that a single television in a church or open plaza will gather the people nightly to define and standardize by example the national dress, music, humor, political state, economic malaise, the national dream, despite the fact that Brazil is immense and variegated. Yet even as it standardizes by example, the *novela*'s story is completely changeable according to the whims of public psyche and approval, although most likely, the unhappy find happiness; the bad are punished; true love reigns; a popular actor is saved from death. Still, the basic elements must remain the same. And what are these elements? Claude Levi-Strauss described it all so well so many years ago: *Tristes Tropiques* — an idyll of striking innocence, boundless nostalgia and terrible ruthlessness. I thank you for tuning in.

Para o Ronaldo: a tua estória

Part I
The Beginning

CHAPTER 1: KAZUMASA ISHIMARU

BY A STRANGE QUIRK OF FATE, I was brought back by a memory. Memory is a powerful sort of thing, although at the time I made my reentry into this world, no notice at all was taken of the fact. In fact, everyone was terribly busy, whirling about, panting and heaving, dizzy with the tumult of their ancestral spirits. This was one of those monthly events under the influence of the full moon on a well-beaten floor of earth on what had once been known, many years before, as the Matacão. That I should have been reborn like any other dead spirit in the Afro-Brazilian syncretistic religious rite of Candomblé is humorous to me. But then I could have been reincarnated, if such things are possible, into the severed head of that dead chicken or some other useless object — the smutty statuette of Saint George or those plastic roses. Instead, brought back by a memory, I have become a memory, and as such, am commissioned to become for you a memory.

But, of me you will learn by and by. First I must tell you of a certain Kazumasa Ishimaru to whom I was attached for many years. It might be said that we were friends, but although we were much closer, we were never referred to as such. I met Kazumasa quite by accident when he was still a young boy, recently born on the back side of Japan, on the shores of the Japan Sea, waves cast away in long arms out to Sado Island.

* * *

In those days, a child racing across the sands in a band with others, Kazumasa felt the Divine Wind ripple through his hair and scatter with the clouds over the ocean's mercuric mantle. One day, on such a race at the shimmering edge of the tide, the wind swept unusually quickly, raising the sand in changing drifts, a heavy comb through the white granules and the stray kelp. Suddenly, an enormous crack of thunder echoed across the shore, and a flying mass of fire plowed into the waves, scattering debris in every direction. There was a sudden burst of steam and sizzle as when tempura dipped in batter is plunged into hot oil. The children ran excitedly in two directions: away to their homes in fear or into the waves with curiosity. Kazumasa could do neither. A tiny piece of flying debris had plummeted toward him and knocked him unconscious. By the time any of the children had noticed his mishap, he was struggling, stunned, up the shore to his home, his bruised forehead a pulsating purple lump of raised skin and blood.

Alerted by some excited children, Kazumasa's mother sped off from her Yakult route, jamming her little red motorbike into third gear and leaving a befuddled grandmother with three six-packs of cold Yakult.

Having fainted at the gate of his home, Kazumasa next felt himself rudely awakened, his head jerked up off the ground. His mother had thrown herself over her wounded son, rested her head on his heart to assure herself of its beat. But there, close to Kazumasa's face, a small object buzzed between the mother and son. She swatted at the object irritably, and, coincidentally, Kazumasa's head was swiftly flung to one side. Stunned, she examined the buzzing thing which was not, after all, an insect, but a tiny sphere whirling on its axis. With the instinctive duty and fearlessness of a mother, she grabbed the thing, wrenching it to one side. Kazumasa's head was wrenched away also, as if by some magnetic force attaching itself to the whirling sphere. Kazumasa's mother drew back in horror, but Kazumasa himself awoke, apparently with no side effects and none the worse for his bruised forehead. He spoke with wonder about the incident on the shore. His mother, not wishing to frighten her son, made no mention of the strange ball whirling a few inches from the center of his forehead and carefully avoided it as she washed and bandaged him.

That evening, she spoke excitedly but quietly with her husband, who was a plant manager in a local dried-fish company. They were simple people who did not wish to have their lives come under any special scrutiny. However, Kazumasa's father wondered if he should not, for reasons of national security, alert the National Space Development Agency. Maybe there was more to this than met the eye, but Kazumasa's mother was cautious. She did not want her son made into a national phenomenon, a guinea pig for experiments. She wanted her son to be like the others, get solid grades in school, get into a good university and then a good salaried job. All of a sudden, a ball, a tiny impudent planet, had come between her and her son, destroying the bonds of parent and child, literally setting them a world apart.

But to Kazumasa, who had gradually discovered the thing in front of his nose, the ball became something of comfort. It was the sort of comfort a child derives from his thumb or an old blanket, and in that respect, his mother's sense of Kazumasa's sudden independence from her was perhaps true.

As the days passed and Kazumasa's head wound cleared, leaving only a slightly pink spot of skin, Kazumasa and his parents began to accept the ball which continued to float before his forehead no matter where he went or what he did. They began to forget their early anxieties as Kazumasa seemed to draw confidence and security from the ball. Like other parents bemoaning their loss of independence when rudely pressed into parenthood, Kazumasa's parents, too, began to depend on the ball, accepting and justifying it as they might a pacifier or a battered teddy bear.

Kazumasa's father forgot to call the proper authorities, and his mother began to readjust her projections for her son's future and to accept those readjustments as mothers usually do all their lives.

Kazumasa was never again in his life alone. During the day, the ball bobbed and bounced and jittered merrily before him in the same wandering pattern of the boy following the intuitive dance of his growing muscles. After school they galloped madly home together. At night, the ball murmured and whirred sweetly near his pillow like a protective buoy. The ball was his pet and his friend, but it required no special attention nor any sort of responsibility on Kazumasa's part. When he felt no particular impulse to do or accomplish anything, he simply followed his ball. On the other hand, when he was busy at work or play, on some new project or activity, the ball was always, faithfully and uncritically, there.

Curiously, the ball had a strange effect on everyone around

Kazumasa. It was a source of wonder, and never, as his parents had feared, of derision. Perhaps this was because of Kazumasa's comfortable acceptance of his difference, his obliviousness to the ball as a special attribute or oddity. He was a happy child, and everyone he came in contact with felt a general necessity to encourage that happiness.

Kazumasa was genuinely proud of his ball. At his suggestion, his mother sewed tiny caps and hats for the ball to match Kazumasa's own. Kazumasa and his ball went everywhere, to school and outings, in matching hats. Even on rainy days, the ball was appropriately dressed under a shiny yellow plastic cap.

The years passed, and Kazumasa's ball became a thing of general acceptance. Most people forgot it was there, just inches from his face, although people avoided looking Kazumasa straight in the eye. They felt the uncomfortable presence of an intruder or even a third eye, and many people struggled with the compulsion to go cross-eyed when talking to Kazumasa. Girls shied away from him; they smiled and waved from a certain distance. This was of no apparent concern to Kazumasa, who was intimately attached to his ball. He did not yet fathom how the opposite sex might supersede such an intimacy.

After high school, Kazumasa took a job with the railway service. He punched tickets and hauled bags of mail. He found things for people in the Lost and Found and waved appropriate flags for passing and stopping trains. He posted train schedules and closed gates and kept the kids behind the yellow line on the station platform when the trains passed. But one day, his true talent in the railway service was discovered.

Occasionally, he was sent on short runs to the next town to collect passenger tickets, wading down the aisles on the moving train, accepting tickets and greeting the passengers. Whenever the train ran over a certain place on the tracks, he could see his ball jerk suddenly, lurched into inexplicable chaos. He decided to mark this place where the train passed and his ball went wild. After several such trips, Kazumasa reported the phenomenon to his superior.

His superior was skeptical but careful, and one day had the train stop just at the place where Kazumasa's ball became visibly agitated. Together, Kazumasa and his boss stepped off the train to examine the tracks below. To their surprise they discovered that the tracks had worn dangerously thin at that point. The train would no doubt be derailed if those tracks were not replaced.

All of a sudden, Kazumasa was the man of the moment. His ball had saved possibly hundreds of lives. Such a person was indispensable to the safety of Japan's national rail system. Immediately he was given a substantial raise and a new title, Superintendent of Track Maintenance and Repairs, and he was called upon by national headquarters to make a complete inspection of the entire national system. From that moment on, Kazumasa rarely saw his home on the backside of Japan, but on the other hand, he saw, peering around his ball, every part of Japan where a train could pass, from snowy Hokkaido in the north to the sunny port of Nagasaki in the south. Kazumasa and his ball rambled, rolled and sped through the Japanese countryside, along the seascapes and through the clutter and crowd of urban Japanese life.

As Kazumasa traveled, he became familiar with the idiosyncrasies and precision of his ball and developed, with amazing exactitude, a system of standards and measurements to calibrate even the most imperceptible deterioration in any length of tracks. Kazumasa, carrying a detailed map and a notebook, would study, with tedious accuracy, the fluctuations of his ball over every inch of track throughout Japan. It was no small task. The Japanese national rail system could now boast of increased safety as Kazumasa and his ball carefully erased the margin of error.

As the years passed, Kazumasa became a sort of one-man/one-ball institution. He required only one assistant, who arranged his daily traveling schedule and punched his records into a central computer. Kazumasa and his ball would appear promptly at the scheduled hour for travel in his national railway uniform, his ball neatly clad in its matching cap. He was treated with extreme respect and care. Boxed lunches, dinners and snacks were always provided for his comfort and convenience.

But one day, the national rail system was dismantled, and the private sector scrambled with contracts and bids to take over portions of that lucrative travel business. At the same time, someone invented an odd-looking device, a sort of electronic box with a ball attached to it by a rod. The box had an LCD digital window which displayed positive and negative readings as the ball balanced delicately. This electronic gadget was sold with a five-year parts warranty and a renewable repair policy — all considerably cheaper than hiring the services of Kazumasa Ishimaru.

The Tokyo City Circular Railway Service, however, took Kazumasa on at a considerable cut in pay, and Kazumasa was relegated to making a continuous circular tour of Tokyo, which he repeated every hour.

One day, Kazumasa and his ball descended from the Tokyo Yamanote circular with a dizzy unfulfilled feeling of repetition. To be a bobbing horse on a merry-go-round was, Kazumasa thought, a better situation than this circular tour of Tokyo. He knew by memory every stop on the line from Shinjuku to Shinjuku, and he even knew many of the people who made these stops. The recorded high-pitched voice of the woman saying, "*Wasuremono nai de . . .*" and the crowds pressing upon him and his ball, sardines-in-a-can fashion, had never really bothered him, but now he felt weary, and his ball, too, seemed to hang sadly over his nose. It was time for a change.

* * *

Well, by now, perhaps, you may have realized that I was that very ball, that tiny satellite whizzing inches from Kazumasa's forehead. Growing up in Japan was for Kazumasa and me a rather predictable existence, compared to the life we would share from that time on. While I could not, of course, control the events that were to come, I could see all the innocent people we would eventually meet. All of them had a past and stories to tell. I knew their stories as you will also know them. There was old Mané Pena, the feather guru, and the American, Jonathan B. Tweep. There was the man they called the angel, Chico Paco, and there was the pigeon couple, Batista and Tania Aparecida. But I am getting ahead of myself.

CHAPTER 2: BATISTA AND TANIA APARECIDA DJAPAN

CHANGE CAME TO KAZUMASA ISHIMARU as suddenly as I had come into his life. Kazumasa realized that as long as he had me for a companion, he would never be alone in life. He would always share the adventure of life with his ball, and with that strong sense of support, Kazumasa stepped away from all his years with the Japanese railroads and took the first flight out of Haneda for what he believed might be a distant but familiar place, São Paulo, Brazil.

Kazumasa had seen an NHK documentary about the Japanese in Brazil. Most of the Japanese who had immigrated there seemed to live in a quaint clump in an urban setting much like Tokyo. Then there were those who lived in the countryside growing Chinese cabbage, daikon and tea. But it was not just the idea of gravitating toward other Japanese outside of Japan nor even that he had seen just about everything there was to see in Japan. Something drew Kazumasa and me irresistibly to Brazil.

Kazumasa had a cousin who had been traveling in South America after passing his college examinations and before entering college. This cousin had stopped in Rio de Janeiro with his backpack and sat out on the beach at Ipanema. He sat there all morning and afternoon and evening, the balmy breeze caressing his thick hair and the sand and salt air peppering his face and arms. The bronzed women and men sauntered by, wet, warm and carefree, and Kazumasa's cousin began to weep. He sent his regrets to the University of Keio and never returned to Japan.

Kazumasa's mother kept in touch with her nephew in Brazil because Brazil seemed to be the sort of place that might absorb someone who was different. Not that her son Kazumasa had not done extremely well for himself in Japan. Kazumasa was, after all, the man who had saved hundreds, perhaps thousands, of lives by his painstaking and accurate calculations of track deterioration. But Kazumasa's mother worried about her son's happiness, about arranging a happy marriage, about the future and the nature of true happiness. While others in the family sneered at her nephew's decision to abandon his studies at Keio for an uncertain future in Brazil, Kazumasa's mother privately praised his courage. It was she who noticed me hanging sadly over Kazumasa's nose and realized that her son's possibilities for happiness in Japan had exhausted the limits of those tiny islands. "Your cousin Hiroshi, remember?" She pulled the address out of a small notebook. "He lives in São Paulo now. Go see him."

Soon after arriving in São Paulo, Kazumasa and I got a job with the São Paulo Municipal Subway System. Hiroshi had arranged the interview and had pulled some strings with somebody who knew somebody else, but considering our background and experience in the field, the São Paulo Municipal Subway System was more than fortunate to retain our services. We also began to get freelance jobs in other states to check out their railways. Once again, Kazumasa and I had the opportunity to go out on the road. Unlike Japan, Brazil was massive, inefficient, encumbered by bureaucracy, graft and poverty. Kazumasa took me, his precision ball, into this tropical and elusive mess like a beachcomber with a metal detector on Coney Island on the Fourth of July. I did not, of course, complain. I was as oblivious to the heat, the humidity, the insects and the stink of sweating humanity as I was to graft and poverty. And Kazumasa met this sudden change in our lives with optimism and resilience; anything was better than that circular Tokyo train.

Kazumasa took his cue from his cousin Hiroshi who seemed nonchalant about the mess and calmly walked Kazumasa through the bureaucratic arrangements of renting a comfortable apartment with a maid on the fourteenth floor of a highrise, not too far from the subway offices.

Kazumasa was drawn to the sunlight flooding his apartment

through the large windows. We stood there together in the window looking out, a prism of light spinning off my shiny surface. Kazumasa looked down at the scenes on the street and in the tenements below. The activity down there was a clutter of street people, children and dogs, women hanging wash from their windows, lovers snatching caresses in the shadows, workers restoring brick walls and tile roofs, men and women playing cards and drinking, dancing and swearing, loving and fighting. As the days passed, Kazumasa found himself observing one scene in particular—the back porch at one end of a tenement house. He found that by focusing beyond me onto the continuing saga of what he soon came to think of as "his" back porch, he began to feel a special intimacy with this new country, to share his cousin's gentle but continuing passion.

* * *

Kazumasa's back porch happened to belong to Batista Djapan, who had rented the room and the porch it opened onto for the past five years. Batista worked in a document processing service as a clerk-runner, which the Brazilians call *despachantes*. Batista caught buses and subways and scurried all over the city with a vinyl briefcase filled with documents needing signatures on as many as ten pages of their forms. He always had a little extra money and a joke to bribe a slow bureaucrat into signing something at the bottom of the bureaucratic stack. Batista handled business for lawyers, small companies and individuals. He knew all the side doors, how far the laws could be bent before they would break, and what anyone from a clerk to a *delegado* might consider enough to buy a beer. Batista considered his business a craft by which he survived, paid his rent, gave Tania Aparecida and her mother some spending money, and had a few coins for a *cafézinho* in the morning and a beer after work.

Batista was a man with a joke on the tip of his tongue, a penchant for gossip, cynical about politics, passionate about soccer, and painfully jealous of Tania Aparecida. He could turn a phrase, sing a song, play the guitar. He was Catholic, cursed the priests and practiced Candomblé. He was an observer of the philosophy of life in the tropics summed up by the statement "There is no sin below the equator." Despite the scarcity of food in the cement metropolis, he continued to live as if mangoes and papayas could be had from the trees, fish from the rivers and manioc from the red earth, all in the abundance of a continuing Eden on earth. Batista was a mellow and handsome mixture of African, Indian and Portuguese, born on a farm near Brasilia in Goiás and raised in the urban outskirts of São Paulo. He was childish and heroic, genuine and simple. He was the sort of man every Brazilian knew and sensed in their hearts.

Batista's wife, Tania Aparecida, came and went as she pleased. When she did not live with Batista, she lived with her mother a few tenements down the street. Her coming and going, however, did not please Batista, who could be seen dragging his wife home at some odd hour of the night or prodding her toward her kitchen with the end of a baguette at dinnertime. "When a man comes home at night, he should have a supper waiting! I'm nearly dead from hunger."

"I took Mama to the movies, poor thing. It was a scary movie. She didn't want to be alone at night, Batista," Tania Aparecida protested.

"It's your fault for taking her to the movies in the first place!"

"Oh, Batista," Tania Aparecida cooed. "You would have liked this movie."

Batista relented, "What was the movie about?"

She grabbed the baguette and jammed it in Batista's stomach. "So you're hungry are you?" she taunted and scurried up the stairs.

"Crazy woman!" Batista yelled after her.

Batista and Tania Aparecida were passionately in love, but they were also always fighting. They had no children, and Batista continually accused Tania Aparecida of never being home long enough to have children in the first place.

Every day, Kazumasa and I peered down from our window on the fourteenth floor to observe Batista's life. We saw Tania Aparecida in the afternoons, washing bundles of clothing and hanging them to dry on the lines on the sunny veranda. We saw

Batista struggle out on Sunday mornings, heavy with a hang-over and cursing his team and that idiot player Pedro-Paulo who overshot the goal on an easy penalty kick. We saw Batista and Tania Aparecida dance on the veranda at night and scream at each other in the morning. We saw Tania's corpulent mother hit Batista on the head with the side of her bag. We saw every-thing—the friends, the good times and the bad—but one day Kazumasa and I saw Batista arrive, balancing his vinyl brief-case on his head and carefully carrying in the palms of his hands a single pigeon.

Batista had found the wounded pigeon on the sidewalk as he stepped off the bus on his way home. The pigeon trembled helplessly as people scurried in both directions without notic-ing the grey thing on the pavement. Batista instinctively scooped the pigeon up from the ground just before a bicycle would have pressed its delicate head into the concrete.

At home, Batista examined the pigeon carefully, taped its ailing foot and tucked it to bed in a box in a warm place above his refrigerator. In the morning he remembered to buy a bag of birdseed and to invest in a small cage. As the days passed, the pigeon grew stronger, hopped around Batista's veranda and took short running flights to the window sill. Soon it was strong enough to fly again, but it did not leave Batista's veranda.

After awhile, Tania Aparecida would come to take down her wash only to find that the pigeon had managed to seat itself on the clothesline and oblige her labor by soiling her clean sheets. "If you don't put that pigeon away, I'm going to cook it for dinner!" she would yell at Batista, but Tania Aparecida did not mean it. She had noticed a change in Batista since the pigeon had come to live with them. Batista no longer tarried so long in the bar after work, but hurried back to their veranda to look after the pigeon. He was always occupied now with the pigeon, giving it a bath, grooming it, mixing some new concoction of vitamins and meal for its supper.

"Isn't this the most beautiful pigeon you have ever seen?" he boasted to Tania Aparecida as if it were his own child. That was it. Tania Aparecida brushed aside a tear. The pigeon was the child they could never seem to have. What a difference a simple bird made to their lives now.

As the days passed, Batista became more and more involved in caring for his pigeon. He wandered into bookstores looking for books about pigeons. He spent evenings in the city library reading everything he could find about pigeons. He searched out and spoke with other people who cared for pigeons, observed their methods and listened to their ideas. He became so immersed in the study of pigeons that Tania Aparecida, who had welcomed the change in him, began to have feelings of envy. Occasionally Batista remembered his old habit of dragging Tania Aparecida home from her mother's, but now he seemed to do it as an afterthought, without the old conviction. Batista, once an avid conversationalist about soccer and women and politics, could now only think, live and talk about pigeons.

One day, it became more than Tania Aparecida could take. Batista had forgotten her birthday and spent the day with a fellow pigeon enthusiast. Tania Aparecida stomped down the steps of the veranda with Batista's pigeon in a cage. She took the pigeon on a bus to the end of the line in Santo Amaro and tossed the pigeon out of the cage. That was the end of her competition, she thought crossly. She was ready to have the old Batista back.

Tania Aparecida took the long bus trip home with a muddled sense of relief and fear. By the time she got off the bus and walked up the stairs to the veranda, she was remorseful. It was only a poor pigeon after all. She met Batista at the bottom of the steps and cried out her apologies. She had really meant no harm. She had been jealous.

Batista looked quizzically at Tania Aparecida and led her up the stairs to the sunny veranda, where the pigeon was flapping around in a pan of bath water after a long flight from Santo Amaro. The sputtering water around the pigeon seemed to bathe it in a soft mist of colored light. It looked at Tania Aparecida forgivingly, nodding its head from side to side. She wrapped her arms around Batista and wept with shame.

"It's all right, Tania." Batista was not angry. "I haven't been able to summon the courage to do what you did. I mean,"—he kissed her lightly on the forehead—"to try the pigeon out in flight. I didn't have enough faith that it would return. Now we know. It is a good carrier pigeon!" Batista was joyful.

From that time on, Batista and Tania Aparecida and the pigeon went everywhere together on the weekends. He would put the pigeon it its cage and she would would pack a lunch. They would board buses and head to the seaside or travel to the hills and fish in the streams. Sometimes they would visit Tania's cousins in the rural interior and spend the day picking fruit and chewing sugar cane. And from every place they went, they sent the pigeon flying home to the tenement veranda in the city.

Batista then got the idea to time the pigeon's flights, making note of the time he let the pigeon free, while Tania's mother and the neighborhood children waited excitedly with a watch on the veranda at home. Batista always sent a message — a riddle or joke — home with the pigeon which the children clamored around to read with laughter and wonder. As the flights became a regular event, Kazumasa could see on any Saturday or Sunday the children gather from every end of the tenement to read the notes brought by the pigeon. For some reason, no matter how simple nor how silly, the messages brought by the pigeon were more wonderful and exciting than a voice on a telephone.

* * *

So it was that Kazumasa and I had come to live in Brazil. Kazumasa had no idea at the time how this simple pastime of staring out his window on the tenement scene below might affect his own future. These things I knew with simple clairvoyance. I also knew that strange events far to our north and deep in the Amazon Basin, events as insignificant as those in a tiny northeastern coastal town wedged tightly between multicolored dunes, and events as prestigious as those of the great economic capital of the world, New York, would each cast forth an invisible line, shall I say, leading us to a place they would all call the Matacão.

CHAPTER 3: MANÉ DA COSTA PENA

IN 1992, two years after torrential rains washed away the tillable earth in one southern region of the Amazon Basin, Mané da Costa Pena discovered the feather. In the years after his discovery, the soil over his small farm and for miles in every direction was scrubbed away. It had begun with the fires, the chain saws and the government bulldozers. Before that, Mané Pena had wandered the forest like the others—fishing, tapping rubber and collecting Brazil nuts. One day, in the usually dark forest, he wandered through a strange tunnel of light in which the damp forest humidity seemed to churn in changing colors. At the end of the tunnel, he found himself in this clearing where one of his rubber trees used to be, and this goverment sort hands him some papers and says, "We've done the clearing for you, sir. Now it's all yours, from that tree yonder to that stick yonder."

"Got nothing on it," observed Mané.

"Couple of weeks, we'll send an agronomist 'round. Get you started; show you how to plant. Whole new way of life, Seu Mané. Meantime, if I were you, I'd get some barbed wire, fence it properly. Congratulations. Just sign here."

The agronomist never did come, but the rains did and the wind and the harsh uncompromising tropical sun. Even Mané's mud-and-thatch house was eventually washed away. What was uncovered was neither rock nor desert, as some had predicted, but an enormous impenetrable field of some unknown solid substance stretching for millions of acres in all directions. Scientists, supernaturalists and ET enthusiasts, sporting the old Spielberg rubber masks, flooded in from every corner of the world to walk upon and tap at the smooth hard surface formerly hidden beneath the primeval forest.

That the primeval forest was not primeval was hardly news to old Mané. He and others had been telling tales of the impossibility of tapping underground water sources for as long as he could remember. Years ago they had even told this to TV reporters when the national network had come over to tape sections of a documentary about the Amazon. The reporters visited Mané's poor farm—the paltry stubble of manioc in an unweeded and eroding garden—and put him and his family (his second wife and all her children and the younger ones of his previous marriage) on national television. Mané complained awkwardly to the cameras about the underground *matacão,* or solid plate of rock that always blocked well-diggers. Mané's old cronies and even Mané himself laughed at the sight of his wrinkled face, eyes dancing about and peering suspiciously into the camera lens. That Mané had said all that in a regional tongue, consonants lost between a toothless grin they could all understand, on real TV seemed to settle the complaint in everyone's minds, and the reporters, who were used to interviewing illiterate, backward and superstitious people, filed the videotape under *fantastico* and let it collect dust until the late 1990s.

There were odd theories about the Matacão, as it became known—that it was the earth's mantle rising to the surface or the injection of a cement layer by a powerful multinational. It was indeed strange that the Matacão was made of some sort of impenetrable material, had a slick shiny surface and seemed to glow in the dark on moonlit nights.

Mané, having discovered the feather, was more fortunate than others who farmed the area and who subsequently lost everything. He had put it this way: "We thought when we came here that we'd farm virgin soil, but her tubes had been tied long ago."

Mané and others did not have much choice. He and his family accepted the government's offer to live in low-cost, riverside condominiums built on the edges of the Matacão, but the government condemned those buildings just five years after they were built, and a private real estate company came in and bulldozed them under, replacing them with American franchises wedged between and under exclusive penthouses with heliports and hotels. Tourists stomped over the Matacão, billed as one of the wonders of the world, and it was considered chic to get a tan on the field.

That was when Mané's feather started to take hold. By now, Mané, his wife and all those children were living in a shack built of construction residue and making a living working on the bulldozing and construction sites along the Matacão. His wife did hand-laundering for hotel guests while the older children slipped off one by one to odd jobs nearby and as far away as Manaus and Rio de Janeiro.

In the evenings, Mané would wash up and lounge around the street bars, sitting at a table in one of the sidewalk cafes, stroking his ear with his feather and cracking jokes with the other old-timers. The others teased him, calling him "Mané feather," but the feather, he claimed, was better than smoking or drinking. Of course, it was not as good as sex, but what feather could compete with that? It had worked wonders on his sleepless children and was completely natural. It was like those copper bracelets everyone used for rheumatoid arthritis: if it didn't help, it sure didn't hurt.

The second time the national network people came by, having pulled out their decade-old tapes on the same geographical area for a historic foothold of some purposeful and continuing saga, old Mané was again a poor, barefoot regional type on national television with another uncredited statement, this time about the feather, which again would change his life forever. To have one's life changed forever, three times, amounted in Mané's mind to being like one of those actors on TV who slipped from soap opera to soap opera and channel to channel, being reincarnated into some new character each time. One story had nothing to do with the other except that the actor was the same. The disjunction of each stage in Mané's life seemed as divisible as the Matacão and as incomprehensible as the magic of the feather. Still, the feather, Mané concluded, was the only tangible evidence of coherence. Like the remote control and the buttons on his new TV, it made things happen.

CHAPTER 4: GGG

MEANWHILE, FAR AWAY IN NEW YORK, I could also see that the great mechanisms of the business world were churning furiously on the twenty-third floor of a smoked-glass high-rise. The conference room for nonsmoking executives was buzzing symphonically. On the other side of the corridor, the conference room for smoking executives was dangerously close to setting off the overhead fire alarm and sprinklers. Nonsmoking and smoking executives communicated between conference rooms via closed-circuit TV. Unknown to anyone, an inconspicuous cable had been hooked by a courier in the interoffice mail run to a private television in the basement. The janitors and the mail couriers drank cokes and ate chocolate chip cookies during quarterly reports and cheered on the opposing teams — smokers vs. nonsmokers.

On the street below, union members paced the street in front of the revolving glass doors with the inevitable signs. A bouquet of helium balloons with the messages "Unfair to Employees" and "Strike!" and "Equal Pay for Equal Mentality" floated in a mass up to the windows of the twenty-third-floor conference rooms. The strikers cheered hysterically. In the basement, the couriers and janitors saw the balloons and cheered too.

Secretaries and administrative assistants rushed to and fro over the spongy carpets outside the president's office, exchanging copies of the same memos and drawing breaths of impatience while queuing up before copy machines. Several fights had already stirred the last hours before lunch break, when certain secretaries had had the audacity to cut in line to make urgent copies for their own files. Consequently, the Human Resources Department was in an additional upheaval, trying to handle the delinquent employees while preparing the paperwork for reopening negotiations with the union after the inevitable and eventual loss of zeal by union members in the hullabaloo over the strike.

Research marketers on the tenth floor were busily putting together their new packaging proposal, along with smaller, sample giveaways and a sleek new brochure. In another room, a couple of managers were editing a series of one-minute commercials while an assistant anxiously pressed the fast-forward button.

A few floors down, dressmakers were hemming gowns on models, while a designer swept around with a clipboard and made monosyllabic comments and gave orders. A woman in tricolor hair coaxed the models to sashay into line and hurried them up the elevator to do their show for the board of directors during dessert.

The Accounting Department was busily printing checks and sifting through and stamping invoices. Their computer spreadsheets had fiscal plans for the next ten years, and the director of fiscal management was wiping coffee off the FY2002 spreads.

The Research and Development Department was deep in conference over a five-year proposal to move into accessory areas—everything from clothing to cars—that would enhance and complete the desired look. The department had drawn up graphs to show where and when infiltration into the domestic and international markets could be expected to peak.

The research theorists had prepared extensive personality breakdowns of potential buyers, their attitudes, credit histories, morals and life philosophies. These theorists had also formulated a new philosophical makeup for potential users based on a combination of computerized biorhythms and earlier editions of Dr. Spock's *Baby and Child Care*.

The commissary was shuttling crepe pans and peach brandy up to both conference rooms, and employees enrolled in the aerobics program were rushing to the showers from the badminton courts. A phys-ed instructor employed by the company was hustling in the 12:30 bunch for stretching and muscletoning. A sign said, "PHYSICAL EXERCISE FOR GOOD MENTAL EXERCISE. —GGG Fit Employee Program."

All in all, it was a normal day at GGG. Except for the strike, the secretaries' tussle and the board of director's luncheon on the twenty-third floor, business went on quite as usual. GGG was one of those business miracles springing from a small one-computer office with two pushbutton phones into a multi-million dollar operation with 100,000 employees in branch offices across the nation, all this in a period of five years. The founding couple, Georgia and Geoffrey Gamble, had already been kicked out of their own business in a simple vote of stockholders and upheld by the board of directors. The chairman of the board looked sympathetically at Georgia and Geoff: "I'm sorry, it's just gotten bigger than you can handle. That's the way of the free market, you know."

Georgia and Geoff Gamble were hardly surprised by the decision. Georgia adjusted her Dior spectacles, and Geoff pushed his hands into the pockets of his tweed coat and smiled blandly. GGG had certainly surpassed their mad brainstorm over albacore at a sushi bar one afternoon in 1990. Georgia had even predicted their forced resignation, but Geoff had sneered at the time. Even so, Geoff had, early on, decided to keep in the pocket of his tweeds a single card, to which he now turned with a vengeance. Georgia looked at Geoff significantly, and the couple took the elevator down twenty-three floors to the revolving glass doors. By the time they reached the bottom, the computer had already deleted their names from the company hierarchy. However, the card in Geoff's pocket was not only deleted but irretrievable, and, although its absence could not destroy GGG, it could wreak its own particular havoc. It was more than the missing microchip in a personal computer—it was the pea under twenty-three mattresses in the bed of a princess, the missing product.

The marvelous thing about the card in Geoff's pocket was that GGG had gotten along without it since the very beginning. In fact, according to Georgia's calculations, GGG could probably go on almost forever without it. That had been the very brilliance of GGG's conception. Geoff tore the card in half and tossed it into a nearby gutter; it was gone forever.

Meanwhile, on the third floor, in one small understaffed department, cryptically titled "Development Resources Research and Viability," a single director and his clerks waded through papers and filed everything in steel cabinets, which were in turn locked in an enormous walk-in vault. Monthly, a manager would wade through the files and remove those containing discarded or rejected subjects and shred them.

There was a second vault with boxes and boxes of junk—everything from silver-plated hole-punchers to quartz shopping-list calculators. At this point, most of the objects were small enough to put in a handbag. The Viability Commission, an outgrowth of Development Resources Research and Viability, had narrowed down product viability to handbag size, and the clerks had had to get the maintenance men to remove the large equipment, such as personal copy machines and chairs with heated seats. The department director was relieved because his request for warehouse space had been denied in the last fiscal budget, and he did not relish the idea of giving up his office space for storage.

Actually, he was not yet aware of the commission's plans to remove even things like the silver-plated hole-punchers because of the price of silver on the international market and costly overhead for insurance and freight. Every week the commission had some new strictures on product viability. They had finally, after five years, however, narrowed the retail price to $9.99 with latitude for inflation. At $9.99, silver-plated hole-punchers were out.

CHAPTER 5: CHICO PACO

"THE FEATHER," Mané had explained on national television in his thick accent, "was my own discovery, my own invention," if it could be called that. The reporter strained at Mané's dialect as if it were another language. No, he did not know if the Indians used the feather for the same purposes, but his great-great-grandmother, they said, was Indian. Even so, he was the first in his family to use the feather, and besides, all his folk said he was crazy. Only the wife and the third daughter believed in him at first. No, there was no particular kind of feather that he used. This was up to individual taste. He himself preferred the feathers of the parrot, but he had been given the wing feather from a very rare tanager by a man who regularly traded with the Indians. In fact, Mané had a rather big collection of rare feathers. The television cameras cut to a scan of his collection, set in empty coke bottles and porcelain vases and strewn over an embroidered and hand-laced cloth on the TV set. The cameras also scanned Mané Pena, who appeared aged according to one standard and youthful according to another, the grizzled grey pepper of his unshaven face, his dark leathery skin and bare feet, the faded Hawaiian shirt splattered with *Aloha*. Mané produced a small, rare, light blue tanager feather and demonstrated its use, sliding it over his right ear. The reporter herself requested that Mané demonstrate the feather on her own ear and also complained of an ache in her shoulder. Mané grinned through his missing teeth and nodded authoritatively, carefully rubbing the soft down over the tip of the reporter's ear. There, on national television, the camera got a rather titillating close-up of the reporter's diamond earring and of the feather's point between Mané's leather fingers poking lightly on her lobe. The reporter exclaimed with surprise that the ache in her shoulder was gone, completely gone!

Mané grinned again and shrugged. No, he did not know anything about Chinese acupuncture. He had never heard of any such thing. He had figured out the sensitive points in the ear himself. Someone had told him about some doctors in São Paulo who poke your body with needles, but he thought that was unnecessary. He frowned in disgust. The feather was, after all, natural, easy to acquire, and above all, it felt good. Mané said he had seen the feather cure everything from seizures to alcoholism. He was beginning to warm up to the interview and started to give an animated account of a little neighbor girl who had asthma, his voice rising and twanging in regional tones. But the reporter smiled, flexed her new shoulder in wonder, and said, "This is Silvia Lopes on the Matacão for National TV."

* * *

Kazumasa saw this on television, but could make little of it. "Ma-ta-kao," he repeated, practicing the pronunciation as diligently as if the documentary had been a language lesson. "Ma-ta-kao."

His maid, Lourdes, came from the kitchen with a small dish of carmelized flan and a demitasse of coffee. She put the dessert on the table and nodded at the television, "There's something about that place, that Matacão, Seu Kazumasa. I just know it. That old man and his magic feather. It's the Matacão."

Kazumasa and I nodded, but Kazumasa did not understand everything. Contrary to what you might imagine, I had no way of enlightening Kazumasa. It was one of those situations often described in children's television dramas where the pet is obviously more perceptive than the master. But who was I—a ball—to say?

"Good," Kazumasa smiled appreciatively at Lourdes, taking a spoonful of the dessert and letting the delicate custard slide down his throat.

While Kazumasa still struggled like an infant with this new language and his new surroundings, there were others, like our maid Lourdes, who made the connection between the Matacão and the strange magic of Mané's feather.

* * *

Far away, in another town on the coast of Ceará, a youth named Chico Paco watched the same TV report with extreme interest. The Matacão, Chico Paco was sure, was a divine place. It was the only possible reason why the feather could have even been discovered by Mané Pena.

Chico Paco thought about old Mané Pena and the feather and the Matacão and walked to the edge of his land and looked over the multicolored sands lifted in great changing dunes, a characteristic of this part of the coast. In his town, there had been a mother who had sent the colored sand in a tiny bottle to her homesick son in São Paulo. It had brought happiness to him in the distant urban metropolis. A young talented boy had then gotten the idea of pouring the colored sand in bottles in such a way as to create pictures. Chico Paco remembered the first pictures in the bottles—the scenes of his home, mud huts, coconut trees and grazing cattle. One day, a tourist brought a picture of the Mona Lisa and asked the boy to duplicate it in a sand bottle, and he did. After that, the boy left the town and went away to be famous, sand-bottling every sort of picture from the President of the Republic to the great Pelé. Someone said he no longer used real sand but some synthetic stuff dyed in every color you could imagine. Someone said he was even making sand pictures in bottles of fine crystal and mixing the sand with gold and silver dust.

Chico Paco shrugged. He, too, would miss the beautiful multicolored sands, that rainbow of changing layers strewn before the azure waves, the salty wind at his back as his *jangada* —a flat raft with sail—thrust itself out to sea, but like the talented sand-bottling youth before him, Chico Paco had a separate destiny.

Chico Paco was nineteen, a thin bony youth with deep green, iridescent eyes and dark lashes set in a gentle face. Despite his youth, he was already a strong fisherman like his father before him. His hair, bleached yellow and orange under the constant sun, could perhaps be traced back to the old Dutch conquerors of that part of the country. Chico Paco had never been away from his home, but now the Matacão seemed to be calling from the great forest. The opportunity to leave home came sooner than he expected.

Chico Paco lived next door to Dona Maria Creuza and her grandson, Gilberto. Chico Paco and Gilberto had grown up and played together from childhood. They had learned about life together, and at one time, both had had dreams of going to the city together. But Gilberto had contracted a strange disease and become an invalid.

Before setting out toward the beach with his line and buoys every morning, Chico Paco carried Gilberto into the early morning sun, leaving him to sit under the veranda, occupied, as most of the women of the village, in the art of weaving lace. From time to time, Gilberto looked up from his handiwork to gaze at the changing shadows of the banana trees and speculate on the occasional passerby trudging along the path to or from the plaza. Gilberto waited for Chico Paco to return from the sea in the early afternoons, bringing in a string of fish — *bujião* and *badejo* — plus something special for Gilberto and Dona Maria Crueza's dinner, maybe a lobster, a small bass or a long sea eel. In the evenings, Chico Paco would hoist Gilberto onto his back and carry him over to watch the big outdoor television in the plaza with the rest of the town. They would share a beer at the bar or buy popsicles, exchange jokes and gossip, predict the outcome of the prime-time soap opera.

During the day, Gilberto worked bent over a small pillow of pins and thread, tossing the ends of the balls of thread skillfully so as to weave a long, narrow and complex piece of finery. Dona Maria Creuza would take the lace ribbon, wound around pieces of cardboard, and dicker the price in the plaza. When the lace ribbon reached its final destination — the trim on a woman's blouse or negligee or the delicate border of a fine linen tablecloth — it had been bought for a hundred times the money Dona Maria Creuza had received for it. Gilberto knew nothing of the price of his lace, which was as ephemeral as the changing shadows of the banana tree and the foam at the edges of the land where he was born and had always lived. Now an invalid, he did not even hope to wander any further.

Dona Maria Creuza, too, had seen the stories told on television about the Matacão. She had held a rosary in one hand and had placed her other hand on her television and prayed to the small saddled figure of Saint George. She had wept and begged and promised and prostrated herself to ask for a miracle: that her grandson, Gilberto, might once again walk. The miracle that occurred was almost more than her heart could bear. Looking up from her tears staining the earthen floor, she saw two bony feet grasping the ground with their toes. Gilberto balanced breathlessly in the doorway and stumbled into his grandmother's arms.

News of the miracle spread through the sleepy beach town in the same way a cool breeze caresses the sweaty foreheads and cheeks of people hiding from the scalding sun. It was murmured and whispered with wonder from house to house and bar to bar. Maria Creuza's Gilberto could walk again.

As Dona Maria Creuza explained the event again and again to everyone who came to hear, it was apparent that there was one small but essential detail that needed attention. Maria Creuza had promised Saint George that if her prayers were granted, she herself would walk barefooted to the Matacão and erect a small shrine in his honor. How did such a woman at her age suppose that she could accomplish such a promise? It was at least 1,500 miles to the Matacão, and Maria Creuza was nearly seventy years old. Certainly, Gilberto, although cured, could not expect to make such a trip in her place. He was much too weak. He might now be able to walk, but he would certainly die in fullfilling the very promise that had been his salvation. The ways of the Lord were unfathomable, but there were limits to human possibility.

Chico Paco heard the news as he dragged his *jangada* to high land and felt his heart leap to see Gilberto's thin, trembling, but indeed, standing figure outlined at the head of the dune before his house. "Chiquinho!" Gilberto was yelling. "Chiquinho! Look at me! Look at me!"

Chico Paco felt the sand kicked up from his heels pelt his back, as he pranced up the dunes to Gilberto's outstretched arms. Chico Paco grabbed Gilberto, hoisting him aloft as usual, and galloped down into the sea, throwing and catching Gilberto in the waves until the sun set.

It was Chico Paco who, without a second thought, volunteered his two healthy legs and promised to take Dona Maria Creuza's place, to make the long trip to the Matacão on bare feet to erect a shrine to Saint George and to give praise and thanks for the miracle of Gilberto's recovery. Chico Paco promised to do this because of his love for his childhood friend Gilberto, and because somehow, this miracle must also be meant for Chico Paco himself.

Within a week, Chico Paco, armed with the handwritten prayers of Dona Maria Creuza on small pieces of tablet paper, a rosary, a locket of Gilberto's hair, a small statue of Saint George and Maria Creuza's hard-earned savings, kissed his own mother good-bye and turned the green iridescence of his eyes toward the Matacão, leaving the prints of his bare feet over the multicolored sands.

* * *

Just as Chico Paco set forward on his journey, Kazumasa and I were on a rickety train somewhere in the state of Minas Gerais coming out of a long tunnel, old Mané Pena was carving a footworm out of the sole of his foot, and Batista and Tania Aparecida were rolling away from their early morning lovemaking. I know these things for a fact. I also know, to make the picture complete, that at that very moment, there was also a certain American in New York, by the name of Jonathan B. Tweep, pensively studying newspaper ads in the last car of a subway train. Well, I am full of such coincidental information, and international at that! But, to continue . . .

CHAPTER 6: JONATHAN B. TWEEP

THE DAY GEOFFREY AND GEORGIA GAMBLE took the elevator down twenty-three floors and passed out the revolving glass doors at the bottom of their ex-empire, an unassuming Caucasian male American by the name of Jonathan B. Tweep pushed his way through those very same tinted-glass doors.

The Human Resources Department of GGG was on the first floor. It was largely a waiting room with clipboards and forms and sign-up sheets. In the old days, before GGG had bought the building, the Human Resources Department had been a temporary placement agency for secretaries and word processors. GGG didn't have to do a thing. It simply bought out the temp agency, changed the nameplates and replaced the pink carpets with a more executive tan. All the temps were immediately given permanent placement on one of the twenty-three floors of GGG.

J.B. examined the clipboards with unusual scrutiny. He collected clipboards or, more broadly speaking, paper clips. (J.B. defined anything that held paper together as a paper clip.) He sat in the waiting room of GGG and filled out the information on one of the clipboards offered to him. Then he flipped through his personal file folder and found a resumé which he had coded "SCWP" (secretarial, clerical, word processor) and pulled it out. It seemed to have the qualifications that matched the requirements for GGG's latest job posting. He had resumés that presented him with the qualifications for every sort of job imaginable, but he read the SCWP-coded resumé again to make sure it did not include any extraneous skills like "supervisor" or "manager."

J.B. turned in his resumé and application and thumbed through GGG's pamphlets on health benefits, group tours and aerobics. He also read GGG's newsletter, which still sported a photograph of Geoffrey and Georgia, and Georgia's "Letter from the President." He looked at Geoffrey and Georgia's photograph with simplistic awe and thought that it might be even possible to apply for their jobs, little knowing that he had in fact passed them on the way in. J.B. slipped the newsletter into a clipboard and surreptitiously stuffed it all into his briefcase folder.

J.B. had handed his resumé to a short, curly-red-haired receptionist with long red nails that matched the color of her hair and a voice like a Dallas telephone operator. The exact same voice, a pitch higher, called out his name, "Mr. Tweep, please come in."

J.B. jumped up and followed this second woman who looked strangely like the receptionist but was not. This curly-red-haired woman also had red nails but was a tad heavier and older. She smiled sweetly and managed to talk about the weather, how busy they were at GGG, where she was going for her vacation, and her dental appointment, all before they got to the office of the personnel interviewer. The red-haired woman who was a tad heavier nodded to a seat for J.B., left a folder on the desk of the personnel interviewer and closed the door behind her.

J.B. looked up at the personnel interviewer in some confusion because she too was a curly redhead with matching red nails and a Dallas telephone operator's voice yet another notch higher. She flipped through the papers in the folder and smiled sweetly.

"Mr. Tweep, can I call you Jonathan?"

"Sure," J.B. nodded.

"Marvelous. We're great believers in making people comfortable. An interview shouldn't be such an ordeal, now should it, Jonathan?"

"No, it should be a straightforward conversation in which the job applicant and the prospective employer converse openly and equally to obtain information to assess whether either, in fact, desires to work with the other." J.B. had once been a personnel interviewer. In fact, J.B. had been many things over the employable years of his life. The resumé the interviewer now reviewed was only one of many resumés, the sum total of which still did not completely describe the man sitting before her.

J.B. was the sort of person who had gone through life trying everything and being second-best at everything. Life was a great elective divvied up into a series of smaller electives. There was nothing he had not tried, but for some reason, there was nothing in particular he wanted to do all the time and forever. If J.B. could have afforded the title, he might have been called a dilettante. But although he was second-best in everything he happened to pursue, no one seemed to really notice. Perhaps it was because he found all tasks so easy and, therefore, boring that J.B. himself was an unassuming projection of boredom. He was what might be called second-best in obscurity or unrecognized talent, but more often, he was stamped "overqualified."

Those who did not know J.B. personally made the assumption that his unassuming manner and obscurity were the protective wall behind which he hid what they believed to be a defect or a freak of nature: J.B.'s third arm. But J.B. was far from ashamed of his extra appendage and only kept it out of sight to prevent hysterical reactions from observers on drugs or those prone to wild hallucinations. He accepted his third arm as another might accept ESP, an addition of 128K to their random access or the invention of the wheel. As far as J.B. was concerned, he had entered a new genetic plane in the species. He even speculated that he was the result of Nobel prize-winning sperm. He was a better model, the wave of the future.

J.B. not only thought his third arm was advantageous, he knew it was. He might have been an acclaimed pianist. He could float three consecutive runs up the keyboard or bang out three octaves, all at the same time, but J.B. lost interest in the piano because there was nothing written for his particular expertise. Chopin and Beethoven were no longer a challenge. In baseball, J.B. was asked to leave the team because there were no rules for a two-mitt player, and besides, no one could get a ball past him. In a factory production line, J.B. was so fast, he threw his fellow workers down the line, who were unable to keep up with such a pace, into chaos. Once he had juggled balls in a circus. The other clowns were jealous, and people laughed every time they dumped water on J.B. during an act. In the matter of love making, well, the advantages were obvious.

Obscurity and an unassuming manner, then, were just part of J.B.'s personality. Maybe it ran in the family. Few people ever suspected his multitude of talents or his additional endowment. But J.B., in his quiet way of sampling everything, was in fact motivated by a simmering enthusiasm for collecting paper clips and the exercise of finding a job. If anyone were to ask him what he was doing in life or what his personal goals were, he would simply answer, "To find a job."

Before entering GGG Enterprises, J.B. had tried an enormous variety of jobs, everything from being a pickpocket to shoveling MacDonald's hamburgers, three at a time, on a grill. Somehow, J.B. had a feeling, a sensation felt in his third arm, that GGG had something to offer him that no other company before had been able to and that he, of course, had something unique to offer GGG.

The interviewer smiled with engaging Southern enthusiasm. They could have been on a front porch, fanning the tepid humidity and drinking mint juleps. She went on. "It says here that you can type 120 words a minute on a typewriter and process 240 words a minute on a word processor. Now, is that possible?"

J.B. said sincerely, "Actually, I'm faster by thirty words on a typewriter and another fifty on the word processor, but you know how it is when you take the tests; you always make more mistakes when you're under pressure."

The interviewer nodded sweetly and even asked the right question, "Jonathan, that's an incredible speed! What's your secret?"

J.B. matter-of-factly pushed the hidden sleeve through his jacket and produced his third arm.

The personnel interviewer blanched slightly but maintained her sweetness. "Oh well, Jonathan, of course," she sputtered. "We are an equal opportunity employer. We employ our personnel regardless of color, creed or handicap." She was about to say that only last week, they had hired a Vietnam veteran who had lost his arm during action in the Mekong Delta, and that J.B. could actually even things up, but she remembered her position as a personnel interviewer. She wouldn't give any indication of their interest in hiring J.B until a decision was made. It was not wise to encourage an applicant's hopes.

When the interview was over, J.B. shook her hand with one of his three hands and gestured amiably with another; this was a clever distraction allowing him to snatch an irresistible handful of heart-shaped paper clips from an acrylic tray on her desk. Then, he walked out with the correct balance of confidence and humility he knew personnel interviewers looked for. He could hear the interviewer pick up her phone and buzz her supervisor, "Can I come and talk with you," she said. "I have a special situation . . ."

Before reentering the waiting room, J.B. could see through an open door into a larger office. Once again, another curly red-haired woman with long red nails in a suit sitting at a large desk picked up her comline.

J.B. felt his throat itch and tighten. The supervisor's voice answered in the same Dallas telephone operator's voice, yet another notch higher in this scale of voices, "Honey, I have my weekly corporate culture meeting in about fifteen minutes, but come on in." J.B. jimmied one of his little fingers into an ear. He could hear the notes in his inner ear rise with every position. Receptionist, secretary, coordinator, supervisor, manager, director, vice president, president. Dropping the heart-shaped paper clips into a pocket, the thumb and index finger of the third hand stretched an entire octave.

Part II: The Developing World

CHAPTER 7: THE PIGEON

WITH TIME, Kazumasa and I noticed, peering from his window at the events in Batista and Tania Aparecida Djapan's back porch, that every weekend, the crowds that gathered to await the return flight of the pigeon were growing larger and larger. Pretty soon, they spread out from the narrow corridors of the tenement and onto the streets, milling with anticipation on the sidewalks and floating back and forth between the bars across the street and on the corner. A slow-moving glut of traffic along with a new taxi stand had invaded the narrow street. Vendors had begun to come regularly on the weekends, selling popcorn, cotton candy, popsicles, deep-fried *pasteis*, lottery tickets, combs, hairpins, key chains and plastic snakes that slithered across the pavement. A few beggars with eternally festering wounds, dark glasses and white-tipped canes, and babies sucking on shriveled breasts, had come to stake out some territory, too. At one of the bars, someone beat out a samba on the congas, and everyone seemed to dance, bounce and walk to its rhythm. There was a tingling sense of excitement in the air that wafted up to us.

Kazumasa noticed me bobbing to the beat of the congas and realized his own physical empathy with the events below. In fact, lately he had had trouble concentrating on his work with the São Paulo Municipal Subway System. As the months passed, he found himself more and more distracted by the pulsating beat from someone's radio or even the memory of the weekend congas on the street below his window. Invariably, he was distracted by me, bobbing rhythmically to a music other than the steady screech of metal against metal or the vacuum-packed sucking and hushing of automatic doors. We were forced to ride our routes several times to get a true reading, and even then, Kazumasa was no longer sure. His mind would wander from his work, and all of a sudden, he would be aware of me bouncing off the last measures of a popular bossa nova.

Kazumasa's maid and housekeeper, Lourdes, came away from her chores and viewed the crowd below, too. He was surprised by the quiet approach of the woman and the sensation of her darker elbow against his own. Kazumasa had never had a maid, and even after nearly a year, he felt slightly uncomfortable, as if he were intruding upon Lourdes, slipping about his own apartment self-consciously. Lourdes imitated Kazumasa, tiptoeing around in bobby socks because she had once worked for a Japanese family who never wore shoes in the house. She thought Kazumasa must appreciate this detail about her work, but Kazumasa thought that maids in bobby socks just came with apartments in Brazil.

"Seu Kazumasa," Lourdes spoke shyly at first, avoiding me bobbing in full swing with the congas. (I could really move in those days.) "It's crazy down there. Everyone is waiting for the pigeon to bring a message."

"Message?" Kazumasa repeated her last word, straining to understand.

Lourdes tucked a strand of dark wavy hair under her scarf. "I don't know," she said. "It is always different. The last time, it just said, 'Eagle.' Everyone ran out and bought lottery tickets on the eagle. And do you know, Seu Kazumasa, they all won! I should have done it, too, but you have to be down there to hear the message. I have tried to have someone telephone me up here as soon as they hear it, but the telephone lines all get jammed." Lourdes sighed.

Kazumasa was still struggling to understand this new language and smiled and nodded and then tilted his head to one side in some confusion.

But Lourdes was not discouraged and said everything again, only more slowly, her gentle eyes glancing merrily off me and my dancing. Kazumasa smiled in wonder. Everyone in this country seemed to be like Lourdes. No matter what it was, they seemed to want, at all costs, for him to understand. He remembered a man who had missed several subway stops on his way to work while explaining to Kazumasa with the utmost patience and consideration that his sister had married a nisei and lived in Campinas and that he was going to take his nephews, who (the man seemed surprised at the results) all looked Japanese, to the circus on the weekend.

"Pigeon!" Lourdes repeated. "The message might make you

rich!" Lourdes rubbed her thumb and forefinger together in front of Kazumasa's face, assuming this mime to be an international sign for money. "Rich!" she repeated.

"Rich," Kazumasa both nodded and shook his head.

Lourdes looked at Kazumasa with twinkling eyes and instinctive generosity. "Come on, Seu Kazumasa! Every day you look down there and watch those people. I watch the soap operas, but you watch those people. I can't get inside a soap opera, but you can go down there. Let's go down!"

The beat of the congas suddenly seemed louder and faster. Lourdes pulled the scarf from her head, her dark hair falling across her forehead and over her shoulders in soft waves. She grabbed Kazumasa by the hand, and together we ran out of the apartment, leaving the curtains flapping in the breeze of the open window.

*   *   *

Down there, waiting anxiously on the Djapan's back porch, was Tania Aparecida's mother with a watch. Her large bosom hovered over everything with an authoritative air. She had personally cleaned the pigeon's cage and put out fresh water and birdseed. She wanted the pigeon's homecoming to be as comfortable as possible. The children from the tenement scanned the skies attentively, each hoping to be the first to notice the pigeon's circling flight. Occasionally, someone pointed at some ordinary pigeon in flight, causing false commotion, a few curses thrown to the wind and lighthearted ridicule. Generally, the pigeon arrived home without being spotted, often circling away from the noisy and expectant crowds below before landing. A tingling bell announced the pigeon's arrival. The word passed through the jostling mass of people, through the corridors and out to the street.

Batista had arranged for three oversized men who worked as bouncers in the local nightclubs to protect the pigeon and Tania Aparecida's mother, who hardly looked in need of much protection. The bouncers stood menacingly against the crowd while Tania Aparecida's mother carefully removed the tube from the pigeon's leg and unwrapped the message.

Batista had been forced to arrange for the bodyguard-types after last week's incident in which a boy ran out from the crowd and grabbed the message from Tania Aparecida's mother's hand before she had even had the chance to unroll it. The boy had climbed over the porch and onto the adjoining roof, skittering over the tiles, down the side of the house and over a wall. Several people tried to follow the boy, pushing Tania's plants over the porch wall, breaking all the tiles on the neighboring roof and bruising themselves badly in the chase. But no one was able to catch up with the boy, even though a few people recognized him and tried to head him off at his own home. The boy's family was not aware of his escapades and became worried when he did not appear for several days.

Batista and Tania Aparecida had returned home to a vigilant crowd and a weeping mother, remorsefully cradling to her breast what she felt to be an abused pigeon. When Batista heard the details of the pigeon-mail robbery, he broke down and laughed until tears dribbled down his cheeks. From his laughter, everyone speculated on the ridiculous nature of the message and the hilarious joke played on the foolish boy, who must have felt sure that he had run off with a veritable treasure map. But Batista never told anyone, not even Tania Aparecida, what had been written on that scrap of paper. Many weeks later, the boy who had stolen the pigeon's mail, came sheepishly to Batista's door and quietly thanked him for never revealing the message.

One could never be sure, then, what the message carried by the pigeon would be. It might bring wealth, some penetrating realization, or it might simply be one of Batista's old jokes. As the crowds waiting to hear the pigeon's messages grew, however, Batista became aware of the necessity to produce messages of greater profundity. He often pondered for hours about what the next message should read, but without success. It seemed to him that the messages came of their own accord when the time came to write them, and it always amazed him that what he had taken a few minutes to conjure and write should have such significance on its arrival.

Today's message was cryptic. The three bouncers cracked

their knuckles, and Tania's mother smoothed the tiny bit of crumpled paper with her thick fingers, reading haltingly, "The Japanese with the ball will find friendship and fortune in Brazil." Little boys scurried through the crowd with the message tripping off the tips of their tongues. Everyone consulted each other, as if mulling over a puzzle to be deciphered.

"It must be some Japanese who plays soccer," someone suggested.

Another scoffed, "They only play baseball."

"Could be that, too."

"They all play baseball!"

"Could be my brother-in-law. He's Japanese."

Everyone ran off to hug a Japanese friend or relative and, then, drag them off to buy a lottery ticket. The lottery ticket shops were soon crammed with Japanese and friends of Japanese all trying their luck. One shop was greeted by a small excited cadre of people moving in a huddle with an elderly Japanese gentleman. "Step aside!" they all yelled. "This is the Japanese with the ball. This is our big winner!" They all pointed at an odd bump growing on the side of the old man's right cheek. The old Japanese gentleman smiled jubilantly.

But this was only one weekend in a long entertaining succession over a period of many months, and while Batista enjoyed the fame he had gained from the pigeon messages, he was still, basically, a pigeon enthusiast. He had already joined the International Pigeon Society and was now the president of the local chapter of the National Pigeon Society. His pigeon had begun to win awards for beauty and flight.

Tania Aparecida now proudly accompanied Batista in his numerous activities and responsibilities. While Batista no longer felt the need to drive Tania Aparecida back to what he considered her proper nest, he was tormented every once in a while by the special attentions she received from one pigeon colleague or another. "He was explaining auto-sexing for whitecocks," Tania Aparecida would protest innocently.

"Ah! Eh? I'll show that bastard an auto-sexing!" Batista raged, strutting around the porch nervously.

But Tania Aparecida ignored Batista's flights of jealousy,

and Batista had to admit that she was becoming as knowledgeable and engrossed in the subject as he. It was Tania Aparecida who had encouraged Batista to invest in an attractive female counterpart to their prizewinner and to establish a pigeon corps. In a short while, Batista and Tania's back porch became lined with cages and feeding troughs and pigeons in all stages of training and development, and Tania's mother came every day, measuring birdseed, cleaning cages, changing the water and lovingly pressing the beaks of the yearlings into her cleavage.

The children in the tenements and surrounding neighborhood, too, were influenced by the activities on the Djapan's back porch. Nowadays, all the children had pigeons which they cared for according to Batista's careful advice. They came regularly to see Batista about some pigeon problem and to buy a few *cruzeiro*'s worth of Batista's famous birdseed blend. Batista noticed that, while all the boys still carried slingshots in their back pockets, they no longer used them to try potshots at the pigeons. Slingshots were now strictly used to scare away stray cats on the prowl. On the weekends, while Batista's prizewinning pigeon still arrived faithfully with messages, dozens of other pigeons were also homing into the tenements with special messages sent by young amateur enthusiasts and students of Batista.

The messages sent home via pigeon by Batista were, for the most part, like those in fortune cookies: aphorisms and pithy maxims, coincidental truths, humor, a thought for the day. Some suggested that Batista got them off the *Seicho-no-Ie* calendar—that dense compilation of daily words of wisdom attributed to a myriad of great teachers (both Asian and Occidental, famous, obscure and unknown), ferreted out of sources as varied as the Bible, Shakespeare, Buddhist sutras and the Koran. Others said he copied them from the newspaper horoscopes. Some speculated that the messages came to him in dreams on Friday nights. Some went so far as to assert that Batista merely sent the pigeon with blank scraps of paper which were miraculously written on during the pigeon's flight. Maybe, some thought, the prize-winning pigeon was literate! Every now and then, however, one of Batista's messages was a prophecy. How could the message "eagle" be explained? Numerous people everywhere claimed to have personally understood and received one or another of Batista's pigeon messages. There was actually a small pamphlet circulating, listing all of the pigeon messages and the subsequent meanings, miracles, fortunes and prophecies attributed to each message.

Batista himself was baffled by the commotion regarding the messages he sent by homing pigeon. What had begun as a simple training exercise to test the talents of his pigeon had ballooned into a massive cult at his doorstep, an institution akin to tracking biorhythms or weather broadcasting. Batista joked and bantered about his growing fame as a prophet/fortuneteller, but Tania Aparecida was not beyond alluding to the special powers of her now-famous husband.

* * *

When Lourdes heard the pigeon message repeated by everyone on the street, she felt a chill run through her body and travel down her arm to Kazumasa, who noticed me, in front of his nose, jittering in excitement.

Lourdes dragged Kazumasa and me from lottery stand to lottery shop. They bought every sort of ticket, from the illegal ones to the state-controlled ones.

"Chose five numbers from 1 to 99, Seu Kazumasa!" Lourdes instructed excitedly. "Five numbers," she repeated more slowly. Kazumasa obediently circled numbers at random. Then Lourdes had him check off random squares next to a series of names. "Corinthians," Kazumasa repeated. "What's that?"

"A soccer team. You check if you think it will win, lose or tie," explained Lourdes.

Together, Lourdes and Kazumasa and I walked though the streets of the city. For one special day, the entire city seemed to become for Lourdes and Kazumasa a great bazaar, an enormous amusement park. We stopped for coffee and cheese bread and wandered on to the next lottery shop. We took buses to no particular destination, got off and sipped cokes or licked ice-cream cones. Everywhere we went, Kazumasa spent his money on lottery tickets, raffle tickets, sweepstakes, and even the horse races. Everywhere Kazumasa went with Lourdes, he gambled and won. It was an immigrant's dream.

Lourdes took Kazumasa and me to the movies, through the shopping centers, in and out of shops and restaurants, through parks and churches, up and down the wealthiest and the poorest streets of the city. Lourdes showed us the great mansions where she had once worked as a maid or a cook or a nanny, and then she took us to the end of one bus line and several transfers further to the outskirts of the city, where she lived with her own family. Kazumasa and I followed her up the dirt road lined with tiny houses, the better of which were cement block structures with tin or tile roofs, but all created out of construction-site scraps and cardboard with plastic wrappings for windows. Some of the houses were stuccoed and painted in bright colors—pink and blue and orange. Oil cans and pots surrounded the houses or hung from the eaves, filled with ferns, begonias, ivy and draping succulents. Barefoot children ran in and out between the houses, stumbling over sleeping or scavenging dogs and scattering the chickens that wandered freely everywhere. The bigger girls all carried babies and toddlers on their hips wherever they happened to go. The boys pulled carts piled high with smashed aluminum cans and old Coca-Cola bottles. Old people sat in doorways or stared out the windows. As evening drifted over the city, men and women poured out of the buses and walked slowly up the paths, greeting and calling to their children as they arrived. Some brought loaves of bread and baskets with fruits or a plastic bag containing a liter of milk. The men were dirty and wet with perspiration, their hands and fingernails filled with the grime of their labor. The women trudged wearily from domestic jobs and piecework in factories. The workday had come to an end.

A young girl met us on the road. She was struggling with a heavy bucket of water which Kazumasa took from her. He was surprised that such a thin-looking child could carry such a heavy bucket of water. "This is my girl, Gislaine," said Lourdes, handing the girl her packages.

"Mama!" the girl looked from the packages in surprise.

"Cheese and *goiabada!*" She held out the large block of sweet guava paste and beamed with pleasure.

"A gift from Seu Kazumasa," smiled Lourdes. "Go on now," she nudged her daughter. "Put the water on for coffee. We have a guest."

Lourdes's home was a small one-room shack built of concrete blocks. Despite its shabby appearance on the outside, it was cleanly swept and cheerful inside. Lourdes had decorated the walls with photographs and bright pictures from magazines. She had hung starched white curtains over the only window and covered the small table with a hand-embroidered tablecloth.

Lourdes poured a demitasse of hot coffee for Kazumasa. The aroma of the coffee filled the small room like a strong spice.

The girl, Gislaine, ran between Kazumasa and a little boy who seemed confined to a cot in the corner of the room. I could see that the boy was lame, his withered legs useless beneath the ragged coverlet. The girl came close to inspect me near Kazumasa's nose and ran back to report everything to the lame boy in the corner.

"That is Rubens," said Lourdes, motioning to the boy on the cot. "Say hello to Seu Kazumasa," she nudged the children who both only giggled. "My aunt looks after them during the day for me. If it weren't for her, I don't know what we'd do. Their papa left us a good while back. Rubens was just a baby. He went north to dig for gold with a friend. You heard of Serra Pelada? The friend came back with some gold nuggets and a pile of cash and this." Lourdes showed him a gold wedding band that she hid in a tiny sack with other trinkets at the bottom of large trunk. "Said my husband got in the middle of a fight. They shot him straight through the heart. Never been sure about that story, Seu Kazumasa. There might have been foul play. All I got was a couple of gold nuggets. Who got the rest? But then again, I sometimes dream that he's still alive, somewhere else with some other woman and kids. This life isn't what it's cut out to be. The Lord only knows how hard it's been."

Kazumasa nodded at the parts he understood. He smiled at Rubens and Gislaine, whose eyes were fixed on me, the strange ball whirling in the air by itself. Gislaine stepped away in fear, but when Kazumasa approached the little boy in his cot, Rubens put his finger up to try to touch me.

"Rubens," Lourdes warned her son. "Don't be a bother. Seu Kazumasa is our guest."

Just as Kazumasa had seen Lourdes apply her talents to his own kitchen, here in her simple dwelling, she quickly had the pots bubbling with rice and beans. Lourdes had terse commands for Gislaine, who quickly ran out of the house. Kazumasa could hear the cackling of a chicken and the excited voices of other children outside. In a moment, Gislaine returned with a chicken, its wings flapping frantically all about, and bunch of collard greens picked fresh from the small vegetable patch at the side of the house. The chicken's neck was swiftly and deftly wrung and stripped of its feathers. Soon the house was filled with the smell of garlic and fried chicken, all cooked with amazing ease on a small stove with a single burner.

Lourdes, Kazumasa, Gislaine and Rubens all broke bread and ate hungrily. Lourdes watched Kazumasa eat with a relish she had not noticed before. She smiled thoughtfully. This was the meal she had been waiting to feed a man who had left so many years ago for Serra Pelada and never returned. She fingered the gold band in her pocket wistfully. Kazumasa noticed me whirring peacefully near his fork, which was loaded with tender rice and beans. He had come to like Lourdes's cooking and her kind, insistent attention to all his needs. He wanted desperately to do something for her in return. He wanted to tell her how much he had enjoyed their day together and how he had suddenly come to feel that this new country was, indeed, his home.

Someone was clapping at the door. "Lourdes! Are you there? Gislaine, it's me, Tia Carolina!" Tia Carolina rushed in, her son Jorge at her skirts, but stopped with surprise when she saw Kazumasa.

"This is my patron, Seu Kazumasa, Tia," Lourdes explained easily, but Carolina's eyes were fixed on Kazumasa and me.

"Lourdes, my God, it's him! So haven't you heard the pigeon message? Everyone has heard it by now. The Japanese. The ball. Who would have thought!" Carolina was sputtering excitedly.

"Quiet down, Tia," Lourdes tried to calm her aunt. "Everyone in the neighborhood will hear you." But it was already too late. Gislaine had slipped out the door with her cousin Jorge, and both were running down the narrow streets to tell everyone. Soon we could hear a noisy commotion outside. People from all over the hillside were converging on Lourdes's tiny home.

"What shall we do?" shrieked Tia Carolina.

Kazumasa looked at Lourdes in confusion, but he stood up calmly and walked to the door. "No worry," he assured her. As Kazumasa opened the door, the crowd shuddered in surprise and stepped back. The little boys who had crawled between legs to get to the front looked up at me spinning, a bright light in the dark, reflected off a lantern from within the house. Kazumasa looked at the sea of curious faces and smiled happily. "Today is the happiest day in my life," he announced. "So many friends!"

All of a sudden, people in the crowd began to step forward to shake Kazumasa's hand, to embrace and kiss him. In an instant he was carried up by this sea of humanity, rocking and singing and cheering. All through the night, the people danced and sang in the road in front of Lourdes's home, and Kazumasa and I were there, in the very center of it all, laughing and singing and crying, all at once.

CHAPTER 8: THE PILGRIM

AFTER WALKING 1,500 MILES barefoot over burning sands, cracked clay soil, slimy mud, steaming pavement and sizzling asphalt, Chico Paco finally stumbled onto the Matacão. He sat down on the edge of it, drew his bloody feet toward his body and winced though his tears. The Matacão stretched before him, filling the western horizon as far as he could see, the heat pulsing through the air in waves into the deep blue skies. It was a desert with no trace of sand, and it was a plain so flat that ball

bearings were said to roll forever into the distance as if in perpetual motion.

Chico Paco stretched his emaciated figure reverently over the
Matacão and prayed for Gilberto and Dona Maria Creuza and
for his own poor wounded feet. A few children nearby were
tossing marbles in a hoop on the Matacão. In the distance, a
dozen boys on low box carts made from discarded wood and
shopping-cart wheels were racing madly toward the finish of
their race. The children tossing marbles scattered in every direction, yelling at Chico Paco as they did, "Hey you! Get out of
the way! You'll ruin the championship!" Chico Paco glanced up
to see the fury of the charging box carts, rolling over in time to
avoid possible decapitation by one cart and causing a second
cart to swerve recklessly into its competitor. The carts shot off
the Matacão onto the dirt, bouncing off the pebbles and weeds,
stopping another hundred feet from the Matacão in a cloud of
dust.

"Damn drunk!" one boy shouted, running from his cart.

"No, he must be a tourist! Sunbathing is on the northwestern
end!" Another boy gestured.

"This invalidates the championship!" said the boy whose cart
had almost separated Chico Paco's head from his shoulders.

"What do you mean? I won anyway by two lengths even
before you came close to that guy!"

The boys confronted each other in a pack, gesturing with fists
and shouting insults over their shoulders. Chico Paco rolled
over in a groan.

One boy turned from the pack, "Hey, you idiots! He's hurt!
Look at his feet! He needs help!"

The pack reorganized itself around Chico Paco, who struggled to raise himself up. After a great deal of scuffling and commotion, the boys succeeded in lifting Chico Paco up on their
shoulders, each boy struggling to lift some part of Chico Paco's
body into the air. They proceeded in a winding amorphous
procession along the edge of the Matacão, slowly carrying
Chico Paco's withering figure under the cloudless afternoon
skies to help.

"Take him to Mané Pena!" Such was the consensus among the

children who began to gather from everywhere, joining the processional first with curiosity and then with a solemn sense of duty and playful pomp. The procession undulated through the poor section of town, down unpaved streets—red dust and urine spattered against the skirts of shuttered buildings, pink and blue paint peeling away in great scabs, graffiti bleeding ultimatums and lost people. Dogs and pigs and chickens scattered from under the marching feet of the children while dilapidated buses filled with tired laborers sat in traffic, sulking in the popular tunes of country music.

Old Mané greeted the procession, with Chico Paco floating on its shoulders, as it approached the outdoor cafe and Mané's favorite sidewalk table. A reporter with a tape recorder was seated there, interviewing Mané for a radio talk show. The reporter anxiously followed Mané and the children and Chico Paco's floating figure to Mané's humble home, recording everything: how Chico Paco was carefully laid in a hammock, his feet bathed and bandaged, and how Mané Pena took away the pain in Chico Paco's feet by applying the point of his feather to Chico Paco's ear. The reporter also interviewed Chico Paco, whose story was equally interesting—the miracle of Gilberto's recovery, Dona Maria Creuza's prayers for her grandson and her promise to place an altar to Saint George on the Matacão after traveling barefoot from her distant home on the seaside, and how Chico Paco had come to take the old woman's place.

Within several days, Chico Paco's feet were healing, the raw flesh drying into a firm crust and the deep cracks in the skin between the toes joining in tender pink ridges. By then, everyone along the Matacão had heard of Chico Paco's courageous journey and Mané's remarkable cure. The radio station had repeated the recorded interview of events once every hour, and far away in the seaside town with the multicolored dunes, even Chico Paco's mother, who had no other way of knowing, had heard her son's name mentioned on a local evangelical station praising the Lord and miracles and Chico Paco's deep faith, generosity and inexhaustible spirit.

Mané Pena's wife, Angustia, filled Chico Paco's plate with fish and a generous ladle of toasted manioc flour. Angustia, like

Mané Pena, was a toothless, leathery woman. She had borne at least eighteen children, too many to remember. Ten of her children had survived so far. The youngest, Beto, a two-year-old, clung to her thick, veined calves as she slapped about the kitchen in rubber thongs. "Suely," Angustia summoned one of the older girls. "Take Beto and give him his bottle."

Suely obediently dumped a spoonful of sugar and some thick coffee into a bottle of milk. Soon Suely and Beto were settled comfortably in the doorway, Suely singing songs while Beto leaned into his sister's lap, sucking on his bottle and examining his toes.

"You'd better eat more," Dona Angusta nodded at Chico Paco. "Put some flesh on those bones," she suggested huskily.

Chico Paco himself had mashed the fresh garlic and salt into a soft pulp for Dona Angustia. "My menfolk won't do any cooking," Dona Angustia commented as she smothered the pieces of fish with tomatoes and onions. "Who taught you to cook?"

"My father died when I was little. I always helped my mother out. There was only my mother and me," said Chico Paco. "Some cilantro and green onions would give the fish flavor," he added.

Dona Angustia nodded, avoiding Chico Paco's glistening green eyes. Those people who lived near the ocean were different she had decided.

Eating the fish and manioc, Chico Paco watched the children and thanked Dona Angustia and Mané Pena through the iridescence of his expressive eyes. "It's been my dream to come to the Matacão, Seu Mané," Chico Paco said earnestly. "It's not just Gilberto's miracle and Dona Maria Creuza's prayers. My own prayers have been answered too. That day I saw you on the television, I knew I must come here. It is another miracle sent from God that I am here in your home with you, a famous healer and inventor of the feather." Chico Paco brushed aside his tears.

Mané Pena grinned modestly, spooning his food down rapidly. He looked up from his plate and said, "But now you, son, are a famous pilgrim and payer of promises." He thought a bit and added with his characteristic humor, "Next time, you ought to wear shoes, or at least, travel at night when the ground is cooler. You might avoid burning those feet. I'm allergic to shoes." Mané pointed to his own bare feet. "These have got their own kind of soles, but I don't do your kind of walking, son." Chico Paco chuckled at the suggestion that he might make the journey on foot a second time, but in less than a week, the radio station was flooded with letters and telephone calls requesting Chico Paco to personally carry out promises made to every saint from Nicholas to the Virgin Mary.

In the beginning, Chico Paco ignored the pleas for his assistance and went about quietly erecting the altar to Saint George on the Matacão, as Dona Maria Creuza had requested. It was a simple structure, no more than a few feet high and wide, but building it was more difficult than Chico Paco had expected. He paid the most attention to the base of the altar, to which everything had to be nailed and cemented, as there was no way of attaching anything to the Matacão. No amount of nailing or drilling could possibly make a dent in its surface. He tried pouring a mixture of common cement around the base, but it did not adhere to the Matacão. The only manner in which he could ensure that the altar would remain in place was to fill the base with cement and heavy discarded pieces of iron and metal to make it too heavy to be moved easily.

By the time Chico Paco was carefully setting a dozen tiles down for the small roof, he had attracted a number of observers and officials who argued about the legality of placing such a structure on the Matacão. Wasn't it like any roadside altar or cross erected by mourners for a loved one killed in a car accident? The roadside belonged to no one, just as no one could put a claim on the Matacão. Government officials, on the other hand, argued that the Matacão was a national park and that allowing Chico Paco to build an altar would be an open invitation for others to do so as well. They envisioned a Matacão cluttered with altars and relics, plastic flowers in porcelain vases and peddlers selling candles and rosaries. The Church was careful in its estimation of Gilberto's miracle, but there was a noticeable scurrying about among the clergy attempting to capitalize on the possible spiritual magnetism of the Matacão

and the miraculous ways of God. A case could be made that the
Matacão was without doubt the natural base for the world's
greatest church. Surely Chico Paco's small gesture was a clear
sign from God. The Matacão, then, belonged to the Church.
Poor Chico Paco found himself in the center of a brewing storm.

The controversy over the altar to Saint George on the Matacão only augmented Chico Paco's fame and popularity. More
than ever now, he was flooded with proposals to walk from one
place or another to the Matacão, in some form or fashion—
barefoot, on his knees, backwards, holding a cross or the flag of
some soccer team, carrying a burning torch or the photograph
of the Pope—to comply with some promise made in return for a
miracle. Moreover, people all over were beginning to rally
around the new cause: Chico Paco's right to establish a shrine in
thanksgiving for a patron saint's blessing.

Far away in the seaside town with the multicolored sands,
Gilberto walked carefully before the cameras with his grandmother, Dona Maria Creuza, speaking of the miracle and the
generosity of his lifelong friend Chico Paco, who had arrived
(Gilberto had seen it himself on TV and heard it on the radio)
barefoot at the Matacão. If the altar to Saint George were de-
stroyed or removed, surely Gilberto would be reduced to his
former state, to being an invalid once again. Was this not a
crime? Who could walk the earth with a clear conscience knowing that, without the fulfillment of Dona Maria Creuza's promise, they had damned Gilberto once again to a life without legs?

Chico Paco nodded, his beautiful green eyes flooding with
emotion. He could not allow such a thing to happen, but a bulldozer, armed with signed mandates, rolled onto the Matacão
anyway to push and scoop the shrine away. Chico Paco bowed
his head sadly while an enormous crowd watched in painful
silence. The TV cameras watched, too, and far away, so did
Gilberto and Grandmother Maria Creuza, who were in turn
watched by other TV cameras. The man driving the bulldozer
crossed himself and drove slowly toward the shrine. Poor Gilberto tottered to one side, but he did not fall. Gilberto, in fact,
stood rooted to the ground. The bulldozer grunted and smoked
angrily, but it could not push the shrine over. It could not budge

the shrine an inch from its site. By some strange magic, the shrine was fused tight to the spot. It was as if the solid base of the shrine clung to the Matacão by some powerful magnetic force. The crowd cheered, running toward the bulldozer and dancing wildly around Chico Paco and his humble altar. The multitude pushed the bulldozer off the Matacão, and the driver jumped off and ran to prostrate himself before Saint George. In the midst of this, Chico Paco was shyly exuberant, and despite his awkward appearance, his eyes shone.

In a miraculous moment, Chico Paco's altar became a place of worship and the destination of pilgrimages. People from everywhere, foreign tour groups and simple farmers, would come to visit the famous shrine, to hear the guides tell about Gilberto, who as the stories were embellished, was even said to have been in a coma for several years, while his grandmother, Dona Maria Creuza, had suddenly become a saint. And the youth, Chico Paco, then came to be called the angel who translated prayers into earthly realities. But this was just the beginning.

Mané Pena scratched the back of his weathered ear with a feather and smiled whimsically, recalling the vision of his own confused figure before the cameras. He had sons younger and older than Chico Paco and certainly more children than he needed or remembered, but Chico Paco got absorbed into the family circle as if he had always belonged there. Poverty made no difference. Somehow, the fruits of everyone's labor got spread around. Chico Paco slept in one large hammock with a youngster cuddled close to him on either side, his long golden hair entwined with the darker locks. Mané Pena stroked his ear and watched the sleeping boys. Maybe this Chico Paco *was* an angel, Mané thought curiously. His wife Angustia had said as much. He certainly didn't look like the others.

Meanwhile, Chico Paco dreamt about his friend Gilberto, now cured, running the long length of beach and riding the waves before sunset. Intruding into this recurring dream was always the face of a young boy; it was not Gilberto as a child nor any other boy Chico Paco could remember knowing. True, it was a common Brazilian face, the sort you always see—the dark mischievous eyes, the unkempt crop of dark brown hair—but the face reappeared night after night, transposed over the face of Gilberto, his bright curious eyes seeming to follow some distant object. Chico Paco thought about the boy's face and looked for him among the boys who had rescued him on the Matacão. He looked among all the children who surrounded him daily but could not find the boy in his dream. Chico Paco wondered what this dream could mean. Maria Creuza's promise had been satisfied, and Gilberto was saved; what more could God be asking?

CHAPTER 9: THREE HANDS

BACK UP NORTH in New York, J. B. Tweep started work at GGG on the first floor in the personnel file cabinets. In less than a week, he emptied twenty cabinets, shredded old confidential materials—unflattering memos, reams of transcribed interviews with internal informants, extensive tables on employee absenteeism and personal habits, moldy employee evaluations, ex-employee personnel folders—and sent into storage countless miscellaneous studies done by outside consultants on subjects such as "Viability of Enlarging Company Commissary," "Coffee, Smoking and the Work Place" and "Natural vs. Plastic Plants and Employee Morale." The efficiency and speed with which J.B. conducted this massive project was indeed remarkable, but after all, he could carry the boxes out and examine the material within, all at the same time. J.B. cut ruthlessly through the thick blanket of dust with one hand, drew out the precious heart of the personnel files with another and reduced it to a single floppy disk with his third. Awarded, finally, with a large pile of rusty paper clips, J.B. knew instinctively that he had surpassed the requirements of his job and that, after one busy week, he was once again a free man in search of a job.

A big company like GGG, however, was not so easily dismissed, even by three hands. Recycling productive personnel was part of GGG's interpretation of the old courses in Japanese corporate business sense. The Human Resources Department immediately sent J.B. on loan to Marketing Development on the second floor as a secretary-receptionist. J.B. could be seen typing memos, answering phones, ordering office supplies (mostly paper clips), and filing all at the same time. The other two administrative secretaries, who shared the same office, felt an unsettling sense of their sudden inefficiency before this whiz of the office. When there was some talk of eliminating their positions, which could be easily handled by one three-handed employee, namely J.B., there was a furor of weeping and backbiting behind closed doors.

J.B. shrugged, took the entire Marketing Development supply of paper clips and was transferred to the third floor of that understaffed department called "Development Resources Research and Viability." He was given the title of Assistant to Assistant Manager, which was odd because there was no Assistant Manager. In fact, the department did not even have a Manager. Everyone told him his title was just a formality for billing his salary, and J.B. sighed with relief at the absence of both managers and assistant managers.

J.B. followed the poor, overworked clerk around the cramped office and in and out of the walk-in vault. So this is where the twenty file cabinets from Human Resources had ended up! The clerk squeezed between them and sneezed, leaning against the file cabinets, which rattled emptily. J.B. examined them. The clerk had carefully typed titles, A to Z, and even dated the cards on all the drawers, but these cabinets were completely empty. J.B. was puzzled, but the clerk replied, "Things are developing, always developing, you know, but the question is, 'Are they viable?'" The clerk sighed heavily as if in answer to his own question.

In one corner of the room, there was an "in" box with stacks of paper in and around it. The clerk pointed hopelessly to the mountain of paper. "That's the latest development. We got that 'in' about 11:15 this morning. The interoffice mail people had to wheel it here in a wheelbarrow. We've got to get that mess cleaned up before the next mail run."

J.B. rolled up each of his three sleeves while the clerk glanced at the top of one pile muttering, "9.99 . . . it's all 9.99." To J.B.'s surprise, the clerk opened one very overstuffed cabinet marked 9.99 and began cramming all the papers in.

Indeed, as J.B. soon discovered, it *was* all 9.99. There were memos about acrylic tape holders, waterproof LCD clocks with suction cups for use in the shower, bookmarks that play music when the proper page is turned to, artificial nonpolluting snow to spread on Southern California and Florida lawns at Christmas, earrings with exchangeable velcro butterflies, creams that had collagen, keratin, turtle oil, aloe vera, PABA, sunscreen 15, vitamin E and a money-back guarantee for complete rejuvenation if used as instructed. (J.B. himself was partial to the large musical clips for closing potato chip bags called "potato clips.") Neither J.B. nor the clerk knew quite where to begin nor how to categorize so much varied material. It was not enough to alphabetize. At one time, 9.99 had been a simple category, a file cabinet unto itself, but now it was the entire department. J.B. and the clerk ran around stuffing folders haphazardly to meet the afternoon mail room deadline. As the clerk had warned, another wheelbarrow arrived at 4:00 PM, and the end was still not in sight. At 5:00 PM, J.B. fumbled for three mittens, stuffed his third arm under his overcoat and went home to think about his first day at his new position and what exactly it all meant.

Early the next morning, J.B. made it known to the Human Resources Department that the backlog of filing in the Development Resources Research and Viability Department was so immense that at least two more employees like himself would be required to make heads or tails of any of it. Human Resources sent over three two-armed temps to satisfy his request. J.B. orchestrated the filing with superb technique, conducting all eleven arms of his newly expanded office into an efficient concerto. As the opening and closing of file drawers reached a steady staccato, J.B. slipped away from the office and whistled down the hall to the office of the Viability Commission.

The secretary to the Director of the Viability Commission

was pounding away madly at the typewriter. A flurry of paper was piled on her desk, and five buttons on her telephone display were on hold. She looked up at J.B. in exasperation and said, "He's in a meeting. He's in meetings all day."

J.B. smiled and leaned over her desk with two of his arms. "How about an appointment tomorrow?" he asked, observing several envelopes clipped together with an unusually large and what J.B. considered attractive, stainless-steel clip, the top envelope stamped all over with the word "CONFIDENTIAL."

"Next week," she answered, "and that's if he isn't traveling."

J.B. nodded, folding his two arms with a mixture of understanding and worry.

The secretary looked up and apologized, "I'm sorry."

J.B. smiled sympathetically. With his third hand, he pocketed the clipped envelopes stamped "CONFIDENTIAL."

That was how J.B. made the amazing discovery that the Development Resources Research and Viability Department and that understaffed mess of 9.99 files was, at this moment, the most important department in the company. J.B. returned to the staccato of filing in his own office. Somewhere in all that paperwork was an answer, the discarded card from Geoff Gamble's pocket, the missing microchip, the very pea of the matter. J.B. thought, excitedly, that it might be paper clips, so he decided to take action.

In the following days, J.B. wrote a series of memos of his own:

"To: B. Carp, Computer Services Department Manager. From: J. B. Tweep, Asst. to Asst. Manager, DRRVD (Development Resources Research and Viability Department). Please make three computer terminals available to our filing department ASAP."

"To: R. Gold, Communications Department. Effective immediately, the DRRVD requires worldwide satellite feeds on 24-hour basis for research and viability scan. Please make necessary arrangements by moving three color-television monitors into room 311 with VHS VCRs and 12-channel memory capacity. Hookup to satellites and decoding devices required."

"To: S. Perkins, Human Resources Director.
Request the status of three temps changed to permanent,
plus request hiring of three more temporary clerical personnel. See attached memo for approved budgetary changes for
critical additional personnel for DRRVD."

J.B. simply attached another memo and marked everything
"URGENT."

It was a simple but auspicious beginning, and for some reason
probably only known to the ex-presidents Georgia and Geoff
Gamble, things actually began to roll. In less than two days,
monitors and computer terminals were rolling down the corridors to the Development Resources Research and Viability
Department. Maintenance men were crawling over and under
the floors and attaching wires to everything. Computer and
electronics experts were interfacing office personnel to software programs, software programs to terminals, terminals to
VCRS, and VCRs to satellite computer systems, which J.B. imagined were probably interfaced with God.

With these enlarged capabilities and the extended interfacing of several more hands, J.B. could now orchestrate a sym-
phony. Sifting with extreme ease and confidence through the
9.99 files, J.B. began to categorize and narrow the options.
That the end result might not be clips of any kind occurred to
him, but he had become, in the process, involved in a new method of thought which he referred to as "trialectics," sorting problems into three options and always opting for the solution in
the middle. His application of trialectics to his job was, he realized, experimental, but J.B. was willing to assume responsibility (something that, heretofore, no one at GGG had been willing
to do). He was beginning to think that trialectics would eventually revolutionize modern thought and philosophy, and he
envisioned, when the time came, backing up his decision by a
firm handhold in the Theory of Trialectics.

J.B.'s gamble (Georgia and Geoff would have been pleased)
paid off. In a short period of time, the Development Resources
Research and Viability Department was the booming center of
the GGG operations, and J.B.'s position became increasingly

powerful, in the manner of a crescendo. Office space and computer terminals—not to mention secretaries, receptionists, clerks, runners, supervisors and assistant managers—were added to the growing personnel of the department. J.B. revolutionized the office routine by setting everyone up in groups of three. The personnel from J.B.'s department were easily recognized because they all went to lunch, coffee breaks and the copy machine in groups of three. J.B. even went so far as to hire a team of triplets for special projects.

But, contrary to the original Gamble plan for a sort of creation in perpetual motion, J.B. was essentially goal-oriented, and he supposed that plans were made for a purpose. Trialectics was simply a way to reach an answer. That is why, one day, J.B. found the very thing in the 9.99 files that was at once the triumph of months of hard work by this now-bustling office and, at the same time, the discovery that meant the annihilation of that same office. And it was not a paper clip.

J.B. sat at one of the many three-terminal settings and punched in the standard input. He could hardly believe the line-up across the monitors. This 9.99 item actually met all the requirements for shape, packaging size, clothing and accessory development; matched the psychological and philosophical makeup of a wide range of prospective buyers; collaborated sympathetically with a high percentile of patented and patent-pending inventions; and met all short-term and long-term planning projections for investment, loan and taxes. The computer terminals blinked and beeped joyously. While the computer spilled its contents onto the printer, zipping back and forth across the pages of tractor-fed paper, J.B. quickly had an assistant pull the stored video material on this item.

To J.B.'s surprise, the video material was in a foreign language. His assistants all gathered around the screen to watch what looked like a documentary report of some sort.

A woman with a diamond earring was saying something while a man held a green feather near her ear.

"What's that language they're speaking?" asked someone.

"Sounds like French, but it's not," someone speculated.

"A Romance language. Cross between French and Spanish, I'd say."

"Where's the transcription on this tape?" asked J.B. excitedly. "We need to know what they're saying. We need an interpreter. Maybe we can get someone from the U.N. This is of
utmost importance!"

J.B. rewound the tape and viewed the entire piece again. It
was Mané Pena on national television demonstrating the medicinal attributes of his wonderful feather on reporter Silvia
Lopes.

"Where are they?" puzzled J.B., looking past Mané and Silvia
Lopes and trying to get a clue from the background. There
wasn't a tree or a shrub, but it wasn't really a desert; nor could it
be a parking lot. The ground around them looked strangely
shiny.

CHAPTER 10: FORTUNE

IN THE DAYS THAT FOLLOWED our descent with Lourdes from
that fourteenth-floor window, the results of all Kazumasa's
gambling became evident. Kazumasa's cousin, Hiroshi, came
over and spoke excitedly with Lourdes and Kazumasa.
Kazumasa had single-handedly won the national sports lottery
and the national numbers lottery, not to mention the numerous
illegal lotteries that Lourdes had had him bet on. Kazumasa's
total winnings seemed to rise with each passing moment, and
Kazumasa's cousin feverishly took Kazumasa in taxis everywhere to deposit the money. It all seemed to be an incredible
dream.

In a country where the disparity between wealth and poverty
is great, the news of instant wealth spread in and out of every
obscure crevice of that massive and unexplored land. Kazumasa became a household name, like a character in a nightly
soap opera, on the tip of every Brazilian tongue. The media
milked his story for everything it was worth, from the story of
his boyhood on the shores of the Japan Sea to weird specula-

tions about the nature and uncanny accuracy of the pigeon messages and their possible connection to me, Kazumasa's ball. When the hysteria surrounding the amassing of the greatest fortune ever obtained through the lotteries and the fear of me, Kazumasa's personal satellite, had undergone the natural process of sedimentation, Kazumasa himself emerged, a simple and solitary Japanese immigrant with a shy smile and a growing desire to experience more of life. Brazilians from everywhere flocked enthusiastically to Kazumasa, adorning him with offers of friendship, both sincere and laced with greed.

I continued to be eyed with extreme curiosity. Most people were sure that I undoubtedly had something mystical, magical or electronic to do with Kazumasa's enormous fortune. A recent graduate of electronic engineering in the southern state of Santa Catarina had happened to make an electronic replica of me (a flattering representation, I might say), which was cleverly attached to one's head by a thin wire and a transparent headband and operated by a tiny battery wired into the inside of the band. When looking at the wearer of this contraption head-on, it did indeed appear as if a ball were spinning free in the air. The graduate student had contrived the replica as part of his costume at Carnival, but a friend immediately recognized the gadget as their ticket to riches. Together, they began to produce the headbands with the electronic whizzing ball by the hundreds and, soon, by the thousands. Soon the lottery shops were filled with people wearing artificial spinning satellites, circling numbers with abandon and indefatigable self-assurance. Of course, when the artificial balls did not produce instant riches, many abandoned the strange headgear, but others, like Kazumasa, found a inexpressible comfort in the ball, a relationship, I can assure you, unmatched by human or animal counterparts.

In the meantime, there was all the money and the problem—if such be a problem—of what to do with so much money. Everyone seems to have an idea of what he or she would do with sudden wealth, but Kazumasa was a true exception. What does a man with a ball need with money? Some people must have realized the value of a ball like me because in a questionnaire asking what you would do if you had won Kazumasa's great wealth, 10 percent of those questioned said they would buy a ball like me.

Kazumasa had Hiroshi and Lourdes read the answers on the questionnaire and listened carefully to every sort of suggestion. There were, of course, the extravagant cars and the mansions with a hundred maids just like Lourdes. Then there were the great causes and small causes, businesses and hotels, plantations as large as the island of Shikoku, great poverty, great politics, great futures. Kazumasa muddled through all these suggestions, nodding and scratching his head in confusion.

"Karaoke bars," suggested Hiroshi. "How about it? You and me, Kazumasa. Open karaoke bars all over Brazil. You'd like karaoke bars."

"Okay," nodded Kazumasa, happy for this suggestion.

"Okay? Just like that?" asked Hiroshi. "It was just an idea off the top of my head."

"Okay. Okay," Kazumasa waved his cousin off maybe because it was just the beginning. "Lourdes, what do you want?"

Lourdes swallowed. "It's not for me to say, Seu Kazumasa."

"I remember what you said that day we went to buy the tickets," prompted Kazumasa. "About Rubens."

"Rubens? A wheelchair?" Lourdes gasped and glowed with delight. "You would give him a wheelchair?"

"Wheelchair? More than a wheelchair," said Kazumasa. "Maybe we can find a way for Rubens to walk again."

"But it is only a dream," Lourdes protested and hoped all at once.

"Maybe we can take him to a specialist," suggested Hiroshi. "Maybe there is a cure."

"Yes," Kazumasa and I nodded. Then Kazumasa walked over to our old window site and looked down at the Djapan's back porch. "And," he said, nodding in the general direction, "Hiroshi, you give money to the pigeon couple. Buy more pigeons."

Hiroshi nodded, "Sure."

"What about the man who said he would buy a hospital bed for his invalid mother?" reflected Kazumasa. "Send him a bed.

And that little girl who wants to own a bakery so her family will always have bread to eat. Buy her a bakery." So it began. Kazumasa instinctively began to give his money away. There were countless people with interesting propositions who began to line up at our door. While crowds filled the back street awaiting the weekend pigeon messages, around the corner Kazumasa faced an ongoing stream of people hoping to find an audience with him and his ball. Kazumasa listened patiently to everyone, and everyone stared at me. He did not turn away anyone; everyone left with something. A group of boys got a soccer ball and team shirts. A man got a prosthetic leg. A young girl got dancing shoes and lessons. A boy got a clarinet. A woman got a gas stove. Kazumasa granted gift after gift like a big giveaway department store. People called him the Japanese Santa Claus. And this was fun for a while.

In the meantime, Kazumasa followed Lourdes and Rubens to doctors and specialists. Rubens was poked and prodded and tested, but all the doctors said the same thing. "Rubens's paralysis is irreversible. There is nothing we can do for him."

Lourdes wept and Kazumasa felt terrible. If he could not give something special to Lourdes, what did it all mean?

Kazumasa shook his head. Every day, there were those who had wishes he could not grant because they wanted things beyond his capabilities, such as health, a lost arm, vision, hearing, babies. Kazumasa could not perform miracles. More than anything else he wanted to share the happiness he felt with others, and it pained him to see so many sick and homeless and hungry people. How many hospitals, how many soup kitchens, how many housing projects would it take? Government politicians, private foundations and a myriad of social agencies approached Kazumasa with great plans. Kazumasa signed check after check, but still, half the people who came to see him needed the impossible.

"Only a miracle, Kazu. Only a miracle can help most of these people," Hiroshi consoled Kazumasa gently. "What can you do about it? You have done more than anyone. Pretty soon, you will have given up most of your fortune!"

"Only a miracle," Kazumasa agreed.

"What I want to know is when are you going to stop? You can't keep on giving your money away like this, can you?" Hiroshi wanted to know.

"Why not?" asked Kazumasa. "Why do I need it? What is it all for anyway?"

"Your retirement? I don't know. Don't you want anything for yourself?"

Kazumasa had to think about this. "I don't know. I don't know," he shook his head. He thought about all the things that people wanted, but he could not think of anything he, too, wanted. He went to the window and looked below on the Djapans and their pigeons. He felt he wanted something that the Djapans had, but he did not know what this might be. No, he thought, it was not pigeons.

Lourdes bit her lip. Balls don't know much about these things, but even I realized that Lourdes liked Kazumasa very much. Kazumasa did not quite know this and would not have known what it meant anyway. In the meantime, Hiroshi was always bringing Lourdes little gifts: tapioca flour to make her coconut tapioca cakes, a ripe pineapple, embroidered handkerchiefs. Lourdes thanked him kindly, but so did Kazumasa. Lourdes sighed. This Japanese with his ball was different from other men.

As one would have suspected, but Kazumasa did not, people were likely to invent their wonderful proposals or their sad complicated stories. In the beginning, people who might have intended to lie were forced, out of uneasiness or perhaps fear in my presence (as if a ball like me could be judgmental), to tell Kazumasa the truth. Actually, I had no way of warning Kazumasa of the truth or falseness of the people he met, but I could see that after a while, people, emboldened by the marvelous stories others recounted of the Japanese Santa Claus, had decided to test the spirit of this phenomenon. Even Kazumasa could see that some people had been through the line twice, that certain stories bore a remarkable resemblance to the current tragedy on the prime-time soap opera, that politicians were using his money for their own campaigns, that the foundations had invested the money in coffee and soybeans, that altruism had been corrupted by greed. By the time Kazumasa realized the sad truth, another year had passed and he had spent much of his great fortune.

* * *

Batista and Tania Aparecida had accepted Kazumasa's gift to buy some prize-winning pigeons and were busily breeding what would soon became known as the finest pigeon corps in the country. To thank Kazumasa, Batista had taken the elevator up fourteen flights with three cages of pigeon couples and personally hung them on the wall just below and outside Kazumasa's window.

It was the invalid boy, Rubens, who took a special interest in the pigeons at the window. At Kazumasa's invitation, he and his sister, Gislaine, had come with Lourdes to live in Kazumasa's spacious apartment. Every day after school, Lourdes or Gislaine leaned out the window and brought up the cages for Rubens. Sometimes Rubens could not wait for anyone's help, and Lourdes would find the boy hanging out the window from his waist and reaching for the cages himself. "Rubinho!" Lourdes would cry. "I've told you! You're going to fall out of that window!" But Rubens was impatient to see the birds. He took each bird from its cage and cradled it in his lap, inspecting it carefully as Batista had taught. He moved back and forth in his wheelchair from the kitchen and interrupted Lourdes's cooking to fill the water feeders and the small troughs with Batista's special seed. Despite Lourdes's protests, Rubens liked to set a pan of water on the kitchen table and watch the birds splatter about in a daily bath.

Rubens also liked to follow the news about pigeons. He had asked Lourdes to frame the glossy cover of the second quarterly issue of *Pigeon Illustrated,* on which Batista and Tania Aparecida's prizewinner was proudly featured. In the most recent National Pigeon Society newsletter, *Columbidae,* there was a feature article in which Batista was quoted at length about grooming techniques, birdseed mix, flight training and homing patterns. Rubens followed all this avidly. Batista was now considered a new authority in the field, and every boy in the neighborhood was proud to say he knew Batista personally. Rubens was even prouder because he had been given pigeons whose lineage could be traced to the original pigeon that Batista had saved from being pressed between the heavy tire of a three-speed bike and a concrete overpass. And, more importantly, this pigeon had brought the message home about the Japanese with the ball.

The weekend pigeon messages continued with much fanfare. No one doubted the story that Kazumasa's great fortune was prophesied by Batista's pigeon message, and the crowds grew and now never abandoned the streets outside the tenement.

Batista, on the other hand, was more concerned with testing his pigeons and with extending the range of their flights. The National Pigeon Society had offered to sponsor a test flight from Rio Grande do Sul to São Paulo, buying Batista and his pigeon round-trip busfare to that southernmost state of Brazil. The pigeon had returned to São Paulo, over 700 miles, in a national record time of 38 hours. In fact, it arrived in São Paulo while Batista's bus was changing a flat, still 300 miles away in Santa Catarina.

Then there was the National Pigeon Society's Racing Homers Division, whose 300- and 500-mile races were consistently won by Batista's champions. Formerly an unheard-of sport, pigeon racing was suddenly followed with enormous enthusiasm by everyone from sportscasters to gamblers. Simple people on the street were soon aware of the difference between a Ptarmigan and a Belgian Voyageur. The latest results of the Belo Horizonte-São Paulo 500 race became a matter of common concern, and the announcement "Djapan's Tropical Dream took first place by five minutes" had some obvious meaning and significance to almost everyone. The 8:00 PM soap had even introduced a popular actor in the romantic role of a pigeon fancier.

Following such pigeon news, Rubens was anxious to try his own birds in flight. He began his birds with short flights from the street, peering into the sky as his sister watched from her post at the window above. All day long, Lourdes saw her son wheeling in and out of the apartment with his pigeon cages. Rubens passed the long lines of people waiting to see Kazumasa, who at the time, held audience in a little office on the same street. Some of the people admired Rubens's shiny new wheelchair and nodded at each other that their wait in line would not be in vain. Each day, Rubens rolled his wheelchair farther and farther away until, one day, Lourdes awaited him at the door with all the fury of a mother expecting a child many hours past his dinner. She sent neighbors and even her patron, Kazumasa, into the dark streets shouting his name. Had anyone seen a little boy on a wheelchair with a pigeon cage in his lap? He left in the morning. Now it is almost ten in the night, and he hasn't returned. *Nossa Senhora!* Where can he be?

But Rubens had simply gone a little too far and returned as unperturbed as his pigeon. The pigeon note had said as much: "Mama, I made it to the Avenida Paulista. It will take me awhile to get home. Don't worry. Your son, Rubens."

After this, Rubens was not allowed to leave the apartment for several days. He rolled around the apartment, cleaning cages, dropping birdseed onto the carpets and bathing his birds in Kazumasa's bath. Still, Lourdes would not let him leave the house. "This will teach you a lesson," she said sternly.

But Rubens had an idea. Nudging his older sister Gislaine into a corner, he convinced her to take his very best bird to the end of the subway line in Jabaquara. "You can take the subway," he urged her. "Here is the money you need. The extra you can keep for yourself. And don't forget to write down the time you release the bird."

Rubens watched out the window anxiously. He saw his sister cross the overpass, headed toward the subway, and smiled. Hiroshi had given him a watch. Rubens watched the time carefully. In the late afternoon, he came reluctantly away from the window when Lourdes called him for a snack. "Cheese bread," she said. "Your favorite."

From the kitchen, Rubens could hear the tiny bell announcing the arrival of his bird. He wheeled out of the kitchen in a flurry, ramming his chair into the wall and checking the time on his watch. He could not wait for anyone to remove the cage from the outside wall. He hurriedly lifted himself by his arms to the window sill. Like others used to depending on the upper halves of their bodies, he had great arm and shoulder strength, even for a small boy, and these days of rolling himself around the city with his pigeons had strengthened him unusually. Misjudging this strength, Rubens shoved his body forward and slipped past the pigeon cages and out the fourteenth-floor window.

Lourdes ran from the kitchen, thinking she would scold him for marking her clean walls with his wheelchair tires, only to see Rubens's withered legs disappear over the window sill. "Rubens!"

CHAPTER 11: SAVED

WITH A TERRIBLE SHRIEK, Lourdes nearly flung herself out the window, but she could not see her son below. She ran hysterically out of the apartment, down the corridor, banging on all elevator buttons and on the elevator doors themselves. By the time she had herself fallen by elevator fourteen floors, gathering apartment tenants at every stop, a tremendous crowd of people ran with her from the elevator, clinging to their pounding hearts and their soundless screams with their bare hands, anticipating a mother's horror.

But Rubens's body was not to be found. Lourdes ran with the crowd up and down the parking lot at the back of the apartment house. Curious tenants were coming from their cars. A boy? Fallen from the fourteenth floor? Everyone looked up at the open window with the pigeon cages and shrugged. This woman had gone crazy. But Tania Aparecida's corpulent mother had seen the boy fall too. She screeched incoherently from the Djapan's back porch and waved a poor pigeon, captured tightly in her fat hands, at the confused and excited crowd in the parking lot: "The truck!" she managed to scream. "The boy fell into the truck!"

Everyone clambered down the driveway in search of a truck. They screamed at and surrounded every truck double-parked along the street. They ran into the refrigerated compartment of a meat truck and searched between the giant cuts of bloody meat, causing the meat man in his bloodstained white apron to topple over in the street with a 100-kilo side of beef. They climbed up the sides of a watermelon truck and accidentally pushed the carefully balanced load of ripe melons onto the sidewalk. Watermelons rolled out into the street and smashed against passing cars. People ran out of the tenements and grabbed the melons. The driver came out of the local grocery and was waving his fists at everyone. The people lined up in front of Kazumasa's so-called charity foundation office stretched their necks to see what the commotion was all about. People stepped in and out of the line, afraid to lose their places. The entire street became a live wire of conflicting information. The story of Rubens falling out of the fourteenth floor into a passing truck was so absurd that people tended to believe the other stories about a man's body being found frozen in the meat truck or about the driver giving the watermelons away because their price wasn't worth the cost of transporting them.

Amidst all this, Lourdes ran to the front of Kazumasa's charity line and burst into his office. Lourdes did not need to say a thing. Kazumasa could see the terror in her eyes. He ran with her to the end of the street, jumping over the watermelons, but not knowing why they were running. "Rubens!" she gasped. "Rubens!"

Beyond the intersection—hundreds of cars and trucks passing from every direction—I could see Gislaine calmly weaving her way home from the subway with an empty pigeon cage, but Rubens and his pigeon, whose cage had also fallen with the boy, were by now speeding away atop a truck filled with bolts of old cloth and bags of sewing remnants. It was one of those open trucks, newly painted dark blue with scrawling designs (probably of Portuguese origin) along its sides and an inscription along the back: *"Carrego tudo no meu peito aquilo que Deus manda de cima."* (I bear in my breast all that God sends from above.)

Lourdes knelt down right there on that busy intersection. Kazumasa, who was always trying to do what was right, knelt down too, without question. Lourdes rocked back and forth as if in a trance, praying for her son, praying. Kazumasa could not understand, but I could hear her praying to a distant and magical place, to the small shrine of Saint George on the Matacão and the angel who had built that shrine, Chico Paco: "Please bring my son Rubens back to me alive. Please, by the grace of God, by the footsteps of the angel, Chico Paco. I will give Chico Paco a good pair of boots this time, and he will make a pilgrimage from this very intersection to the great Matacão and make your glory even greater. I promise it. I promise it."

Hiroshi and Kazumasa ran around the city, in and out of every police station and morgue, pulling strings and making promises to anyone who might be able to find the boy. They did not have hopes of finding Rubens alive. It was a long fall. They were searching for the body of a dead boy with withered legs.

But it was the pigeon who saved Rubens.

Rubens was awakened from the shock of his fall by the driver of the truck. The driver had not believed the nonsense of a boy falling from an apartment window with a pigeon. He angrily told Rubens that he wasn't taking any hitchhikers and that Rubens could get off. When Rubens didn't move, the driver swung the child, who clutched desperately to his pigeon cage, onto the crumbling edge of the asphalt road and drove away.

A drunkard stumbled from the bar where the truck had stopped. "Where is this place?" Rubens asked the drunkard without fear. "Where are we?"

The drunkard swung around. "Godforsaken place. You don't know this hellhole they call Freguesia do Ó?" The drunkard made a rude circle with his fingers. He made a fist at the trucks and automobiles rumbling by, one after another. "Know what's good for them. Don't stop here!"

It seemed to Rubens that a cloud of black oil and rubber soot never ceased to churn around the drunkard. Rubens fumbled for the small pencil he kept in his pocket. He snatched a dirty gum wrapper from the ground and scribbled the name of the place on the wrapper. The wrapper went into the pigeon's carrier tube.

"Mighty fine bird you got there," snarled the drunkard, coming closer, but the pigeon flapped its blue-grey wings in a sudden flurry, dispersing the putrid fumes of the drunkard's dissipation, sailed up and, circling its lost owner, was gone. Well, that was how Rubens came back to Lourdes's arms alive, but there was also the small question of the promise made to Saint George on the busy intersection of that São Paulo street. Lourdes wrote a simple letter addressed to "the Angel Chico Paco, in care of the shrine of Saint George, the Matacão." She enclosed a small photo of Rubens, glued the envelope closed, licked the stamp and kissed the whole thing with another prayer.

*　*　*

Meanwhile, back near the Matacão, the angel Chico Paco was toying with the idea of returning to his home on the multicolored dunes of the northeastern coast. He missed his mother and Gilberto. The Matacão was amazing and sacred and stretched into the horizon in one smooth shiny immensity, but it was still not like the sea. He missed the salty spray of warm tropical waters and the cool breeze running through the coconut palms and the thatched roof of his mother's house. On the Matacão, the wet air often stood still, a great cooking sauna, and everything—people and animals and even the thousands of species of insects—seemed paralyzed by the dense atmosphere. When it rained, Chico Paco would race with the children out to the Matacão to listen to the drops spatter against the smooth surface and to slide with wild abandon across the slippery surface of that tropical skating rink. At least it was wet then, but it was still not the sea.

When Lourdes's letter arrived, Chico Paco's first impulse was to toss it into a pile of others he had received. He had accumulated a small pile of fan letters containing requests that he walk for some miracle or other, like he had done for Gilberto. In the evening, he read these letters to Mané Pena and Angustia, who could not themselves read. Mané and Angustia both nodded: "There's great work for you out there. Great work."

But Chico Paco thought the idea of complying with any one of these requests more than absurd.

Mané insisted, "What about that one there? It says that the man had a sick mule, and he prayed to Saint George and promised that he'd get you," Mané pointed at Chico Paco, "you to walk from where was it? to the Matacão. And, poof, his mule stood up and hoed an entire field. If that isn't a miracle . . ."

Angustia agreed. "God has chosen you, son."

Chico Paco shook his golden head and laughed. "I'm just an ordinary man. Saint George did this, not me."

"No one is arguing that. But it's you that has to keep the promise. You're the key!" insisted Mané, rubbing his ear with his feather to help him think this matter through.

But Chico Paco could not see this reasoning until he opened Lourdes's letter and the photograph of Rubens fluttered from the pages. Chico Paco dropped to his knees and stared into that face—the dark mischievous eyes and unkempt crop of dark brown hair of a common Brazilian boy—the very face that returned night after night, imposing its memory until the dream stared back, a living reality.

The next day, Chico Paco bid Mané Pena good-bye from the dusty window of an old bus. Mané Pena handed him a handful of feathers. "For the trip," he insisted. "Seven days they say. Rainy season. Could be more. These buses get stuck. You have to all get out and push."

Chico Paco nodded. Going by bus to São Paulo was the easy part.

Mané Pena continued, "They say São Paulo is a big city. I seen it on TV. It don't all fit into one TV screen. It's that big."

Part III:
More Development

CHAPTER 12: THE FEATHER

TWO DAYS AFTER CHICO PACO left the Matacão on a slow bus headed for the great city of São Paulo, the American J. B. Tweep jetted in from New York, representing that big company which I have already described in some detail, GGG. Mané Pena thought this American was a strange sort, slightly lopsided, and that his name was funny. Mr. Tweep, Mané called him. Mr. Tweep spoke to Mané Pena through an interpreter, asking a lot of questions about feathers. He wanted to know everything: names of birds, feather size and color, methods of use, positioning of the feather on the ear, how long a particular feather was effective, historic use of the feather, how to the use the feather in conjunction with other remedies and apparatus, feather power in Indian and local folklore.

Mr. Tweep and the interpreter went with Mané Pena to one of the classy local hotels, which had a large aviary with every sort of tropical bird. He pointed out the various birds to Mr. Tweep, describing the feathers and their particular attributes. Some, Mané Pena admitted, were purely ornamental. Peacock feathers, he said, were an example. Too big and fluffy. Made you sneeze.

The next day, Mr. Tweep showed up again at the sidewalk cafe with his interpreter and a French bird professor (Mr. Tweep called her an ornithologist) who happened to be doing her thesis on the rare Brazilian tanager. (The Thraupidae family, she had said.) She was also studying the migration patterns of the red-eyed vireo, taking intermittent trips into the forest and banding one of the few species known to migrate to the Amazon region.

The French bird professor wore binoculars around her neck and had a talking parrot, which perched on her shoulders and seemed to go everywhere with her. Mané decided that the parrot talked in some funny language different from the one Tweep spoke. It said things like, *"Bonjour, messieurs-dames!"* and sang a tune the bird professor called the *Marseillaise*. Mané kept staring at the parrot's green primaries. Their particular iridescence reminded him of Chico Paco's eyes. The self-conscious bird screeched at him angrily, *"Monsieur, parlez-vous Français?! Parlez-vous Français?!"*

The professor took careful notes on everything Mané Pena had to say about tanager feathers. Mr. Tweep also took notes and tried to record everything on a small tape recorder that kept jamming and chewing up the tape, which was strewn in garbled brown ribbons over the cafe table. "It's the humidity," Mr. Tweep fumbled in exasperation. "Nothing seems to work in this country!" The interpreter did not translate this, but it was not necessary. Both Mané and the interpreter thought nothing worked either. The interpreter had gone to pick Mr. Tweep up at the hotel, where Mr. Tweep was hopelessly yelling into a broken phone. Then there were no taxis to be found, and when at last the interpreter located one, six arrived all at once. The taxi Mr. Tweep chose broke down before they had reached Mané Pena's outdoor cafe, and they were forced to walk the rest of the way.   ·

Mr. Tweep was in a visible sweat, and at some point, Mané Pena noticed that Mr. Tweep, in his excitement, was actually untangling the spaghetti of tape with two hands and thirstily gulping down a glass of Guaraná soda with a trembling third hand. Mané Pena and the professor looked on in astonishment. Americans certainly were more advanced! Mané jittered his feather back and forth over the lobe of his ear, like the bow on the strings of a violin in a high c. This was Mané's way of absorbing shock, but the professor fumbled for her sunglasses and went crimson in confusion while the parrot sang, with a certain fervor, the *Marseillaise*.

As the days went on, Mané Pena grew accustomed to, and reverent around, Mr. Tweep's third arm. He shared his experience with his old cronies at the bar, who all scooted their chairs around to Mané's table when Mr. Tweep arrived, gripping their cold beers, to get a full sense of the phenomenon. There was, indeed, in the beginning a sort of quiet awe, rather like, Mané thought, seeing television for the first time. In the beginning Mané and the others noticed that Mr. Tweep's third arm had a sort of twitch or tremble to it, as if it were not quite well. Not understanding third arms, they assumed this was a normal third-arm characteristic. They discussed third arms at length. Did other Americans have three arms? How about three legs? And better yet, three penises?

The French professor and her parrot now seemed to accompany Mr. Tweep everywhere. She had the glazed look of someone with a miraculous discovery. It was announced that she had been chosen as the first recipient of the GGG Fellowship for Scientific Studies in Ornithology and the Relationship of the Feather to Human Health. She was all aflutter with talk about hummingbirds. But Mané Pena understood intuitively that her studies had moved on to topics tertiary.

J. B. Tweep had been, with the dissolution of the Development Resources Research and Viability Department, transferred to the GGG International Research and Funding Division and sent on assignment to the Matacão, where he was busy collecting data on the 9.99 selection of the feather. J.B. had never been to a foreign country and was initially alarmed at what he felt to be a sudden listlessness in his third arm. Upon examining himself in the hotel mirror, he actually thought his third arm might be atrophying in this hot tropical weather. And it exasperated him that things did not seem to work in this country. There was no organization. And they didn't use plastic clips; the metal ones absorbed the humidity and rusted onto his papers. How could a third arm survive in such a place anyway? By the time he had located Mané Pena and exposed himself to the natives and the French ornithologist in an untypical show of ineptitude, J.B. was beginning to have serious doubts about his effectiveness in the Third World. J.B. would have left Brazil then and there, but the Matacão, like GGG, had a way of recycling everything.

J. B. Tweep, after he had begun to feel a sort of revival in his third arm (reasons for which I will explain later), went about with his usual trialectic efficiency to build GGG Enterprise's International Research and Funding Division into a major division, with the major investment and budgetary considerations it truly deserved. Suddenly, for reasons that, as I've said before, were known only to the original founders Georgia and Geoffrey Gamble, a tremendous and, since Brazil's debtor-nation

IMF agreements, unheard-of amount of capital poured from the U.S. GGG Enterprises into its Brazilian counterpart on the Matacão. This capital was likened to amounts loaned Brazil for Itaipú, the largest dam in the world, or Angra dos Reis, a nuclear-powered reactor that never worked. Anxious to duplicate GGG's New York offices on the Matacão, J.B. made a trialectic decision to import an entire building, all twenty-three floors, to the luxurious Matacão Row, overlooking the Matacão itself. J.B. had no time for the handmade mortar-and-block construction, which would have provided jobs for and fed hundreds of people for several years. He wanted GGG's presence to be felt immediately. After all, he reflected, there were historic precedents for such a grandiose move: the grand opera house imported in every detail from the iron fixtures to the parquet floors from England to Manaus on the Amazon River; or Ludwig's ship, which sailed from Japan down the Amazon River to dock as a great factory in the dense tropical forest for the purpose of churning everything into tons of useful paper. J.B. simply had a twenty-three-floor office building constructed in Florida and flown in piece by piece, office by office, secretary by secretary, manager by manager. He even had the Human Resources Department, complete with red-haired Texas-accented clones, re-cloned and flown in. Except for the fact that power failures were frequent and caused chaos close to hysteria (Human Resources had several ongoing seminars to help shocked employees: "Working in the Third World," "Controlling Emotions in Dysfunctional Elevators and/or Dark Copy Rooms," "What to Do When the Air Conditioning Fails" and "Sexism in a Friendly Country"), everything seemed to fall into place. And, if you have the strange sensation that all of this happened just like that, it did.

With a bustling, twenty-three floor office building to back him up, J. B. Tweep became nothing less than a king and nothing more than a CEO. Of course, he would not think of appointing himself CEO of GGG. He continued to manipulate everything via memos while promoting and demoting himself to the various departments that might need his three-armed expertise. Titles meant nothing to J.B., and as Mané Pena had said of the angel Chico Paco, J. B. Tweep had great work to do.

Everyone got an office at GGG. The French bird professor got an office, of course. Even Mané Pena became what he heard was called a "consultant." "This sort of work," he explained to Angustia, "is like when the TV people came and asked about why we couldn't grow anything, and I told them that her," he pointed at the earth, "tubes were tied. It's like that. Telling people things they already know."

Angustia remembered. "Imagine. I was more fertile than this piece of land. Twenty-six children. God works in strange ways."

"Angustia," Mané looked at his wife meaningfully, "I don't know if this Matacão isn't fertile. I mean it is a strange place. Fertile not for manioc or tomatoes, but fertile in a different way. Do you see what I mean?"

"Either a place is fertile or it isn't," sneered Angustia.

"But don't you see? It grows a different kind of thing. Buildings for example. It grows buildings!"

Despite his amazement at the Matacão's ability to grow buildings, Mané Pena did not like to venture much inside the GGG offices. He did not like to ride the elevators; he could feel the whirring of the machinery on the balls of his bare feet and feared his toes would get stuck in the automatic doors. He preferred to walk up the stairwells, so J.B. kindly sent a memo out to put Mané's office on the first floor. J.B.'s memo provided Mané with a computer and a secretary and an expense account. Mané Pena padded in barefoot to the offices once or twice to look at his desk, the ample supply of plastic clips and the computer, and to meet the secretary, but he could not think of anything else to do there. Occasionally he charged a beer or a cup of coffee in the coffee shop on the first floor and returned to his outdoor cafe table in the old section of town to banter with his cronies. If J.B. wanted to talk to Mané, he had to go down to that outdoor bar. J.B. tried to make Mané wear a pager or walk around with a mobile phone, but these things invariably got lost or broken. For a while, Mané's cronies in the bar put money in a jar and passed around the pager everyday, wearing it conspicuously on the belts of their pants. If the pager went off while a crony was wearing it, he got the winnings in the jar.

Still, Mané Pena was an enormous help to J.B. and GGG Enterprises. Consulting with Mané Pena and the French ornithologist, J.B. began narrowing down his selections and closing contracts with key feather distributors. The value of a feather depended, of course, on the availability of the source. The rarer the bird, the more expensive the feather. J.B. wanted to limit the selection to parrots, whose availability was generally good. Although Mané Pena praised the attributes of the common pigeon feather, J.B. knew that parrots had the reputation of being exotic and that the colors of these birds would give the Accessories and Design Department, as well as the Publicity Department, a lot of room for imagination. The value of feathers was rising with this new demand, but J.B. could still cut a deal to get high-quality double-A parrot feathers in blue, green, red and yellow for $150 a kilo. J.B. wanted to close a series of five-year deals to beat the rising prices, but no one was willing to extend themselves for longer than a few months. Feather distributors could see the future heaped in gold feathers, speculating that it could be the biggest rush on Brazilian resources since gold was discovered in Serra Pelada back in the eighties.

As J.B. sent his high priority dispatches back to New York, the Export-Import Department and the Legal Research Department were preparing paperwork, looking up customs regulations and discovering loopholes through which feathers might make their entry into the American marketplace. GGG lobbyists were busy in Washington and in Brasilia, feting politicians and handing out expensive feathers. GGG had already made some initial thrusts into the marketplace with enormous success. People were beginning to talk about "The Feather," and GGG was touting it like a sensation akin to Coca-Cola. GGG public relations people were promoting their product as one of those projected to become a part of American life, like coffee and orange juice at breakfast or potato chips and dip. Talk-show researchers were trying to line up guests with some knowledge or experience in feathers, and a few magazines were beginning to develop feature articles.

Back on the Matacão, the creative center of this brainstorm, it was becoming commonplace to see people walking and talking with feathers slipped comfortably above or behind their ears. Some people carried feathers in their pockets or purses. Others had small feather-carrying cases. It was not unusual to see people in bars, offering each other feathers and casually stroking their ears with them while carrying on animated conversations. The tourists who came to visit the Matacão were easily drawn to the use of the feather. They spent a great deal of time selecting from feathers under glass cases, asking about the birds from which the feathers originated and the type of feather best suited for their particular ailment or temperament.

Mané Pena, now the feather guru, was so frequently accosted by feather enthusiasts and salespersons about the nature of the feather and its proper uses that he was finally summoned to give classes and lectures at the local college. Lectures were not, after all, difficult for Mané Pena—he divided his knowledge into a series of topics and simply chose one to talk about for an hour. In the beginning, he likened being at a podium to his sidewalk cafe table. He sprinkled his lectures with anecdotes: every sort of story from the one about the girl with hiccups to the man with a twitch in his eye.

"Some say they feel funny holding this feather," Mané pointed out. "But it's no more funny than some people sucking the smoke of charred leaves. And you talk about pollution of the earth—what's more polluting than a plantation of tobacco?"

Mané Pena had a way of putting together information that people found ingenious. "There's a guy I heard about says we got sensibilities from way back before we were ever born. I mean back generations and generations. So take this other theory I heard about the dinosaurs, that these dinosaurs been changing and changing every generation until now they're birds. Think about it. Bird sensibilities coming from way back millions of years. Now, that's a power."

And Mané had answers for his skeptics. "Well, they say I'm a primitive. But you suck smoke—that is primitive. After all, you can see smoke. Look at TV—they say the pictures are sent through the air by invisible waves." Mané pointed at the feather. "Principle's the same here—invisible waves, a force you can't see."

After outsiders got used to Mané's regional tongue and accepted his bare feet, they began to feel that there was really no other way of talking about feathers. Everyone raved over Mané's charm and erudition disguised by his humble appearance, the bare feet and those foreign university T-shirts he liked to wear. This was, someone said, science in the guise of folklore.

CHAPTER 13: PILGRIM'S PROGRESS

IT TOOK MORE THAN SEVEN DAYS for Chico Paco to reach São Paulo. It took a week just to get a few hundred miles outside the Matacão and another to reach Brasilia. As Mané Pena had warned, the rainy season was the worst time to travel. Water and the red silt of the earth ran through the newly cut forest in open veins. All along the way, the roads were clotted with broken and stalled vehicles, tractors sinking in the mud, abandoned Volkswagen Beetles turned on their sides. Small groups of stranded passengers ran out in the rain from their stalled vehicles and waved down the moving vehicles. Chico Paco's bus quickly accumulated new passengers, their cargo, their animals—both living and dead, and their hopeless stories of the road. Chico Paco gave up his seat to an old lady and her chicken and sat in the crowded aisle until it was soon necessary to stand. It was common to get out to push or heave the bus from the gutted road or to walk up an incline rather than risk having the bus slip backward or into a ravine. It was necessary to do this in the rain, sometimes at intervals of only two or three miles. The poor but well-groomed passengers were soon caked and spattered with mud, and by the end of the trip, the outside of the bus was indistinguishable from the inside. Chico Paco felt as if he had, in fact, walked to Brasilia. When he could later compare taking the bus to walking this piece of God's earth, he often praised the virtues of walking and was apt to suggest this alternative to the stranded and wet travelers he met along the way.

When Kazumasa looked up from his paperwork, I immediately recognized Chico Paco. But to Kazumasa, this was just another muddy, green-eyed, dark-skinned, blonde northeasterner who wanted some of Kazumasa's lucky money to ease his suffering on earth. After so many months, Kazumasa continued to give away his money as a matter of course. It ceased to concern him whether or not people had legitimate requests. No matter what, Kazumasa smiled and listened carefully, thoughtfully. Although much of his fortune had been spent, there was, by Hiroshi's private estimates, a fortune to last a lifetime. Cousin Hiroshi, who would have been a business and economics student at the University of Keio, was an entrepreneur and investor par excellence. No matter how much money Kazumasa gave away and despite Hiroshi's harangues about Kazumasa's giving, Hiroshi was able to triple whatever remained, so there was virtually no end to it. Many people stopped referring to Kazumasa as the Japanese Santa Claus and began to call him the Japanese Robin Hood. It was, they said, just a more modern way of stealing from the rich and giving to the poor. Hiroshi himself explained the phenomenon to the press as "recycling capital." Kazumasa would not have thought of any of this. He was simply listening to people's stories and their desires, trying to figure out what it was that people wanted or should want out of life. After so many months, you would have thought that Kazumasa had finally gleaned something important from his research, but there we were, still listening when Chico Paco's turn in line came up.

"I'm looking for a particular woman and her child," said Chico Paco.

"I see," said Kazumasa, smiling understandingly but fearing immediately that this was one of those desires that money could not buy. Kazumasa was ready to put this request in the category he called Miracles, but Chico Paco insisted.

"Her name. The woman's name is Lourdes, and her son is called Rubens. I believe Rubens, the poor boy, is handicapped."

Kazumasa smiled and then, realizing that Chico Paco had spoken about Lourdes, was suddenly taken aback. "Lourdes?"

"Yes, this is the address I was given. I've been in this line for three days now," Chico Paco explained. He did not explain how he had also been lost in the city for another two days, taking buses and subways twisting around what seemed to him a dense concrete jungle, no different from the living jungle he had left behind, where the sun barely filters through a tight network of skyscrapers trapping a thick layer of carbon monoxide, electric and telephone wires grasping tenaciously at everything. "Everyone has said that you will be able to help me." Chico Paco's iridescent eyes glistened pleadingly.

For the first time in his life, Kazumasa felt a sudden twinge of something one might call, at this point, possessiveness. "Why?" he asked cautiously. "I mean, why do you want to find Lourdes?"

I knew that this Chico Paco was a young man, not even twenty perhaps, but Kazumasa could only see the mud on his feet and clothing. The men who went to Serra Pelada to dig for gold were all muddy, and perhaps this was the man, the husband that Lourdes had lost to that gold rush back in the eighties. It did not occur to Kazumasa that Chico Paco would have been a young boy, maybe Rubens's age in those days. Kazumasa looked at Chico Paco intently, not knowing what to think, what to hope for. He had not been very successful at making Lourdes happy, he thought. Money could not cure Rubens's paralysis, but at least, the boy was alive. That was something to be grateful for. He sighed.

Finally, Chico Paco produced Lourdes's crumpled letter and the faded photograph of Rubens, which Chico Paco had so often gazed upon before he dropped off to sleep. The photograph had become very important to him. It was a sign from God. It reminded him of his purpose. When he looked at the photograph before he fell asleep at night, he seemed to sleep better. He could then sleep with the memory of the boy on his mind but the picture of his friend, Gilberto, in his dreaming. The boy's face no longer superimposed itself on his dear friend, and Chico Paco felt at peace.

"Shiko Pako!" Kazumasa jumped up. "The prayers! Of course!"

People at the front of the line could hear the jubilant commotion.

"I told you," someone said. "It is him. It is the angel Chico Paco!" Pretty soon there was a great hubbub of people, and Kazumasa's sleepy charity line disintegrated in an excited mass of people repeating the suspicions of one bystander. "Didn't you see those green eyes? Who could forget them?" One woman began weeping joyously. "It is God's will!" she cried. "I prayed that I would be able to come to São Paulo from Rondônia to see the Japanese with the ball to ask for the money to buy an ice-cream cart. And I am here only fifth in line. Then, I prayed that if my prayer was granted, the angel Chico Paco should take my promise to the Matacão. And he is here!" The woman was close to fainting, and the people in line around her had to brace her up.

When Kazumasa appeared, smiling with Chico Paco, people followed us down the street to Kazumasa's apartment building. Ever since Kazumasa's sudden winning on the lottery, the building supervisor had had to double the guards at the door in order to keep eager people away from Kazumasa's apartment. We slipped past the guards, while the crowd clambered at the door. Kazumasa was used to this; he had to run from everyone, smiling and nodding every morning and evening. Lourdes found it easier to bring lunch down to Kazumasa at his office. Kazumasa nodded at Chico Paco, who could not help staring at me. "Nothing to worry," he assured Chico Paco. "People very friendly. Very friendly," he explained. "My friends."

When Chico Paco recognized the boy in the wheelchair, all of his doubts and confusion vanished. Here was the very boy, the vision of whom had been sent to Chico Paco on the Matacão. This was the magic of the God-given mind, greater than TV, as Mané Pena had said. Chico Paco stared carefully at Rubens. Better than a faded photograph was the boy himself, saved by a pigeon and a slow-moving truck full of rags. Everything about Rubens reminded Chico Paco of Gilberto. Despite the paralysis in his legs, Rubens was a restless child, always moving here and there in his wheelchair, his hands constantly occupied with some project or another, some curiosity, some prank to play. Gilberto had been the same way; he could not be without some activity. Chico Paco wondered what Gilberto must be doing now that he could walk, now that his legs could follow his hands and his mischievous mind. How many times had Chico Paco refused to carry Gilberto somewhere to perform some ridiculous task, like painting the old Turk's white horse with black stripes to resemble the zebras Gilberto admired in the movies, or agreeing to strap some handmade wings to Gilberto's back and throwing him off the edge of the dunes.

"I can't walk, Chiquinho," Gilberto explained. "But I will fly!"

"You're crazy. I won't be responsible for the death of a cripple like you!" Chico Paco had refused. Now he thought with amusement that the boy Rubens had even flown. Gilberto would be interested to hear this story.

In a matter of three days, Chico Paco announced that he was ready to return on foot to the Matacão to comply with Lourdes's promise to Saint George. In preparation for this trip, Lourdes bought him a pair of very sturdy boots, but Rubens had been preparing zealously for Chico Paco's trip as well. Rubens announced with determination, "I am going with Chico Paco."

"Don't be silly," Lourdes laughed.

"I will wheel alongside of him," he insisted.

"What are you talking about?"

"The pigeon and I are both going. I have feed for a month."

Hiroshi laughed, "I suppose you want to send the pigeon home from the Matacão?"

Kazumasa and I thought about this idea. It was an interesting one, but we knew Lourdes would not allow it.

Chico Paco smiled kindly at Rubens. "Your mother is right. It is not a trip for you. The rainy season is not over. I would have to carry you and your chair through the mud."

Rubens wanted to cry. "No one has done this before. My pigeon would be the first to travel from the Matacão. Perhaps you will take my pigeon with you and release him when you arrive?" He looked earnestly at Chico Paco.

"Well, if you trust me with your animal," Chico Paco hesitated, "I will try."

When the word spread that Chico Paco would be leaving for the Matacão on foot with a pigeon, Batista was immediately interested. "Tania," he said, "this idea of the boy's is brilliant.

Of course, he needs to send more birds than just one. It's a treacherous trip for animals. You can't expect all of them to make it. We have some birds who can make it, no doubt."

"Maybe we can help him out. Send more birds. A dozen."

"Chico Paco can't carry and care for all these cages filled with birds. He will never make it to the Matacão."

"Well then, someone should go with him. Maybe go ahead in a truck."

"Tania Cidinha!" Batista kissed his wife. "Of course!"

In a week, Batista had arranged for a truck, loaded his birds, kissed his wife and mother-in-law good-bye, and as the truck pulled away, zealously watched the figure of Tania Aparecida in the truck's rear-view mirror until she was a small speck. A flood of doubt welled up in his heart as he turned the corner. "Leaving that woman behind may be a great mistake." He shook his head and almost turned back.

Over the radio, Batista heard the news about Chico Paco's progress. Chico Paco had already left several days before with a small crowd of people, who stuffed his pockets with money for the trip, the names and addresses of relatives and friends along the way, and notes filled with other promises to be fulfilled by this same walk. A jeep with the words "Praise the Lord" and "Living Moments in Sainthood" also followed slowly behind. A reporter rode or walked alongside of Chico Paco with a microphone and a tape recorder, interviewing Chico Paco as he walked toward the Matacão. It was this radio show that Batista listened to in his truck. Chico Paco was in Ouro Prêto today. It would not be long before Batista and his pigeons would overtake the walking angel.

CHAPTER 14: KARAOKE

"Karaoke is a style of nightclub invented by the Japanese. It generally consists of a sound system with a stage, lights and microphones, with a sophisticated video system to boot. This sound system creates an entire orchestra for a myriad of selected popular songs. The sound can be controlled to move up or down to any octave, according to the needs of the amateur singer. The sound is accompanied by a video with some appropriate story line—lovers walking, smoking, arguing, gazing longingly, etc., a sort of mood commercial to go with the song—and under all this are the words of the song printed in the language of your choice. You choose a song from a selected menu, grab the mike, read the libretto on the video and sing, accompanied by a full-bodied orchestra. An operator adjusts the sound and the octave to your voice, and suddenly you are Frank Sinatra or Dionne Warwick. At the end of the evening, your waiter hands you a bill for your drinks and your songs."

INEVITABLY KAZUMASA BECAME DISILLUSIONED with the charity business, but not because people took advantage of him or because they were greedy or because they lied. Despite his innocence about human nature and character, he did not believe that people were or should be perfect. With me in the way, he could not, even if he wanted to, have a vision of perfection. Everyone he met had something missing, some part of them that needed filling in. A lack of character was no different from a physical lacking. What disillusioned Kazumasa was that, given the opportunity to imagine happiness, people could only imagine things, and so many of the things they imagined were basic to their well-being: food, shelter, clothing, medicine, health care. He gave to everyone, from the poor beggar on the street to the big foundations, hospitals and schools. No matter who they were, they all had to stand in Kazumasa's charity line. The need was so great, so big and so deep that it boggled the imagination. It was a great crime that so many came to swindle a kind man's goodwill, but it was a bigger crime that so many were in so much need. The list of people who required miracles got longer and longer and longer until Kazumasa began to feel the hopelessness of a wealthy man whose giving was eternal and, therefore, whose vision of suffering would also be eternal.

Hiroshi was incapable of allowing Kazumasa's fortune to dwindle away to the predictable nothing, the absolute zero that Kazumasa envisioned. This money that came out of a poor people's dreams should thus return to those very dreams, but Hiroshi did not see it that way. He learned very quickly that great wealth generates greater wealth, that the stakes were greater and the returns greater yet. There was a greater lottery, an international lottery that could turn thousands into millions and millions into billions. Without knowing it, Kazumasa began slowly to have international holdings, real estate in Tokyo and New York, hotel chains, entire islands with all their flora and fauna, stocks in everything from computers to cars to chips and clips. Hiroshi had even invested Kazumasa's money in those computerized balls that measure railroad track wear. All of this was unknown to Kazumasa, who asked Hiroshi wearily from time to time, "When will it be done?"

"Not yet. Not yet," was always the reply.

Back on the Matacão, it was J. B. Tweep who, with one hand on the GGG stockholder reports, another flipping through the current issue of *Forbes* and another massaging the handle of his morning coffee cup, noticed the name Kazumasa Ishimaru. He eyed the blurred picture in *Forbes* of Kazumasa, who seemed swept up in the throngs of a Brazilian carnival. I'd never been very photogenic myself, and I was slightly hidden from view and blended in unattractively with the grey background. J.B. clipped the page and read the blurb on Kazumasa: "An obscure Japanese immigrant known to have a strange personal satellite the size of a golf ball whizzing inches from his forehead, probably some sort of bogus invention intended to complete the eccentricity of this man who, since making his great fortune on the Brazilian lotteries, now calls Brazil his home." But the thing that really concerned J.B. was the notice in the GGG Enterprises quarterly report that showed that Kazumasa was now GGG's major stockholder.

All of this would have come as an enormous surprise to Kazumasa, who only thought that Hiroshi dabbled in the karaoke business. Kazumasa was particularly fond of karaoke, and he often took me out to bob and sing for an evening at one of Hiroshi's hotspots. You might have thought that Kazumasa was a shy sort, hardly given to singing on stage in smoky bars to tipsy audiences, but karaoke is after all a sport for the shy—those closet, or rather, shower performers who let it all out while sudsing and rinsing. Where else could you belt out a song with a full orchestra into a mike with its reverb set to match the acoustics of your tiled shower? Despite Kazumasa's fondness for karaoke, it was not always easy to sneak out and sing incognito with a ball obviously pointing at your nose. Even though we were often mistaken for one of those who wore the artificial balls attached by transparent headbands, people would invariably rush up to Kazumasa's table and form a charity line. To assuage this problem and to feed Kazumasa's hunger for karaoke, Hiroshi had a shower stall built with a waterproof karaoke system, stereo, mike, video and all. Every morning, Lourdes could hear us singing. Depending on the choice of songs, she knew how Kazumasa was feeling and even what he might like to eat that day. In time, Hiroshi successfully glutted the market with karaoke shower stalls.

In the beginning, Hiroshi's karaoke business was confined to three small bars in São Paulo. But after awhile, they began to sprout up like hamburger stands. The neon signs scrawled in deep blue with the words "HIRO'S KARAOKE" popped into the evening sky in major cities like Rio, Belo Horizonte, Salvador, Recife, Manaus and moved on to Buenos Aires, Santiago, Lima, Bogotá and Mexico City. Hiroshi sold the karaoke bars as franchises, and pretty soon, almost every town in South America had one. People burst from their showers to sing.

Kazumasa was very proud of his cousin's success and envious of Hiroshi's obvious happiness with his new business, but he could not, for his part, find happiness in his self-proposed career. It was beginning to feel much like traveling around in the Tokyo Yamanote circular train again. The sad stories began to run together, everyone getting off at the same stops with the same desires. Every day, we passed the same suffering. The depression of these stories began to show in Kazumasa's face. "When will it be over?" he asked Hiroshi every day, but Hiroshi was merciless.

"Not yet. Not yet."

When Kazumasa's holdings in GGG Enterprises hit 50 percent, J. B. Tweep decided to call the eccentric Japanese with the personal satellite. Kazumasa and I nodded on the phone.

"Mr. Ishimaru," J.B. spoke from the Matacão. "This is J. B. Tweep from GGG Enterprises. I'm—," J.B. paused. What was he this week? "er, Vice President of our International Division, and since we're both on the same end of the hemisphere, I figured you might be interested in taking a short hop up here to see what we're about."

Kazumasa hesitated. He had no idea what GGG Enterprises could possibly be. He figured they must be some foundation in need. "Please Mr. J.B.," Kazumasa answered politely. "I know it is a long way, but to be fair, everyone must stand in line. I am here every day. If you don't need a miracle, I'm sure I can do my best to help you."

J.B. looked at the phone. It was not a bad connection; it was the Japanese's odd Portuguese. "Yes, well, we don't need a miracle of any sort, Mr. Ishimaru. We are on very sound ground. As you know, we're up 11 percent this week and climbing. Your investment is in good hands." J.B. examined the nails on one of his three hands.

Kazumasa and I nodded again. "Mr. J.B., you make a mistake. I don't invest. I give my money. I trust you completely."

"Yes, yes," J.B. nodded too. "I understand your way of doing business. Some people just watch those numbers, but since you now play such a large and critical financial role, I suppose it is incumbent upon us, as well as you, to develop a relationship, don't you agree?"

Kazumasa thought about this.

"Now I know you're a busy man, but I'm proposing to send down our private plane. You name the time and date, and a vehicle will be there to pick you up. It's the least GGG can do, Mr. Ishimaru."

That is how Kazumasa and I left São Paulo for the Matacão. Lourdes saw us wistfully to the elevator. "Please take care, Seu Kazumasa," she said softly. "Don't you worry about anything. We will take care of everything here just fine. And please come back soon," she added.

Kazumasa looked at her with his kind eyes. Suddenly, it was hard to leave for some reason. He looked beyond me at Lourdes, her dark shining eyes pressed upon him with all the love she could muster. What was it about this woman? He nodded at her and smiled warmly. Hiroshi was a lucky man, he thought. He knew Hiroshi was in love with Lourdes. She and Hiroshi would be very happy together. Kazumasa still could not see that all Lourdes's love was meant for him. Something tugged at his heart, the sweet sadness of feeling another person's joy. He missed Lourdes already.

"Seu Kazumasa," Lourdes said breathlessly because she could wait no longer for this man to come to his senses, but the elevator door closed and parted us for the time being.

CHAPTER 15: PRENDAS DOMESTICAS

TANIA APARECIDA WATCHED HER HUSBAND Batista leave with a mixed feeling of longing and relief—longing because Batista was the epitome of Brazilian good looks and charm, and relief because he would not be around for a while to follow her every movement with a tenacious and jealous eye. She could go out with her friends, take in a movie, visit her sister in another town, drink and laugh with abandon, enjoy the looks and stares of other men without having to justify anything to Batista. If they wanted to look, if they liked looking, what was it to her? If she were an ugly witch, then who would look? Surely not Batista. Why did he have to make such a big deal about every little thing, as if she were some sort of prostitute lifting her skirts so that anyone could see? She was a respectably married woman. Was it her fault if she was also attractive? She didn't go around making a scene whenever some silly woman came along and made eyes at her Batista. She didn't blame Batista even though he smiled too. She just gave the other woman a cold look that cut her off. What was the point of making a scene, of blaming Batista if he were handsome? And he was so handsome, her Batista. Tania Aparecida sighed. She missed Batista, but she was not going to let his absence spoil her vacation from him.

In the meantime, Batista was on the road with Chico Paco. Sometimes he drove ahead and waited for Chico Paco to catch up. Sometimes he stayed behind, biding his time with a bottle of beer in some corner bar, feeding and watering his birds, exchanging small talk with the locals who also dabbled in pigeons.

After awhile, Batista preferred to be ahead or behind Chico Paco, who always brought crowds and tumult to the sleepy towns and hamlets. People who never left the shade of their front porches or the fabricated world of their nightly soap operas were bound to come out to see the walking angel, the keeper of promises. They showered him with gifts of food and drink, and there was no lack of sheltered places to lay his sleepy golden head. The "Praise the Lord" radio station faithfully followed him from town to town. They got into every story, every miracle, every blessing that a town could produce. All along Chico Paco's route, people listened for his coming and told stories of his passing.

And along the same route, every few hundred miles or so, Batista released a pigeon with a message, carefully noting its name and time and place of release. Tania Aparecida and her mother had strict instructions to watch for these birds, to note their time of arrival and their condition after flight. It was all very scientific. Batista did not want to miss a thing. These flights were historic in nature. Everything must be carefully documented.

Tania Aparecida left these details up to her mother Dona Gloria, whose affection and pigeon-mothering was beyond reproach. Despite whatever Batista might have thought of his mother-in-law in the past, he could never have found a more caring pigeon keeper. Dona Gloria knew all of the pigeons by name. She knew their histories and parentage, remembered their birthdays and had her favorites. Some pigeon could always be found nestled in her hair or on her shoulders, or if she were reclined, snuggled warmly in her bosom. She carried the young ones in her apron pockets, took the sick ones to her home, and talked what Tania Aparecida called "pigeon talk" all day long.

While Dona Gloria tended the pigeons, Tania Aparecida kept the records, haggled over the price of feed, and did the bookkeeping. It was Tania Aparecida who set up a breeding program to sell a line of potential prizewinners. It was Tania Aparecida who set the fees for mating prizewinners. It was Tania Aparecida who set up the concession stands on the street on weekends to sell pigeon cages and Batista's special feed, which brought in a nice profit. It was Tania Aparecida who furnished the information for the *Pigeon Messenger*—a weekly pamphlet that listed the famous pigeon messages, their possible meanings and the people who benefited from them—in return for free advertising and a small consulting fee. And it was Tania Aparecida who put their winnings from pigeon flights into the *poupança*—a money market that pays interest while promising to keep up with inflation.

In the beginning, of course, there was not a great deal of money, but it was enough that Batista no longer had to work as a dispatcher. Tania Aparecida discovered that she liked to haggle over prices, to make deals and even to watch the inflation index. Compared to washing clothing, cooking and sewing, this was so much better.

It was Tania Aparecida's idea, therefore, that great money was to be had in the pigeon business. Unlike Batista, who was really an enthusiast and sportsman, Tania began to see pigeons as a profitable source of income. With Batista away, Tania Aparecida's mind began to wander to new ideas. She toyed with a bar of sweet-smelling soap that had the impression of a dove pressed into its oval shape. Within the week, Tania had put on her very best dress and shoes and matching purse and was knocking at the door of the Pomba Soap Company.

When an enormous truck filled with more pigeons—the words "Djapan Pigeons Incorporated" and "Pomba for Lovely Clean Skin" painted across it—drove up behind Batista, he was already approaching the Matacão. Chico Paco was about a week behind, walking in the rain, and Batista just wanted to get his remaining batch of pigeons to the Matacão and into some dry place. He had hoped that the timing would be better and that he would be able to release his pigeons upon arrival at the Matacão. But if the rain did not stop, he would have to wait. He thought he would wait at least until Chico Paco made it to the Matacão. He had an idea that it would be a special event to send the pigeons off just as Chico Paco arrived. God willing, it would be a sunny day.

Batista squinted through the rain at the truck in wonder, unable to acknowledge his own name painted across its side. Two men got out and sauntered up to Batista importantly. "Seu Batista?" they asked.

Batista nodded.

"Dona Tania sent us."

"Tania Cidinha? Has she gone out of her mind?" Batista surveyed the truck full of pigeons. "Where did she get all these birds?" he cried.

"We did our best, Seu Batista," one of the men assured Batista. "Not a one of them is dead. Dona Tania said you'd confirm it."

"We've been giving it the gas, and if it weren't for this rain, we would've caught up sooner."

Batista scratched his head in confusion. "What do I need with another truckload of pigeons?" he asked.

"Well, sir," said one of the men. "The way Dona Tania explained it to me, it's what they call a joint venture. See now, look at this." He went to the cab of the truck and pulled out a handful of tiny pigeon-carrier tubes from a large box.

Batista took a tube from the handful, opened and unwound the tiny message. He read, "Pomba for Lovely Clean Skin?"

"They all say that," said the other man.

"Pigeon advertising," nodded the other. "Dona Tania invented it."

Batista read Tania Aparecida's letter that came with the shipment of pigeons: "Batista, honey, how I miss you. Mother and I have been very busy. You can check your release times but Gugu came in at 2:30 PM on Tuesday the 4th, and Kaka came in at 6:00 AM the next day. Well, to get to the point, I met Sr. Carlos Rodrigues, who owns the Pomba Soap Company. What a cute old man!" (Batista cringed.) "Well, he really liked the idea. I mean, really, it's very brilliant. He is sure to sell more soap than anybody else. Imagine people all over Brazil will get the message about Pomba Soap. We got a very nice commission, you know, and a year's worth of Pomba soap. What do you think? Kisses and hugs, your Tania Cidinha." (Batista pulled at his hair. What was that woman doing anyway? You just don't go and make a deal with one of the largest soap companies in the country!) "P.S.: Good news! Gigeta's Pizzas and Hiro's Karaoke want an account with us. Anyone who finds a pigeon with a message gets a free pizza or a night at Hiro's! More later."

CHAPTER 16: THE MATACÃO

> They wept like anything to see
> Such quantities of sand:
> 'If this were only cleared away,'
> They said 'it would be grand!'
> 'If seven maids with seven mops
> Swept it for half a year,
> Do you suppose,' the Walrus said,
> 'That they could get it clear?'
>   — LEWIS CARROLL
>   *Through the Looking Glass*

SINCE EVERYONE IN THIS STORY seems somehow headed for the Matacão, perhaps it would be appropriate to stop for a moment and discuss it. I don't claim to be an expert on the Matacão, but I did gather some interesting facts.

The Matacão has been, since its dis-covering, a source of curiosity and confusion in the scientific world. Geologists, astronomers, physicists, archaeologists and chemists were suddenly thrown into an unsettling prerevolutionary state where the basic parameters of scientific truths were undergoing a shift similar to that experienced when Einstein redefined the Newtonian world. Nowadays, scientists cannot present papers or new findings without having to answer the now-common retort, "But what bearing does the Matacão have on your findings?" or "How do you reconcile your hypothesis with the Matacão?"

How or why the Matacão came about is a puzzle for which no clear answers exist. The speculations about its origins have been as varied as the people who came to visit, gasp, grovel, get a tan, pray, relax, study, wonder, hang out, make love, worship, meditate, or pay homage to its existence.

In one comprehensive survey, 18 percent of the people questioned believed that the Matacão was the creation of a highly sophisticated ancient civilization that inhabited the area thousands of years ago. This fraction believed that the Matacão, once penetrated, would produce one of the greatest treasures of ancient civilization. Another 9 percent of those surveyed believed that the Matacão was the result of a hot molten substance within the earth that had managed to seep into the upper layers of the its crust.

A mere 3 percent believed the Matacão was the work of the CIA, that it was one of a number of air bases hidden in the tropical forest for staging short-range raids into Central America and exporting arms to fallen dictators and terrorist freedom-fighters.

About 13 percent believed that the Matacão was a miracle from God, the great foundation for a great church or a new Vatican, while another 11 percent believed that the Matacão possessed supernatural powers, not necessarily from a single God, but beyond the ordinary realm of human reason or contemporary science. Those of the supernatural bent believed that unknown powers that were life-giving and rejuvenating emanated from the Matacão, and that these powers could be

used to benefit humanity or to wreak havoc, depending on who
was able to harness them. Of course, many of this latter group
felt that the powers of the feather were only the tip of the ice-
berg. A few expressed genuine concern that the free world
should maintain control of the Matacão.

But the largest group, 33 percent, believed that the Matacão
was of an extraterrestrial nature, a sort of runway prepared for
the arrival of aliens. Of these, about half believed that the aliens
were of a friendly or benign nature, while the other half believed
that military precautions were necessary to prevent invasion.
An insignificant number were undecided, and the rest had never
heard of the Matacão.

Numerous public and private entities other than GGG Enterprises were funding a variety of scientific research projects
on the Matacão. The Brazilian Ministry of the Interior had to
create a department to keep track of the projects and to act as a
intermediary for overlapping projects. In order to keep a tab on
these findings, the government had created a series of legal requirements and official documents to keep the wealth and value
of the Matacão within its control. This, in fact, contributed to
a growing system of favors and outright graft associated with
getting concessions to study areas of the Matacão. Still, a number of congressional members were beginning to argue for
greater restrictions on the use and study of the Matacão. Brazil
had once before emptied its wealthy gold mines into the coffers
of the Portuguese Crown and consequently financed the Industrial Revolution in England. This time, if there was any wealth
to be had, it had better remain in Brazil. Some scoffed at the
pretensions of certain congresspersons, saying that the treasure of the Matacão might, at best, make a small dent in their
continuing interest payments to the International Monetary
Fund.

A few of these research studies actually did produce some
significant findings. One study, after 5,381 hours of human input and 3,379 hours of computer output, was able to reproduce
the complex molecular structure of the Matacão's material
composition. The computer was completely straightforward
in proclaiming the nature of the material: "NHCOO linkages

indicate rigid, tightly bound polymer. Polyurethane family commonly known as plastic."

Another study was finally able to arrive at a method of penetrating or cutting through the Matacão's rigid plastic. It involved a complicated combination of laser cutting with amino acids and other chemical compounds. When the process was refined, a core sample was extricated from the Matacão. It was discovered that the Matacão was a solid piece of plastic. This agreed with sonar information, which revealed a continuous block of plastic five feet deep. Subsequent tests showed that this plastic material was virtually indestructible, a substance harder than stainless steel — or diamonds, for that matter. This news excited the NASA researchers who were naturally at the forefront of these studies, anxious to find new materials for their space vehicles. This was a breakthrough tantamount to Teflon. Some people even believed that the Matacão *was* Teflon.

There was, however, one significant but unaccounted-for property of this highly rigid polymer: it was for some reason magnetic. That would be the only explanation for the fact that Chico Paco's altar to Saint George stuck to the Matacão. However, no one was certain what substances the Matacão attracted. Scientists studied with great care the nature of the strange altar and its physical properties in order to ascertain what caused the altar to "glue" itself to the Matacão. They discovered that Chico Paco had gathered an enormous amount of iron refuse, nails, aluminum cans, plastic wrappings and plastic containers from a garbage dump. He had filled a large base with all this trash, which he, in turn, melted down into a solid mass with a welding torch. The combination of these materials, in fact, simulated the physical structure of the Matacão itself, creating a magnetic attraction that proved irresistible. Of course, most people still held the belief that Saint George's altar was a miracle sent to Earth by the saint himself.

All of these findings were presented in an atmosphere charged with excitement and arguments. Where did the Matacão originally come from? How did it get there? What enormous force could possibly have been present in the Amazon

Forest, other than decay, to mold such a perfect block of plastic? How was it possible that plastic could have magnetic properties? What did such an enormous magnet near the equator mean to the Earth? to the Earth's gravitational pull in the solar system? to sunspots? to ecological systems in the forest? to human civilization? to extraterrestrial life in the universe? to the apocalypse? The questions seemed endless and fraught with speculation and wonder and outright fear.

Of course, the area surrounding the Matacão had been in question ever since international ecological groups discovered that the Amazon Forest was enormously photogenic and made beautiful calendars. Then, there had been that debate in the late eighties and early nineties about holes in the Earth's ozone layer and the greenhouse effect. In those days, everyone, whether they understood anything about it, seemed to blame Brazil for burning down the forest and replacing oxygen-producing plant life with roaming cattle and carbon dioxide. The big problem, people said, was that Brazil hadn't asked permission to destroy the Earth. But who had? At one time, there were as many "save the rain forest" groups as there were *lambada* clubs in L.A. and New York. People were madly grinding their loins in that lascivious dance and gasping and moaning about the dying forest thousands of miles away. Never mind the poor homeless forest people, the Indians in extinction, and most of the species of life on Earth. What about the air? But like *lambada,* all that became passé; the emergence of the Matacão changed everything.

Still, the forest itself continued to attract interest. Teams of researchers with sophisticated measuring equipment, cameras, tape recorders, nylon tents, machetes, insect repellant, dictionaries, dried food and native guides were constantly bumping into each other while contemplating the canopy. There were also teams of tourists looking for the tropical paradise, the opportunity to swing on vines, wear orchids over their ears, slide down cataracts into cool pools, hold monkeys on their shoulders and teach parrots to speak in English, French, German or Japanese. These safaris became so numerous that a series of outposts were established at key locations. Tourists soon discovered for themselves what Mané Pena and his family had felt in their guts, that the Amazon Forest was a great decaying hothouse where all sustenance was sucked up immediately by the voracious flora and fauna, leaving nothing for the poor soil. This did not make the forest uninteresting, but after three days of 218 species of mosquito and other swarming insects; of tarantulas, foot worms and itching welts; of trudging through an enormous sauna in drenched clothing; of poisonous snakes and 35-foot anacondas; of sloshing through streams harboring piranhas, alligators, electric eel and giant catfish known for devouring entire arms and legs; of competing with monkeys, toucans and fungi for forest fruit—after all that, the outposts presented to many a tired traveler the inestimable pleasures of a shower, an air-conditioned bar, a hamburger and a coke. The franchise owners who managed a series of these outposts, called "Bromeliads" (named for the tropical plant that can draw sustenance from a leafy water cup filled with dead matter), found that they could charge just about any price for things as common as toilet paper, a bar of soap or a cube of ice.

There was, however, discovered in one region, about seventy-two kilometers outside the Matacão, an area which resembled an enormous parking lot, filled with aircraft and vehicles of every sort of description. The planes and cars had been abandoned for several decades, and the undergrowth and overgrowth of the criss-crossing lianas had completely engulfed everything. On one end of the field, a number of the vehicles seemed to be slipping into a large pit of grey, sticky goop, a major component of which was discovered to be napalm.

One of the many safaris, this one made up of entomologists, had mistakenly discovered this metal cemetery while chasing after only one of several thousand rare forms of butterfly. The machines found all dated back to the late fifties and early sixties—F-86 Sabres, F-4 Phantoms, Huey Cobras, Lear Jets and Piper Cubs, Cadillacs, Volkswagens, Dodges and an assorted mixture of gas-guzzlers, as well as military jeeps and Red Cross ambulances. After so many years in the forest, the vehicles were slowly crumbling, piece by piece, bit by bit, into a fine rusty dust. Occasionally, a loud clanging noise echoed up into the arching trees, scattering the parakeets and sending a family of monkeys screeching into a panic. But it was only the door of a '63 Plymouth banging off its hinges into the Thunderbird parked next to it or the rotor of a helicopter bouncing off the roof of a camouflaged jeep.

The shiny bumpers from some of the cars had been torn away, and most of the rear-view and side-view mirrors had been stripped from the cars. This would account for the curious use of reflective materials in the masks, headpieces and necklaces of some Indian tribes. It would also account for the odd tales and primitive drawings left by Indians, which has led to the intense debate about whether these Indians had in fact had contact with extraterrestrial life, that is, UFOs, or whether flying objects and moving vehicles could be classified as archetypes of the unconscious. Meanwhile, some anthropologist ran about frantically re-editing and annotating a soon-to-be-published article about the primitive use of mirrors in ancient religious rites.

What was most interesting about the discovery of the rain forest parking lot was the way in which nature had moved to accommodate and make use of it. The entomologists were shocked to discover that their rare butterfly only nested in the vinyl seats of Fords and Chevrolets and that their exquisite reddish coloring was actually due to a steady diet of hydrated ferric oxide, or rusty water.

There was also discovered a new species of mouse, with prehensile tails, that burrowed in the exhaust pipes of all the vehicles. These mice had developed suction cups on their feet that allowed them to crawl up the slippery sides and bottoms of the aircraft and cars. The color pattern on their bodies was impressive; the females sported a splotchy green-and-brown coat, while the males wore shiny coats of chartreuse, silver and taxi yellow. The mice were found to have extremely high levels of lead and arsenic in their blood and fat from feeding on chipped paint, yet they seemed to be immune to these poisons. Most animals who happened to feed on these mice were instantly killed, except for a new breed of bird, a cross between a vulture and a condor, that nested on propellers and pounced on the mice as they scurried out of exhaust pipes.

Finally, there was a new form of air plant, or epiphyte, which attached itself to the decaying vehicles and produced brownish sacklike flowers. The rare butterflies and other insects, attracted to ferric oxide, fell prey to these carnivorous flowers; slipping down into those brown sacks, they were digested in a matter of minutes.

There were, along with these new forms of a life, a myriad of traditional varieties of flora and fauna that had somehow found a home, a food source or way of life in this exclusive junkyard. It was an ecological experiment unparalleled in the known world of nature. One of the more exciting studies being undertaken was the documentation of the social behavior of a tribe of monkeys that had established territory in the carcasses of the bomber planes and their relation to a second tribe whose territory was decidedly the fossil remains of former gas-guzzling automotive monsters. A number of monkeys' skulls were found riddled with machine-gun bullets, which gave credence to the theory that the tribe established in the bombers had somehow triggered the mechanisms that led to their omnipotence in the monkey world. All this was naturally being documented in the authoritative and measured tones of NHK, PBS and BBC.

In the meantime, back on the Matacão, human life was adapting itself to the vast plastic mantle in ways as unexpected as those found in the rain forest parking lot and as expected as the great decaying and rejuvenating ecology of the Amazon Forest itself. A number of travel agencies had found it lucrative to expand their activities to include the promotion and sponsoring of events on the Matacão. The Ringling Brothers Circus had already come and performed on the Matacão, as had the Peking Acrobats and the Shakespearean Summer Festival of Kansas City. There had also been a Live Aid event with at least 100 big-name entertainers to raise money for the victims of nuclear fallout in Nevada, Utah and Arizona. The World Hockey play-offs were scheduled to be played on the Matacão this year, and there was even talk of having the skating events of the Winter Olympics on the Matacão. And the Pope himself had chosen to meet his South American flock on the Matacão. The place where he had kissed the surface, easily identifiable by the indelible smudge of his lips, not unlike an impression on a glass or mirror, was now permanently encircled by a decorative wreath.

There were, of course, smaller events of less than international significance: Candomblé affairs and the wild, exuberant presence of African gods, weddings, folk-dancing, operas, stand-up comedy, scenes provided for daily television soap operas, prayer meetings, magic shows, intrigues. Many couples claimed that they had experienced love at first sight on the Matacão. One mother and father decided to have their baby born there, while an old woman insisted on fasting there to complete the cycle of her life on what she considered sacred ground. The Matacão had become a stage for life and death.

Part IV:
Loss of Innocence

CHAPTER 17: THE BALL

UPON ARRIVING at the Matacão, the tug on me was so strong that Kazumasa had difficulty at first in securing his balance. After several hours, he found himself plagued by pains in his neck and a splitting headache. In the early days, when we first arrived in Brazil and while traveling the Brazilian trains in the north, we had experienced a similar sensation of being jerked inexplicably in one direction or another. But this had never lasted for any period of time, and as the train sped on, the sensation disappeared altogether. We could never account for this problem; it was not due to track wear. Kazumasa supposed it to be one of the quirks of my otherwise good-natured personality. A ball cannot be expected to be perfect—round, but not perfect. But here, near the Matacão, Kazumasa felt me jerking in a direction opposite the one in which he wished to direct himself, his head yanked around by some odd force.

Kazumasa confessed his discomfort to J. B. Tweep, who had personally gone up to the heliport on the roof of GGG headquarters to meet him. We should have realized that something was wrong when J.B. had to grab Kazumasa and physically push him inside the building to prevent us from falling off the building. J.B. thought Kazumasa was just a little off-balance, nodded understandingly and calmly tossed Kazumasa's concerns aside. "Probably jet lag," he remarked matter-of-factly. But after escorting Kazumasa into a room in a plush hotel on the north end of the Matacão and having to grab the Japanese with all three arms to prevent him from tumbling over the balcony overlooking the vast plain, both J.B. and Kazumasa realized my undeniable attraction to the large slab.

"This is first time has ever happened," said Kazumasa feverishly. "Only other time, I feel something like it when working in Pará, but I thought it was because no sleep."

J.B. nodded, "Pará? Is that so?" J.B. took a feather out of his pocket and rubbed it over his ear with one of his hands. "What do you think is going to happen if you go down there to the Matacão?" J.B. asked.

Kazumasa sighed and pressed his lips together. He imagined

himself with his face plastered to the floor of the Matacão and me, his ball, hugging what he imagined to be my true mother. Here then was a force greater than himself, Kazumasa, my lifelong friend and brother. Kazumasa wanted to cry. He had often thought of himself as my mother or father or closest earthly relation. He felt crushed at the suggestion that I had a family of my own that, having been attached to Kazumasa, I had been denied all these years. Kazumasa suddenly felt guilty. Of course, I should be allowed to join other material of my own kind. It was only just. Kazumasa stood up resolutely and said, "Mr. J.B., I must go down there. It is my duty."

J.B., too, stood up with alarm, setting his body and three arms squarely between Kazumasa and the open balcony. "Now, Mr. Ishimaru, let's be reasonable."

Kazumasa ignored J.B.'s ridiculous stance before the open balcony and said, "Mr. J.B., you will accompany me down the elevator. You will be my witness. Whatever happens, you let my cousin Hiroshi in São Paulo know. I remove you from any responsibility."

"But, but, I don't understand. What on earth do you mean by 'your duty'?" protested J.B.

"Perhaps there is great reason for my coming to Brazil and to this Matacão," answered Kazumasa. "Perhaps this is moment of truth. This," Kazumasa pointed to me, "is not ordinary ball."

"Well, I'm well aware of that," said J.B. "But I can think of a number of reasons why going down there might be dangerous."

"I'm not afraid of danger," said Kazumasa.

"Well, if not dangerous, then, complicated, embarrassing!" exclaimed J.B.

At that Kazumasa sat down. Together, they examined all the possibilities of what might happen once Kazumasa was actually on the Matacão, everything from the possibility that I would be permanently torn from Kazumasa's sphere of influence to the possibility that Kazumasa might be flung bodily into the Matacão, crushing his skull in an untimely death. The physical, psychological and social damages might be irreparable.

"You don't have to go down there," J.B. asserted. "Think of it this way: Your ball's obvious attraction to the Matacão is something that should be studied. We can't subject you to some unknown danger. You and your ball might be the key to a lot of unanswered questions!" J.B. was getting excited as he spoke. "Didn't you say you felt this way in Pará?" This time, J.B. stood up. "Think of it! There may be other uncovered Matacãos! That's it! You've got to discover them, Mr. Ishimaru! Your ball knows!" J.B. threw up all three of his arms in genuine excitement.

"My ball knows." Kazumasa smiled, even as he had to grab the sofa to stay seated.

J.B. sent down for several rolls of sturdy velcro and a bottle of aspirin. He velcroed Kazumasa to the sofa and poured him a drink. Even then, we were being pulled with the sofa imperceptibly toward the Matacão. I felt sorry for Kazumasa, but there was nothing I could do.

"Well," said J.B. "This will do for the time being, but we really have to find some other accommodations for you, Mr. Ishimaru, farther away from the Matacão. My people are looking into it right now. I wonder how far away you must be to be comfortable?" J.B. pulled out a silver case in the smart shape of a paper clip. "Well, Mr. Ishimaru, these are really unforeseen circumstances, but I had intended to present you with this." He gave the silver paper-clip case engraved with the letters GGG to the velcroed Kazumasa.

Kazumasa opened the case. Inside was a rare tanager feather. The light glistened off it in iridescent shades of black and blue.

"That's what we're about," J.B. nodded proudly. "We captured the market, and no one can match us. We've anticipated everything. Cases, accessories, post-yuppie tastes. We've been studying this very carefully. We're the best. Now, that is the top of the line, for the more affluent customer, you understand. But we've got a sort of "Bic" line, you might say. We sell it in a shiny package, very chic, but less expensive, and by the pack. We're also looking into a line of disposable stuff using dyed chicken feathers."

Kazumasa nodded carefully, the pain in his head still throbbing. He thought the feather was beautiful, but he did not understand what it was for. He had seen the commercials on tele-

vision with the beautiful women and the handsome men casually enjoying themselves in different posh situations with feathers
held elegantly like antique fans. He noticed that Hiroshi had
been given to taking out a feather from time to time and rubbing
it inconsequentially behind his ear while he enjoyed Lourdes's
coffee after dinner.

The phone rang, and J.B. picked it up with his third hand.
"Sheik who?" he asked the phone. "One of Mané's friends? Ah.
Well, I see." J.B. nodded. From the balcony window, we could
hear the roar of a growing crowd of people from below. J.B. ran
to the balcony in time to see the Matacão flood with a great mass
of people. They ran around and pressed upon a single man at the
center of the commotion. When the crowd was just below the
balcony, J.B. could see from above that the man at the center
was blonde and seemed to be carrying a cage of some sort. The
man was Chico Paco, just arrived from his long pilgrimage from
São Paulo for the promise of a small crippled boy named
Rubens. Suddenly, Chico Paco was lifted on the arms of crowd
into the air, and the whole mass of humanity seemed to sail
away in smooth waves above the Matacão toward the distant
shrine of Saint George.

J.B. returned to the living room where Kazumasa and I were
still velcroed tightly to the sofa. He turned on the television, and
we watched the commotion on the Matacão with great interest.
"That is Shiko Pako," nodded Kazumasa. "He arrived safe!"

"You know him?"

"Yes. He brings prayers from Lourdes for her son Rubens.
Rubens, a very nice boy."

"Rubens?"

"Yes. Rubens fell from window. Fourteen floors." Kazumasa
made a ducking motion with his head and let me fall symbolical-
ly fourteen floors to demonstrate. Then with his free hands, he
showed the truck catching the falling boy. "A miracle from
Saint George, Lourdes is convinced." Kazumasa concluded.

The reporter on the television concluded the same thing, only
that it was a much greater miracle. They said Rubens had become crippled from falling out of the window of an apartment
house; that the boy, playing with other children, got left behind

in a truck full of rags, which drove out of the city; that the frantic mother Lourdes prayed to Saint George; that she promised the angel Chico Paco would walk to the Matacão if her prayers were answered; and that Rubens was suddenly cured and miraculously walked all the way home, 18 kilometers from the Freguesia do Ó.

Kazumasa scratched his head. "I don't understand." It was true. Kazumasa really didn't. It was hard to follow the fast talk on newscasts. Still, he thought the reporter had gotten things mixed up. "I see Rubens only this morning. He still can't walk," Kazumasa assured himself and then wondered. He smiled wistfully, "But Lourdes would be very happy."

J.B. thought the television report was so much more coherent than Kazumasa's illogical tale, that he assumed the Japanese had explained it poorly. J.B. said, "It's a superstitious country, Mr. Ishimaru, but if it works, I'm for what works, you know." J.B. found a particularly delightful spot on his ear to scratch. He pressed the feather there with special attention.

"Ah," exclaimed Kazumasa, pointing at the television screen. "The pigeon!" Sure enough, there was Rubens's pigeon, the very one that had saved his life. Chico Paco took the pigeon ceremoniously from its cage, held it steadily for the cameras and then tossed the bird into the air. The pigeon circled the sky and sailed away over the forest. After the single pigeon disappeared, there was a sudden swoop of feathers and flapping. In the background, you could see Batista's truck with the words "Djapan Pigeons Incorporated" and "Pomba for Lovely Clean Skin." For a moment the sky above the Matacão seemed to reflect the same grey with a multitude of pigeons circling ever higher and higher. In a matter of days and hours, São Paulo would be sprinkled with exhausted pigeons, all carrying the same message: "Pomba for Lovely Clean Skin."

*   *   *

In the next few days, J. B. Tweep had a memo sent to himself ordering him to make every sort of arrangement for the very important stockholder of GGG Enterprises, Mr. K. Ishimaru.

Even though all the best hotels were on the Matacão, J.B. managed to find a suitable place a good distance away. For precaution's sake, J.B had the furniture screwed down to the floors in the hotel room and had an assistant come in and velcro Kazumasa to his bed at night, but this was probably unnecessary. Kazumasa and I were quite ready to leave the Matacão for an easier life of surer gravity, but J.B. was insistent that Kazumasa stay to take the special GGG Enterprises tour that had been arranged. J.B. was also curious about my strange attraction to the Matacão. GGG had a sort of side foundation devoted to the study of the Matacão, something called Matacão Scientific Research Institute, which claimed to be studying the origins of the Matacão and for which GGG got a substantial tax break. J.B. was privy to some important, but very secret, breakthroughs about the nature of that smooth mysterious plain. It was possible that my relationship to this place could be the the missing link.

In order to provide Kazumasa with some comfort during his tour of GGG, J.B. had key areas recarpeted in velcro. He also had furniture upholstered in the same material. On the day of the tour, Kazumasa was given special velcro shoes and clothing. This must be, Kazumasa thought, what astronauts experience on the moon or how insects feel crawling up a wall. Kazumasa stuck to everything at GGG. He had to pry himself away from floors and chairs. At the same time, every time we passed a window overlooking the Matacão, Kazumasa would flail wildly off balance—his head jerked toward the Matacão while his feet were glued to the carpeting. It was a very tiring business.

Kazumasa tried to listen politely to all the explanations about what this or that department did, who this or that vice president or director was. Kazumasa noticed that all the desks had a large supply of plastic-covered clips, that managers generally had stainless-steel clips, directors silver-plated clips, vice presidents pure silver clips, and that only the president used gold clips. He noticed that all the women on the first floor had red hair and nails, while all the women on the second floor had black hair and gold nails. As you went up the floors at GGG, the similarities between people were less conspicuous, until they actually became rather subtle on the upper floors. Kazumasa, who was so busy trying to keep his ground, could hardly appreciate these details, but I had nothing else to do but observe. The employees on the tenth floor all did crossword puzzles, while those on the eleventh were into pornographic video games. Everyone on one floor had secretly written a screenplay, and the vice president's secretary on that floor was really a Hollywood agent. On one floor everyone was politically left, and on another politically right. The people on these floors only used the left or right elevators, depending on their political preference. The left elevator was swamped with protest posters and articles cut out of *Mother Jones*. The right elevator had the photographs of great conservative icons—Nixon and Reagan—under glass. Occasionally, someone from the left elevator would sneak in and draw little mustaches on the glass under Nixon's and Reagan's noses. By the time you got to the top floors, the clone factor was so subtle that only I could have noticed it—the middle initial P. for Peter or Pedro or Pietro or Pierre, or congenital lobotomies, for example.

For some reason, J.B. never thought it important to point these things out, and I suppose he was right. GGG was a great functioning miracle, a living, breathing organism that fell to the Matacão from the sky. J.B. would not have had it any other way. He had to move in and around it from the top to the bottom. Cloning helped him to remember what floor he was on. What was there to explain? Like the miracles associated with the angel Chico Paco, it worked, and J.B. was concerned with what worked.

Kazumasa watched the videotape slickly produced in several languages for the astute stockholder. Kazumasa listened to the Japanese version and finally understood the feather business. GGG touted feathers as a natural, healthy habit, an intelligent replacement for tobacco and coffee and a variety of nervous tics. People who had smoked for years claimed that they had given up the dirty cancerous habit within a day, an hour, or a moment: it was that good. The Surgeon General was even recommending it.

And it was not simply healthy; hundreds of medicinal values were attributed to the feather. Where else but on the Matacão, could one expect to find such a miracle drug? This alone was testimony to the great unknown value of tropical plants and animals still unclassified among thousands of species in the Amazon Forest. There was a romantic shot of Mané Pena, the feather guru, walking barefoot across the Matacão at sunset, contemplating this wonderful world and the great mystery of the Amazon Forest. Everything was enveloped in New Age music, and Kazumasa, who had a ball for a companion, even felt that feathers might bring him closer to this great ecological wonder.

GGG's marketing strategy was pure. You will recall that before J.B. arrived, GGG had no product on which to test its strategy; therefore, GGG developed a strategy that simply created a miracle product that would bring the greatest returns if GGG could control all the markets relating to that product. GGG had wrapped up the entire marketplace; there were no inroads, no avenues that had not been foreseen. GGG simply produced, controlled and sold everything. Georgia and Geoffrey Gamble, inspired by raw halibut, were the rare geniuses of this impeccable phenomenon. But J.B. was still not satisfied.

"Now," said J.B., when he had accompanied Kazumasa up twenty-three floors to the conference rooms overlooking the Matacão and seated the Japanese with the ball securely in a velcroed chair. "About that ball of yours. I've been instructed to let you in on some of our newest developments in Matacão research. This is very secure information, but under the circumstances, we believe you are the one to help us fill in the missing parts of our research. We've discovered that the stuff that the Matacão is made of is a sort of, well, sort of miracle plastic — Matacão plastic, if you will. We've discovered that it is extremely resistant stuff; we're the ones that have cracked the code in drilling and extracting the stuff, and now we're on the verge of controlling it."

Kazumasa nodded.

J.B. continued, "We know how to remove it from the earth, mine it, you know, but we're also involved in researching how to use it. We've got the contract from NASA to develop a space material that won't burn up when passing through atmospheres. This Matacão stuff is incredible. It is stronger than steel, resistant to extremely high temperatures and," J.B. emphasized, "totally moldable!" He threw up his three arms in excitement.

Kazumasa was wondering what it was that J.B. wanted of him. He listened carefully.

"But, this Matacão below us is a sort of, well, you've seen it, that shrine of Saint George, that Chico someone and those pigeons. People think it should be preserved. It's practically a national monument—no, an international monument. The piece we got hold of was not easy to come by; we had to pull a lot of strings to convince the Brazilian government that this was scientific nonprofit research. When they hear that we want to start mining this place, we'll have an uproar similar to the one Exxon had back in '89 with that Alaskan spill or even this old hubbub over the destruction of the rain forest or what's left of it. Don't get me wrong, Mr. Ishimaru, GGG is committed to environmental conservation. You've seen our promotion; we want to bring people back to nature, back to health. We want them to be ecologically responsible, too. Every time a person puts a feather to his ear, picks up the primary of a rare tanager or a scarlet ibis, they've got to think about the birds, about nature. My wife's an ornithologist, a real bird fanatic. So I know what I'm talking about. What was I saying?" J.B. paused to gather his thoughts.

Kazumasa thought birds were important too.

J.B. continued, "But this Matacão, this is even a bigger find than feathers. You can't imagine the possibilities. Sure we could start to chip away at one obscure end of the thing, but this place is crawling with scientists and environmentalists, with tourists to boot. Someone's bound to notice, and when we get going, we are going to need a lot of the Matacão." J.B. leaned forward, as if to get the full sensation of what it was like to be a few inches from me. "This ball, Mr. Ishimaru," said J.B., "is the key. If I'm not mistaken, it should lead us to other deposits of Matacão plastic."

Kazumasa nodded, "My ball knows."

CHAPTER 18: FEATHEROLOGY

MANÉ PENA HAD RUN BAREFOOT to the Matacão with the others to greet the young man who was called an angel but was like another son to him. Angustia had heard the news on the radio, and she had sent one of her young ones to the university, where he interrupted Mané's story-telling lecture to whisper the news in his ear. When Mané ran from the classroom with the little boy at his heels, his abandoned class followed him out and ran with him to the Matacão. Seeing the barefoot guru of feathers running with a small cadre of people caused others to run as well. It made no difference to where or from what, but only that it was important enough for that old man to run.

On the other hand, many people had joined Chico Paco for the last portion of his walk, convinced by the Praise-the-Lord radio station that Chico Paco's arrival on the Matacão was a historic moment on the Christian calendar. They came with their candles and rosaries, their caged pigeons, with babies in their arms and old people on their backs.

Batista, waiting with his two truckloads of pigeons on the Matacão, could see the collision coming from both directions. He felt momentarily frightened to see what seemed to him two armies of excited people approaching. What was one to think? Batista and the two truck drivers ran to their respective trucks, ready to bolt into reverse and hopefully watch a momentous riot from a proper distance. But nothing more momentous occurred than what J. B. Tweep observed from his balcony or the velcroed Kazumasa on TV—the significant convergence of two great rivers of believers: featherologists and pilgrims.

* * *

It would be 1,500 miles and at least seven days, Batista predicted, before the homers might arrive in São Paulo from the Matacão. He wondered if Tania Aparecida would even be at her post to await the birds, if she would be somewhere making those infernal deals. He could feel the irritation of his jealous thoughts just below the roots of his hair, which he scratched in frustration.

Mané Pena handed him a feather. "I think you might try one of these," he suggested to Batista wisely. "You were saying about your birds?" he prodded Batista to continue his conversation.

"On long distances like this," Batista gestured, "the female is usually faster than the male. You see, the female goes to sleep later and rises earlier; she gets in the habit of it from taking care of her babies. Now, she'll get an earlier start and then stop later to rest. She's got better flying time on the whole. I'd bet on a female every time for distance. Naturally, we've got more females out there than males." Batista nodded at the skies above them.

Mané Pena thought about this. "That so?"

"Now the young males do better on short runs. You let him in with a hen for a few minutes before the basket. Let him get a taste for some ass and pull him out just when he's dragging the old tail feathers. Then, oow," Batista snapped his fingers to accentuate the lusty speed of his males, "they come panting back faster than the devil."

"Heh heh, would've known it," Mané Pena grinned.

"That first batch, not that Pomba stuff," Batista inserted, "they're all our very best." Batista was proud of his birds. "Strong wing formation. Muscular. When you hold them in your hand, the feathers feel like silk stretched over hard wood." He paused, that tactile sensation still radiating from his fingers. "That comes from a lot of training on the short runs. We've been long-distancing them gradually. This is the big test." Batista rubbed the feather over his ear and smiled at his sudden relief from that taut feeling in his gut, from that necessity to soar back with his homers to São Paulo and that woman with those crazy ideas. He looked at Mané Pena quizzically.

Mané grinned. "That's a pigeon feather," he said. "They want to use the bright stuff—parrot feathers—you know, but these greys can give a man tranquillity. A man needs tranquillity of mind."

Batista shot a look at the old man; what did Mané Pena know about him, Batista? Did his mad jealousy show? Batista looked at the feather. "What about pigeon feathers?" he asked hesitantly.

"Well," Mané Pena spoke with authority, "take this feather. Not too big or too small. Quill's stout and the vanes just wide enough. A pigeon feather's just about the right size," Mané nodded knowingly. "If it's the wrong size, you have a hard time working it around. True, a lot of people like the parrot because of the colors. They don't care how feathers work. They think color counts. But a feather's an instrument. You need a little skill as well."

Batista nodded, approving Mané Pena's expertise. "I can give you some primaries from our next moult. Maybe you could give us your opinion on the Djapan champions."

"From the looks of those birds," Mané Pena gestured to the southern skies, "there's some firm feathers, strong barbs."

"You can be sure of it." Batista urged his flock home.

"Those champions might not be for everyone," Mané Pena speculated, sucking air through the spaces in his grin. "Might be best for athletic types, football players. See what I mean? I don't suggest the strong flyers for everyone. An eagle feather can get you in trouble, for example. Give a fool more guts than he can negotiate. Nope. A simple man like me sticks to simple feathers."

"What did you mean about tranquillity," Batista still wanted to know.

"Well, some feathers provide tranquillity. Don't know why, really, but they do. Pigeon feather's one, specially the female. Suppose because they say pigeons marry for life. Domesticated sorts and stuck to each other forever after. There's birds that get a new partner every season. Some's got various. Talk to that French bird professor; she'll tell you stories get your mind to thinking. Nature's like the TV. You take a good look at it; it'll tell you something new all the time."

Batista wanted to know about those French bird professor stories, but a tiny buzzer went off. Batista noticed the fancy digital watch with all sorts of buttons on Mané's wrist.

"They've punched this up so when it buzzes I know I've got to go somewhere." Mané thought for a moment. "It must be that TV lecture. That's it."

"TV lecture?" asked Batista.

"Funniest thing. I talk for two, three hours, see. Then when it's finished, they do something, make it come out 'bout one-half hour. Speed everything up. That's how come you can watch a story, guy gets born and dies in one hour." Mané Pena nodded gravely, then grinned and left for his TV lecture. Batista watched the old barefooted guru walk away. He wanted to walk away too. He wanted to get in his truck, press the gas pedal for home and sing all the way back to the rattling of his empty cages. He wanted to be there when the homers arrived. He wanted to take Tania Aparecida in his arms and dance on the back porch all night. He wanted to make love to the sound of their cooing pigeons. But he could not. Even as the sky above the Matacão was grey with those Pomba pigeons, another two truckloads had arrived. There were pigeon messages for Gigeta's Pizza and Hiro's Karaoke and some popular politician named Evandro Alves. Tania Aparecida had sent detailed instructions so that the arrival of certain pigeons would coincide with such and such an advertising campaign. And then Evandro Alves himself was supposed to come to the Matacão to make a long rhetorical speech and to let the pigeons out himself. It would be months before Batista could even think of returning to São Paulo.

*   *   *

In the meantime, Chico Paco had once again returned to the Matacão, his sun-bleached hair a shade lighter and the iridescence of his eyes glistening brighter than old Mané had remembered. Chico Paco seemed somehow stronger, too, as if this pilgrimage had somehow filled out the boyish places in his youthful build. It had been a little over a month of serious walking, and the boots provided by Lourdes had barely survived the trip; they were worn thin and flapping open at the toes. But this trip had been different, a comfortable change from the first excruciating trek from Chico Paco's hometown. This time, a national radio station had accompanied him, following him in a jeep and making updates every few miles. The radio station interviewed Chico Paco, taped telephone conversations he had with his mother or with the former invalid, Gilberto, or even with Lourdes and Rubens back in São Paulo. In between everything, the station played religious songs and pressed forward with evangelical messages and pleas for money to continue to make possible these broadcasts of "Living Moments in Sainthood." As a result of so much publicity, Chico Paco received free room and board and was greeted with excitement and anticipation all along the way. As before, he continued to receive pleas for his assistance in meeting promises made in exchange for miracles or desires, everything from curing a case of chronic worms in a beloved goat to securing a job after college. The radio station kindly gathered all these letters in a growing sack in the jeep, which they dumped off with Chico Paco as they drove away from the Matacão.

Back again, recuperating from his walk in the home of Mané Pena—where even more letters of the same nature awaited him —Chico Paco patiently opened each letter, reading the contents with sympathy, pity and amazement. Many of the correspondents sent money, often the precious savings of a lifetime, to support Chico Paco's mission. In fact, there was a great deal of money, more money than he had ever seen in his life.

"What does this mean?" Chico Paco asked Mané Pena for advice.

"Don't really know," Mané Pena scratched the scruff of his unshaved face. He walked over to a drawer and pulled out an envelope. "There's this, too." He handed the envelope addressed "To Chico Paco."

Chico Paco pulled out a check from the Kazumasa Ishimaru Foundation and signed by Kazumasa himself. A small note was attached to the check. "Mr. Chico Paco: I'm very happy you arrived at Matacão safe to pray for Rubens. Please use this gift to continue your good work. Your friend, Kazumasa Ishimaru."

Chico Paco's green eyes blinked with disbelief. "It's a lot of money, Mané! I didn't walk to get money. I just did it because it was God's will. What will I do with all this money?"

"Some people wouldn't have a problem answering a question like that." Mané Pena grinned at the young fisherman now so far from the sea.

Chico Paco pulled the tiny photograph of Rubens from his pocket. "You didn't see this boy, Mané. He was the very boy in my dreams. Once you see something real like that in front of you, you know you can't do wrong by God."

Suddenly the buzzer on Mané's watch went off. "Now what is it this time?" Mané had to think. "I'll have to call Carlos to find out. Good thing there's Carlos." Carlos was the secretary who came with the office provided by GGG Enterprises. "Carlos is what they call 'efficient.'"

Chico Paco looked with confusion at the old man, searching his thoughts for an idea. "Mané, please help me think about my problem. I can trust you."

Mané Pena pulled out a feather. "Here, try this one. I'm sure you will think of something."

Chico Paco laid back in the hammock, rubbing the soft fluff at the end of the feather over his earlobe. He thought about the radio station that had accompanied him for the past month. It had made a tremendous amount of money from their program, "Living Moments in Sainthood." The radio station had given him nothing for his central role. Of course, they had paid for the telephone calls to his mother, had scouted places for him to eat or sleep, and he had been grateful for their friendship on that long journey that otherwise would have been quite solitary. Chico Paco had not thought of his walk as something that required payment; it was his duty to God and to his fellow human beings. It would seem, however, that all these letters and all this support must require some sort of answer and action on his part. If he were indeed a chosen angel—and all of these letters and requests seemed proof in themselves—he must take on these God-given responsibilities and invest these gifts for God. He nodded to himself, scratching on this point with the tip of the feather.

Then, he thought about his amazement at the possibility, the very miracle, of being able to send his voice through the air over invisible waves. It had taken a while to become accustomed to the presence of the radio people, their announcers, tape recorders and microphones. But after a while, he began to enjoy giving interviews. He liked hearing himself on the radio, squeezed in between the commercials and gospel news. He liked the music. Yes! Chico Paco pecked his ear excitedly with the feather and sat up with sudden resolution. If he could have anything, he would like his very own radio station.

* * *

Mané Pena pressed the buttons on his phone. He had to learn to use a pushbutton phone.

Carlos answered his call. "Oh, Seu Mané. It's that television talk show. Mr. Tweep has a memo that authorizes you to take the GGG plane to fly to Rio. You do the show and come back the next day."

"Fly?"

"Yes."

"Likely those metal birds fall from time to time." Mané sawed a feather anxiously over his ear.

"I wouldn't worry about such things. They say flying is safer than getting on a bus."

"I'm not much for buses either. If God had meant people to go faster, he woulda built us with wheels and wings."

"It's the only way to get to Rio today, Seu Mané. I'll come by in a bit and pick you up. If we're going to make the show, we'd better hurry."

Mané Pena sighed. This feather business had gotten rather complicated. Mr. Tweep said education and research were the most important things. Mané Pena owed it to the world to spread his knowledge about feathers. If he didn't want imitations and misconceptions to crop up, he'd better keep the matter straight and do his bit for the good of the feather and its good to society. But everyday, they had something else for him to do. If it wasn't what they called a seminar, it was an interview or a press conference. One day, they had him going everywhere and taking pictures all day. He had to stand in front of banana trees, on the Matacão, off the Matacão, in front of this or that building, under bright lights, in front of a sunset, posing for picture after picture. The photographer had this mechanical camera that spit out the shots like crazy. There wasn't one conceivable expression or pose they hadn't caught of the old man. After this, Mané had a better respect for those people he saw in magazines who posed for this or that. "It's harder work than meets the eye," he would tell Angustia.

And then there was Carlos, who seemed to be busy writing down everything that Mané Pena ever said. He was always transcribing video and audio tapes of Mané's interviews and lectures. Mané could not read the transcriptions, but he thought Carlos worked awfully hard. "Carlos is always pecking away at that machine in the office," he told Angustia. "Says he's writing a book. Pecking. Pecking like this with the fingers," Mané showed Angustia how Carlos typed.

"He gets paid to do that?" asked Angustia.

"There's many ways to make a living, Gustia," asserted Mané. "Who woulda thought I could live off of talking about feathers?"

"Don't know it's worth the trouble," pouted Angustia. She was getting tired of Mané's buzzing watch and not being able to send a young one over to the corner bar and cafe to fetch the old man for supper.

Very rarely now could Mané Pena be found at his favorite spot at the old cafe. Once, Mané Pena had been a rubber tapper in the forest, then a simple farmer on infertile soil. Then he had been a mason on construction sites along the Matacão. Now he had left the labor of his former days for a different kind of toil. He had to be places at a specific time. He had to get on airplanes to get there. He had to squint into bright lights. He had to talk about the same things over and over. The stress and tension of this new life was a constant challenge to the effectiveness of the feather. Mané Pena had once found the proper balance of relaxation and excitement in the simple feathers of the parrot or pigeon, but lately, he had discovered that his needs were met only by the more sophisticated feathers of rarer birds. He was not sure what this meant, but he knew it was significant.

CHAPTER 19: MICHELLE MABELLE

J. B. TWEEP WAS IN LOVE. It was true he had known other women, but never a French ornithologist with three breasts. Here, then, was that indescribable meeting of hearts and minds where two overqualified human beings find their romantic match. It was a dream come true. All those years, excelling from one job to the next, the satisfaction of a job overdone, which invariably soured into boredom, and the extraordinary chance to work for a company like GGG where the chances to extend the possibilities of overqualification were infinite—all of this no longer seemed to matter. Michelle. Michelle. Michelle. J.B. proclaimed his love in triplicate.

Michelle Mabelle, different from J.B., had always harbored extreme embarrassment and shame about her unusual trinity. But like J.B.—who always retained, despite his successes, an unassuming air, that of an obscure bureaucrat—Michelle was a sort of wallflower, albeit a French one. But while J.B. had, like most Americans, no known ancestry to which he might trace his working-class dilettantism, Michelle came from a long line of bird lovers. It was said that her great-grandfather, while studying a strange species of cockatoo, had met Paul Gauguin in Tahiti. And drawings of North American birds by her great-aunt, who had immigrated to French Canada, predated those of John J. Audubon.

In the beginning, J.B., occupied as he was with feathers and the pursuit of the excellence of his obscurity through GGG, only saw before him a French ornithologist with an encyclopedic knowledge of pertinent details. Little did he realize that this bird professor with the French-speaking parrot on her shoulder was the very salvation for his third arm, otherwise doomed to tropical atrophy.

As for Michelle, she had long ago decided to revive the memory of her French-Canadian aunt in the history of women ornithologists. She had no time for the song and dance of male suitors and was certainly averse to the humiliation of being exposed to any instincts she might arouse in a possible admirer. It was not until J.B. innocently fluttered his additional plumage that Michelle felt her own instincts awaken, her three (heretofore disinterested) mammaries mellow like papayas, ready to burst with new-found succulence. Had it not been for the presence of Mané Pena, sawing abstractly at his right ear with a feather, Michelle would have torn her blouse open in a similar gesture of unabashed honesty.

J.B., who had maintained, even in Brazil (the home of Sonia Braga, Jorge Amado and the Girl from Ipanema), a life of routine amenities—sorting his beloved clip collection into complicated classifications known solely to J.B., viewing old videotaped movies and National Geographic specials while eating microwaved leftovers, soaking in a hot tub filled with some green mineral powder imported from Japan, a solitary evening at the keyboard with a midi synthesizer after a hard day at the office—suddenly discovered his capacity for insatiable lust. Night after night, one wild weekend after the next, J.B. and Michelle attempted to exhaust the possibilities of unmitigated pleasure.

"I never knew life could be like this," sighed J.B., who finally thought he had discovered an activity at which he excelled, but for which his interest would never diminish. His third arm swelled with muscular virility.

"*Moi non plus,*" admitted Michelle whose three nipples grazed his chest like the concerted beaks of a trio of sea gulls skimming the waves for perch.

"Liberty. Equality. Fraternity," J.B. spoke and pointed lovingly to each mammary from left to right as if these personal designations were tattooed to each breast.

Michelle's parrot, observing J.B. from the foot of the bed with a certain hostility, suddenly began to scream the *Marseillaise* with exaggerated pride.

"Polly want a croissant?" J.B. asked warily.

Michelle crawled over, pulling the sheets with her, to speak to the parrot. "Ah, *mon cheri,*" she said soothingly to the bird. "You aren't jealous, are you, Napoleon darling?" Michelle cut a piece of Camembert from a round on the bed stand and held the particularly moist and pungent cheese in front of Napoleon's beak. After a pause, the parrot pecked at her fingers, ate the cheese with wounded pride, then perched with its head poised to one side and defecated over the side of the bed.

"Do they all eat that stuff?" asked J.B.,gesturing with one of his arms at Michelle's collection of parakeets, cockatoos, doves and rare birds, all staring from a spreading array of cages now crowding his apartment. He thought a clip collection was much more pragmatic; he could get most of it into a few boxes. The important part of his collection he could actually toss into his pockets.

"Oh no, Jonathan, darling. Of course not." Michelle said seriously. "Did you see the mangoes and the papayas that arrived yesterday? Those are for the toucans. And I've been very fortunate to get an exceptionally good blend of well-seasoned seed from that Djapan acquaintance we met the other evening. How do you say? Batista was his name."

In the mornings, J.B. got used to being awoken by the chatter and screech of what seemed to him a jungle of birds. Michelle explained that among tropical birds, constant duetting was necessary to maintain their bonds in the dense forest. With the advent of Michelle, J.B.'s apartment began to seem like an aviary, his clip collection relegated to a few insignificant shelves along with some old 9.99 objects that J.B. had grown accustomed to. Michelle hired a full-time birdkeeper, who was endlessly filling water troughs and seed feeders and cleaning cages.

Michelle had names for all her birds, besides the Latin classifications, which J.B. could never remember. The cockatoos were Mimi and Charles, Genevieve and Pierre. The parakeets had names like Guy, Jean-Jacques, Catherine and Phillipe.

The toucans were Sartre, Rousseau and Voltaire.

Besides Napoleon, there were other talking parrots whose repertoires were equally impressive. Some parrots spoke as many as five languages. Michelle also received as gifts a couple of mynahs who spoke Portuguese. Neither Michelle nor J.B. understood the Brazilian slang, and the bird caretaker wouldn't explain any of it. "Nonsense," the caretaker excused himself while the mynahs mocked with gleeful enthusiasm, *"Arara fresca só fala français!"* (That snob of a parrot only speaks in French.) *"A perereca da vizinha 'tápresa na gaiola!"* (Literally, the neighbor's frog is imprisoned in a cage . . .) or *"Ei meu amigo, a terçeira e prá coçar saco!"* (Eh my friend, the third one is for scratching his balls.)

J.B. sympathized with the American magpie, Butch, who spoke only English. Often Michelle would find J.B. conversing with Butch. "Hey brother," Butch would be saying, "Chill out. Jus' chill out and cruise, baby!"

And J.B. would insist, "Butch, it's not like you think. I mean, what if GGG begins to actually appreciate me. Up until now, I've had the security of a Japanese businessman but the advantages of an American worker with mobility and the added excitement of instability."

"Jus' cruise. Jus' cruise," was Butch's standard advice.

"But I don't want to be appreciated. I want to be left alone! I want inconspicuous control!" complained J.B.

Michelle surprised J.B. from behind and forced herself into his embrace. "What is it you are discussing with Butch? Always talking with Butch. Perhaps you have forgotten poor Michelle?"

"I'm worried about my job at GGG," confessed J.B.

"Worried about GGG?" Michelle tittered with amusement. "Whatever for?"

"I think they're beginning to notice me."

"And why shouldn't they? You are probably the most important person in the entire company! You do everything!" said Michelle enthusiastically.

"No, Michelle," groaned J.B. He did not want to know that he might have, in fact, maneuvered himself to a height from which one could easily be kicked off. "Tomorrow morning, I'm going to send out a memo and demote myself back to Associate Director," J.B. said resolutely.

"It will just cause gossip," Michelle said knowingly. "People will say that so-and-so was jealous and slept with so-and-so and you got a raw deal. They will love and notice you even more!" Michelle smiled.

J.B. sighed. He had always admired, not the visible presidents, but those people behind the scenes, the national security advisors and aides-de-camp, the former chairman of the board, the anonymous party who held 51 percent of the stock, influenced crucial decisions and sometimes, unknown to others, secretly controlled everything. With this in mind, J.B. worked incessantly to retain anonymity and to keep everything and everyone flowing past him into the limelight. After all, J.B. admired the simplicity of the clip, something that held papers together in a neat batch—nothing fancy, taken for granted but indispensable. But it was indeed true that J.B. was responsible for the enormous success of GGG Enterprises, for its pioneering activities in featherology and plastics, its singular control of those markets and GGG's skyrocketing stocks on Wall Street. That J.B., flitting from one position and project to the next, clipping papers together within GGG, had a hand in everything and somehow controlled and wielded enormous power had never been apparent to anyone, until Michelle, the French ornithologist, appeared.

It was not that Michelle spoke up in public. The simple presence of that suddenly radiant Frenchwoman was enough to make anyone notice the man at her side.

* * *

Certainly Batista questioned the presence of the strange, lopsided American. Batista had first noticed Michelle one evening at Hiro's Karaoke. Hiro's Karaoke had naturally opened a place on the Matacão to capture the evening tourist trade. After a day of doing the Amazon jungle tour or tanning oneself on the north end of the Matacão, people were ready for an evening of Matacão enchantment, as the tour guidebooks all talked of it. Hiro's was a five-star sort of place. You could meet celebrities there actually paying to sing their own songs. Michelle loved to go to Hiro's in the evening, coaxing J.B. away from his clip collection so that she could dedicate and sing for him the theme song from *Umbrellas of Cherbourg*. Batista noticed the Frenchwoman singing because of the parrot on her shoulder. When he was away from his birds, he missed them and felt pleasantly surprised to see the parrot at Hiro's. In fact, the parrot Napoleon was a kind of karaoke fanatic himself. Batista watched with amusement when Napoleon sang along with Michelle or even agreed to a solo. Batista made his introductions by sending a bag of his special Djapan birdseed over to Michelle's table.

Michelle was quite impressed with Batista's birdseed, especially since the very picky Napoleon, who would usually only eat Camembert, actually ate the stuff. She had heard of the Djapan champions and knew of the world records set by his birds in long-distance flying time from the Matacão to São Paulo. She was also aware that it had been the first time that homers had ever been sent out from the center of the Amazon. It was an exceptional triumph, and she called Batista over to their table to tell him so. "I have been telling J.B. about your champions and we would like very much to meet them," Michelle said sincerely.

"Well," said Batista, "Most of my best birds are at home in São Paulo. I'm only here temporarily." Batista paused. He had been saying this for the past six months, but he was still here on the Matacão, and Tania Aparecida was saying something about branching out the operation and setting up a post on the Matacão. She had sent several champion couples via airplane to the Matacão, saying she knew how much Batista must be missing his birds and suggesting that his idea about homing birds to the Matacão was a brilliant one. Batista rubbed a pigeon feather madly over his ear, trying diligently to control his anger. Brilliant idea? What brilliant idea? But Batista knew that she was right. He had her to thank for making Djapan Enterprises a real business. They were actually becoming very successful. So he went to work, leasing the roofs of several buildings on the Matacão and setting up his pigeon cages. Tania Aparecida had set a goal of five hundred birds to start, eventually growing to a couple thousand more. It wasn't impossible, she said, if you worked it out on a calculator. Batista sighed. In time he would have pigeons procreating on, and flying to, almost every roof on the Matacão.

"Who takes care of your birds in São Paulo?" Michelle asked.

"My wife. She's takes care of everything," Batista almost groaned.

"How good it is to have a partner who can handle both your business affairs and the affairs of love," said Michelle snuggling closer to J.B., who simply nodded at Michelle's bird conversation.

"I suppose," wondered Batista. The last time he'd seen Tania Aparecida, she was a reflection in the rear-view mirror of his truck. He had talked to her on the phone once or twice, but more often, a truckload of pigeons would meet him somewhere on the Matacão with a longish note of instructions and her fluttering love banter, which only made him more anxious. Batista's gaze grazed the Frenchwoman's double cleavage; he watched the perspiration break out on his beer glass and wondered how he was going to get some relief. All of his pigeon couples were busy copulating on the rooftops all up and down the Matacão. If he could just be released from his invisible cage, he could beat the human record for getting back to his nest. Batista fumbled for his feather. He would just get back to work, moving from rooftop to rooftop, running those birds in and out of the Matacão.

It was his turn to sing. He smiled at J.B. and Michelle and stood up. The women in Hiro's all gazed with longing at his handsome features, all internalized the sound of his voice and understood the meaning of his emotions to be as their own.

CHAPTER 20: PROMISES

AFTER SOME INQUIRIES, Chico Paco soon got a hold of a fledgling station which broadcast country music near the Matacão. Presently, Radio Chico was on the air with country music and a new show called "Answered Prayers."

Chico Paco went over with his pile of letters and a look of confusion on his face to see Mané Pena's secretary, Carlos. Carlos, who was as efficient as Mané Pena had said, quickly sorted out the letters. He pointed out that the letters could be classified into several catagories: fan letters and personal questions about Chico Paco (the color of his eyes, et cetera), pleas for carrying out promises, requests for advice and some hate mail. Finally, there were a few letters from people who claimed that they, too, had made similar journeys to satisfy promises for the sake of some miracle or answered prayer. Carlos prepared a form letter on the computer and answered most of the mail himself. Many letters of support were simply read over the air on Radio Chico.

The letters from persons who had spoken of making similar pilgrimages for answered prayers were answered personally by Chico Paco:

> "Dear Brother/Sister So-and-So: I was pleased to read your letter and learn that I am not alone in my mission to walk for answered prayers. Everyday I receive requests from the blessed who need our help. I am only one man with two feet. Can you help me?"

To Chico Paco's surprise and delight, the response to his own letters was overwhelming. Past pilgrims from all over Brazil converged on the Matacão and the headquarters for "Answered Prayers" to commit themselves to new pilgrimages. In a matter of weeks, Chico Paco surrogates were marching forth from every possible place in Brazil, some walking barefoot, some on their knees, some lugging crosses, others waving banners, bearing abandoned crutches, pushing empty wheelchairs, heading processions with saints carved in wood and plaster of Paris, all in a direction toward the Matacão, all complying with some promise to walk for an answered prayer.

Back at Radio Chico, a growing number of personnel, volunteers and Chico Paco enthusiasts carefully followed the progress of each pilgrim on enormous wall maps. Radio Chico was kept informed by several jeeps with long-distance connections that were employed to track down and follow the pilgrims and update the show's listeners. Chico Paco himself hosted the show.

"Brother Zé!" Chico Paco would speak to the pilgrim in some remote town in Goiás. "Hallelujah! You are nearing your destination."

"That's so!" Pilgrim Zé would proclaim. "And I want to send my abiding love to my family and to Dona Mariamelia Rosa for whom I am making this great walk."

"Praise the Lord!" said Chico Paco, hailing his distant pilgrim on. "I believe Sister Clara, who is marching from Paraná will be meeting you in a few days. Our reports show that she is not but a few miles from where you are."

"Sister Clara and I will walk to the Matacão together!" announced Brother Zé.

"And I will meet you personally as you arrive!"

The popularity of Chico Paco's "Answered Prayers" was so enormous that shows were re-broadcast or pumped live to a growing number of stations all over the nation. As Chico Paco's pilgrims marched to the Matacão, money poured into Radio Chico, "Answered Prayers" and the new parent institution, the Foundation for Votive Pilgrimages.

Everywhere, people were proclaiming the new church on the radio waves, the living angels marching toward the Matacão and the growth of a new and popular faith based on the renewed belief in prayer itself, Chico Paco as a new religious leader and his pilgrims, now referred to as the New Disciples.

* * *

Lourdes, back in São Paulo, listened to the radio with great interest. She had followed the progress of Chico Paco to the Matacão and, weeping tears of joy, observed his arrival for the sake of her son, Rubens. Rubens himself was ecstatic to learn that Chico Paco had released his pigeon from the Matacão. When Radio Chico went national, Lourdes, like so many others, became an avid listener, almost abandoning the prime-time television soap operas. Besides the live updates of "Answered Prayers," Chico Paco hosted another popular show which interviewed various pilgrims and the actual people whose prayers had been answered, recounted numerous stories of pilgrimages and gave accounts of famous pilgrims in history. There was also a show in which members from opposing positions on religious issues—usually regarding miracles or answered prayers, saints and blessing techniques—were invited to debate their opin-

ions. There was also a call-in show in which listeners telephoned and expressed their concerns and experiences on live
radio. Throughout the programming, by calling in and giving
the correct answer—often the name of a pilgrim or saint for the
week—listeners could win free trips to the Matacão or certi-
ficates entitling them to one surrogate pilgrim for any answered
prayer.

This was how Lourdes won a trip to the Matacão.

Now, Kazumasa and I had not returned to São Paulo. In fact,
besides a postcard or two, Lourdes had not heard anything at
allabout Kazumasa for several months. She had asked Hiroshi
about Kazumasa, but Hiroshi had received only a cryptic note
about Kazumasa's having to stay longer in the north. "Don't
worry about him. He's used to traveling, that ball and him,"
Hiroshi told her. "Come out with me for an evening of karaoke," he urged Lourdes.

But Lourdes shook her head and made excuses. "No, I just
can't get away from my radio program." But Lourdes missed
Kazumasa. She even missed me. Little did she know that J. B.
Tweep had made complicated arrangements to send Kazumasa and me up and down and all over the state of Pará to find the
very spot where I had been pulled, presumably by another deposit of Matacão plastic. These arrangements were steeped in
secrecy; J.B. was taking no chances. GGG Enterprises would
have Matacão plastic, or nobody would.

When the deejay announced that Lourdes had won a trip to
the Matacão, she was ecstatic, but there was no way to contact
Kazumasa to tell him that she would be coming to join him on
the Matacão. Lourdes called Tia Carolina to have her take over
her duties in that fourteenth-floor apartment. She kissed Rubens and Gislaine good-bye. "I'll call you when I get there," she
assured them.

Hiroshi saw Lourdes off at the bus station. "Why didn't you
tell me you wanted to go to the Matacão?" Hiroshi asked. "We
could have gone together by plane."

"The bus is fine for me," Lourdes smiled. "I don't think I'm
the sort to go by airplane. Besides, I won this trip."

"When you get there," said Hiroshi, "go to my place on the
Matacão. You'll see the Hiro's sign in blue neon just like here.

You can't miss it. My people will find you a place to stay. I've got some business here, but I should be there by the time you arrive." Hiroshi looked at Lourdes hopefully, but she felt shy and uncomfortable. She was thinking about Kazumasa.

Lourdes nodded, but four days later, when she arrived on the Matacão, Lourdes made her way to the offices of Radio Chico. Chico Paco was very happy to see Lourdes. He asked about Rubens and Gislaine and even Kazumasa. "Did you know," he asked Lourdes, "that your patron Seu Kazumasa gave me the money to buy this radio station?"

"So many people have been helped by Seu Kazumasa," said Lourdes proudly. "He is the most generous man I have ever known. He's not like anyone I have ever met." Lourdes sighed. "I haven't seen him in several months, you know. I am afraid that something may have happened to him."

Chico Paco detected the urgency in Lourdes's voice.

Lourdes did not want to lose Kazumasa to the north in the same way she had lost her husband. "I wonder if there is a way to find him. He was supposed to come here to the Matacão, but even his cousin Hiroshi doesn't know where he is."

Chico Paco smiled kindly at the woman whose letter had started a whole new way of life for him. "Maybe I can help you find Seu Kazumasa," he suggested. "If he listens to the radio, maybe he will answer your prayers."

Lourdes decided to volunteer her time for Radio Chico and the Foundation for Votive Pilgrimages. She would wait to see if Kazumasa could be found, and in the meantime, help Chico Paco out. It was such a big mission for such a young man. It was Lourdes's idea to start something called "Telephone Pilgrimages." Lourdes helped to compile a list of answered prayers of more modest nature, such as the recovery of some lost article or treasured possession or the blessings of a raise in pay, which could be telephoned in to the Matacão. "Not everyone has such great needs," she argued. "But everyone, every day, has some small prayer that God answers. They should have a way to show their thanks."

Trained "telephone pilgrims" were soon waiting to receive these calls and to place the blessed person's promise on the Matacão in the form of a lighted candle, prayer or statuette, any one of which could be purchased by a small donation to the foundation. Lourdes made sure that a certificate or prayer book signed by Chico Paco himself was sent out to assure the caller of a completed act of devotion on his or her behalf. And every day, Lourdes herself set a candle at Saint George's altar, praying for Kazumasa's speedy return.

Then there came the idea of using pigeons as votive messengers. Batista had lent Chico Paco a pigeon couple to try the idea out. "Where did you get such an idea?" Batista asked Chico Paco.

"There was a woman who called the show from São Paulo the other day. I don't remember her name."

"Woman from São Paulo?" Batista bristled. She could only be Tania Aparecida. Was she trying to kill him with work?

Of course, the foundation was quick to see the possibilities in homing pigeons, symbolic representatives of the Holy Ghost, and immediately contracted with Djapan Enterprises for 500 "pigeon pilgrims." Batista worked day and night to breed pigeons until there was no more room for cages on the penthouse roofs off the Matacão. People below them were beginning to complain about the pigeon droppings on their windows, cars and incoming guests. Batista had to buy a small plot of land not too far from the Matacão and continued breeding pigeons there.

The pigeons earmarked as the foundation's votive messengers were carefully packaged in special cages with complete instructions and sent by air to requesting parties within the suggested radius of the Matacão. Pigeons returned from everywhere to the Matacão with votive messages and prayers. As the messages arrived, a Radio Chico announcer read them over the air. "Chico Paco," said the announcer, "I think I hear the bell. A votive pigeon has arrived!" Every day, dozens of new callers telephoned in with donations and requests for pigeon pilgrims. The votive pigeon was becoming almost as popular as the telephone pilgrimage. In time, Batista would count as many as a thousand pigeons homing in from various places to the Matacão.

* * *

One day, Chico Paco answered a call from a small northeastern coastal town. He could almost hear and feel the sea breeze sifting through his golden hair. "Chico Paco," said a familiar voice, "this is Gilberto. I have sad news to tell you. My grandmother Maria Creuza is no longer with us. She has gone to heaven."

Chico Paco felt the tears well up in his green eyes, not so much for the old woman, who was after all very old, but for the memory of his friendship and the strange empty place in his heart which could only be filled by his dreams. How hard it was to comply with God's will.

"How long has it been? Almost two years? I miss you, Chiquinho," said Gilberto. "So does your mother. I've been thinking that your mother and I could come to visit you."

Chico Paco's heart leapt. From that moment, it would be held aloft until the waves engulfed it and the tide would take it out to sea.

CHAPTER 21: HOMING

IT WAS A WORLD RECORD akin to the eighteenth-century record of 7,000 miles to the West African coast in 55 days. The Djapan pigeon had flown 1,500 miles from the Matacão to São Paulo in 5 days, averaging 300 miles per day and 20 miles per hour. Congratulations came from every corner of the pigeon world. Photographs of the famous Djapan pigeon, Azulzinha, reunited with its pigeon mate and brood on the Djapan back porch, were on all the front pages of the major newspapers. Batista read the newspaper articles with a mixture of pride and jealousy. Tania Aparecida was in most of the photographs, her hair cut and waved in some new style. Batista stared at her features, trying to find the woman he loved within the black-and-white newsprint. He looked at the pigeon Azulzinha; she was the culmination of months of hard work, study and training. Batista and Tania Aparecida were the proud parents of a world-record-winning champion. He and Tania Aparecida should be there together basking in this glory, cooing lovingly at their brood of pigeons and at each other in a honeymoon of bliss. He slumped back in depression but continued to read.

Of the pigeons sent from the Matacão, one had arrived in record time, and two days later, two more birds straggled in with likewise respectable times. Three birds were discovered in varied stages of their trip, for the most part on target. And Rubens's bird, to the boy's joy, straggled in, not a record-winner but certainly a survivor. Five of the Djapan birds were never accounted for, probably lost, killed or waylaid somewhere in the great expanse of Brazil.

Finally, long after the commotion of the world record had subsided, one bird arrived in New York at the revolving doors of GGG Enterprises, carrying one of Batista's cryptic notes, which simply read, "Feather."

J. B. Tweep called Batista at his pigeon farm to tell him the news. "I can't tell you what a sensation your pigeon has caused," he spoke excitedly. "It means more to GGG than anything our publicity people could devise. We've got lines of people filling the New York lobby to see your bird. How did you plan this? I mean, it was a stroke of genius to put in that note."

Batista listened to J.B. in confusion. "Seems she went the wrong way." He scratched his head. "That's my bird all right. You say the ring on her leg reads DJAPAN?"

"We're trying to make the most of this. The publicity people will be contacting you to do a short interview," said J.B.

Sure enough, as old Mané Pena knew all too well, the GGG publicity people came through with their cameras and questions. After an hour of questions and another hour of wandering around the pigeon farm, they produced a five-minute piece that was interspersed with material on the Matacão and GGG's inroads into the science and development of the feather.

Batista's New York pigeon caused a commotion in the business world, those repercussions eventually reaching Wall Street, sending GGG stocks shooting upward. Not only people who had an inside track on the market, but also those without an iota of business acumen were throwing their money "on the feather"—GGG Enterprises.

Overnight, the fame of the Djapan pigeons had spread around the globe, and Batista was suddenly accosted by business proposals, pigeon enthusiasts, and reporters from all over the world. A market astrologer from New York, anxious to propose regular pigeon flights carrying Batista's messages direct to his Wall Street office, called daily, trying to develop a proposal that would appeal to Batista. "Just start something up for me. Anything," the market astrologer pleaded on the phone. "I've heard all about your prophetic messages. About that Japanese and his ball. Well, what he did is peanuts compared to what we can do together. This is Wall Street! You name your deal!"

Another odd fellow from Las Vegas came around in a pinstripe suit. He said he was the friend of a Brazilian dancer who did a follies show on the strip. He showed Batista pictures of the Brazilian dancer in an enormous headdress with rhinestones and feathers. "Come to Las Vegas," he nudged Batista. "I can show you a good time." Batista looked at the pictures of a tall shapely *mulata,* but he was not impressed. Tania Aparecida was several times more beautiful, he thought. What if this fellow were to meet Tania Aparecida and she in turn were to see this stuff, all this glamour and whatnot? Batista fumed. He waved off the foreigners and their foreign proposals. He had enough work from Tania Aparecida's crazy ideas. There was bird feed to negotiate, cages to build, water troughs to clean, pigeon dung to cart away. He had nearly a dozen full-time workers, expensive incubating machines, barns, silos, and trucks. The pigeon votive and advertising business alone was work for another dozen people. He was already plagued by deadlines in several cities to raise substantial broods. He didn't like to leave it to an assistant. He wanted to be there to let the birds out with their advertising messages. He didn't have time for any nonsense.

But as Batista suspected, Tania Aparecida would not have brushed off the man in the pinstripe suit so easily. It was not because of the rhinestones or the headdress on the *mulata* or because of any gifts of gold watches and diamond earrings, but because Las Vegas would have sounded like a nice place to visit. Tania Aparecida looked at the map to see where the Djapan pigeons were flying, and she compared this with so many other exotic places in the world. Brazil was a big country, and their pigeons were flying everywhere. It would not take much more to get them to fly even farther. After all, one had reached New York. New York, thought Tania Aparecida. Somehow, she would find a way to get to New York.

It was thus that Tania Aparecida got the idea to provide special services for special occasions, a sort of greeting-pigeon business. Her marketing approach was to sell pigeons as monogamous, familial, dependable and loving creatures, the perfect messenger to send one's love, best wishes or condolences. She set up an experimental pigeon route between São Paulo and the nearby city of Campinas. Special homing posts were created where customers could write their messages and direct them to and from São Paulo and Campinas via pigeon. It was an immediate success. Grandparents sent Happy Birthday pigeon notes to their grandchildren in São Paulo, while lovers sent discreet messages from Campinas to São Paulo and so forth. In no time at all, Tania Aparecida was opening new homing posts in towns everywhere. The entire state of São Paulo was soon crisscrossed with Djapan Greeting Pigeon routes, and other states were eager not to be left behind in this trend. Tania Aparecida could hardly get to the next town fast enough to establish another homing post. Soon she found herself as far from her home as Rio Grande do Sul, thousands of miles away at the very southern tip of Brazil. From there, it was a short hop to Buenos Aires in Argentina. Djapan Pigeon Communications went international.

"Where are you?!" Batista shouted into the phone. "Who is watching things in São Paulo?"

"You needn't shout, darling," Tania Aparecida talked calmly into the phone. "Mother has everything under control. We had to move out of the tenement, you know. It was much too crowded. I got her a nice place in Suzano, you know where all the Japanese live. Thirty acres. It should be enough, don't you think? I'll give you Mother's new number . . ."

Batista scribbled the number on a scrap of paper. "What about the champions?" he asked. "Did they go to Suzano too?"

"Of course," Tania Aparecida assured him. "Oh, I almost forgot," she said. "There's a publisher that wants to put all of your messages in a book."

"Messages?" Batista had not relinquished his own weekly pigeon-message flights, which now flew into the Matacão and were announced on Radio Chico. People still followed with sustained ardor Batista's famous weekly pigeon messages, which continued to provide surprising strokes of luck for some and profound wisdom for others.

"They are going to call you. I've got to go, but I'm sending you a surprise. I miss you terribly." She hung up.

The surprise was that instead of communicating by telephone, he could now communicate with Tania Aparecida via their pigeon communication service. "The airways are ours," she exclaimed. "And it's completely free!"

Batista's jealousy still attempted to spread its clinging web through the communication system. "Tania Aparecida: Where were you when I called at 2:00 AM yesterday? What were you doing at such an hour?!"

"Darling, 2:00 AM your time is 10:00 AM here. I was in important negotiations," Tania Aparecida returned.

"Do you know how long it's been?"

"It's only temporary. Look how far we've come!"

"It's going to be a year!"

"How time flies!"

Batista raged impotently as Tania Aparecida wove the Djapan Pigeon Communications network farther and farther over the globe and, as she had always wished and dreamed of, traveled abroad for the company to New York, London, Paris and Las Vegas.

Part V:
More Loss

CHAPTER 22: PLASTICS

As KAZUMASA AND I took off to search for other Matacão locations, research concerning the nature of the Matacão's plastic structure was constantly churning up new information. As J.B. Tweep had explained to Kazumasa, after the first succeses in actually cutting the rigid plastic of the Matacão to obtain core samples, new breakthroughs establishing the means of molding and shaping the plastic were made. The new technology associated with the Matacão plastic would rapidly become the wave of the future, and GGG Enterprises was definitely leading this wave with most of the technology under wraps. J.B. had foreseen the eventual stabilization of feather sales and was eager to find new and dramatic sources of revenue. Once Matacão plastic technology became cost-effective, GGG would revolutionize the plastic market with one incredible novelty after another.

One of the great breakthroughs in plastics had to do with the magnetism of Matacão plastic. Not only did this open up new possibilities for refrigerator magnets, it was also discovered that this magnetism could be programmed in an infinite number of "addresses," making possible GGG's personalized credit cards without numbers or names. Matacão plastic magnetized credit cards were virtually indestructible and impossible to counterfeit. GGG, of course, would provide the computerized scanner to read the magnetized, coded information held within a seemingly blank piece of plastic. Instantly, a wealth of data regarding the purchaser — card number, license number, social security number, address, home and business phones, credit rating, checking account number, simulated signatures and recent photographs of authorized users — could be made available on a monitor. Magnetized credit cards, known as MCCs for short, would suddenly replace the antiquated stuff and send the credit-card insurance business scurrying for some new gimmick like a toll-free number to restore lost cards through an express mail, 24-hour service. Magnetized credit cards were so reliable that people would be able to use them to purchase things like real estate, stocks and gold bullion. GGG, it would be claimed, had accomplished what no one before had been able to achieve: it had turned plastic into gold! But for the compromising system of computer records, some had even considered the replacement of cold currency with a nationalized MCC system a real possibility. Some even predicted that currency would cease to be used by the year 2020 or even sooner.

The wonderful thing about the Matacão plastic was its capability to assume a wide range of forms. When the means of molding and shaping this marvelous material was finally discovered, the possibilities were found to be infinite. Matacão plastic could be molded into forms more durable and impenetrable than steel; it was harder than diamonds and, at the same time, could be spread out in thin sheets, as thin as tissue paper with the consistency of silk. Every industry from construction to fashion would jump into Matacão plastics. At a plastics convention, all sorts of marvels were displayed—cars made completely out of Matacão plastic, from the motor to the plush velveteen fabrics of the seats; imitation furs and leathers made into coats and dress pumps; Danish furniture made of Matacão "teak"; and all sorts of plants, from potted petunias to palm trees. The remarkable thing about Matacão plastic was its incredible ability to imitate anything. In the past, imitation leather had always had a telltale vinyl appearance, and silk flowers only seemed real until one got close and noticed the dust collecting in the stamens and pistils. But Matacão plastic was so true to reality that, even upon touch and a lot of palpating examination, one could not tell the difference. At the plastics convention, two tiger lilies, one natural and the other made from Matacão plastic, were exhibited for public examination. Few, if any, of the examiners could tell the difference between the real and the fake. Only toward the end of the convention, when the natural tiger lily began to wilt with age, bruised from mishandling, were people able to discern reality from fabrication. The plastic lily remained the very perfection of nature itself. Matacão plastic managed to recreate the natural glow, moisture, freshness—the very sensation of life.

Plastic surgeons would be quick to recognize the practical uses of Matacão plastic and adapt the new technology for use in facial rebuilds. Complete facial masks could be created and applied permanently to patients because of the Matacão plastic's novel capability to be breathable. Suddenly, people in all walks of life would appear to be facially younger, glowing with a constantly dewy freshness. Some would also appear to be not at all the way anyone remembered them.

Matacão plastics in a form harder than steel (some referred to it as flexible steel) could, of course, be immediately applied in housing and civil engineering. Anxious to experiment with this new moldable plastic, architects and engineers were scurrying about to design structures that would spread and jut incredibly into the modern skyline. Bridges, overpasses, skyscrapers, domes, coliseums, hamburger stands, parking lots, shopping malls, tract housing, would all suddenly take on miraculous forms. Bookstores everywhere featured books on Gaudi architecture and the Matacão plastic that was enabling his vision to become a reality.

In the next few years, Matacão plastic would infiltrate every crevice of modern life—plants, facial and physical remakes and appendages, shoes, clothing, jewelry, toys, cars, every sort of machine from electro-domestic to high-tech, buildings, furniture—in short, the myriad of commercial products with which the civilized world adorns itself. Matacão plastic would even be used to create artificial food (sushi samples, etc.) A few people had mistakenly eaten artificial food samples with no bodily discomfort or detriment; this signified to some researchers that if imitative and satisfying tastes (plus minimum daily requirements of minerals, nutrients and vitamins, less the calories) could be injected into plastic food samples (with the approval of the FDA, of course), plastic food might be touted as healthy, nonfattening and noncholesteric. Plastic food, of course, could not spoil. One would merely have to brush or wash off the dust and enjoy a juicy steak or chocolate mousse pie injected with only the necessary calories to maintain bodily functions. There was absolutely no risk of ptomaine poisoning, and astronauts could take it into space.

This new era, which some historians would refer to as the Plastics Age, was all made possible because of me, Kazumasa

Ishimaru's ball, without which new deposits of Matacão plastic could not be found. As J. B. Tweep had suspected, Kazumasa discovered new underground sources of Matacão plastic at several new sites in Pará, Amazonas, Maranhão, Ceará and Rondônia. The north of Brazil was a gold mine in plastic. Although GGG endeavored to keep the discovery of new sources of plastic a secret, unofficial leaks sent speculators from all over the world flocking to denude the forests. It seemed to be of no consequence that those who uncovered a piece of Matacão plastic in most cases did not have the technology to cut even a splinter of the stuff away from the mother lode. Some people wept at the sight of the shiny stuff, which reflected back a dull image of their happiness. Most people slipped away disconsolately, with only photographs of themselves near an uncovered site. Others remained resolutely camped on their handiwork until the government or GGG, with its laser-chemical-acid system for cutting the Matacão, came along and had to pay these squatters handsomely to leave.

As advanced as the technology behind Matacão plastics was becoming, the means of discovering new sources of the material eluded scientists. Kazumasa and I, alone, were the key to this incredible source of wealth.

In this great task of combing the countryside for Matacão plastic, J.B., with his usual thoroughness, sent Kazumasa and me out with a team of specialists, their assistants and their gofers to map out entire areas—every road, every railway, every waterway, every path through, by, under and over we must walk, swim, ride, float or hover—leaving no piece of that portion of Earth unknown to me, the ball. In this, J.B. was ruthless in his expectations, weaving and tossing GGG's net farther and farther, oblivious to any obstacles in our path: acres of flooded forest—dolphins leaping into the canopy, giant *pirarucú* waiting in the shallows for dropping fruit; great government hydroelectric dam projects—hundreds of species of plant and animal life bulldozed under, rotting and stinking for miles in every direction; Indian homelands, their populations decimated by influenza. Kazumasa saw, smelled, felt and tasted everything. He saw the beauty of the land, smelled the stink of its decomposition, felt the heat of the great forest fires, tasted the sweat of human labor. And still we moved on, searching for plastic.

That Kazumasa and I were the key to Matacão plastic was a secret which even Tweep could not keep under wraps for long. There were spies of every description—a motley and shady crew of CIA, KGB, international and industrial spies—in every corner of the forest, every Bromeliad, every Indian outpost or missionary's home, every public place, restaurant, men's room and hotel lobby that Kazumasa and I ever went to. In the beginning, Kazumasa was mildly aware of these people, and as he was always eager to make new acquaintances in this new home of his, he was openly friendly toward those spies he recognized frequently. J.B. had to step in with his own spies and whisk Kazumasa around to throw everyone off his tracks. There were days when, in order to shake some obstinate tail, Kazumasa and I were checked into and out of a dozen seedy hotels in a dozen towns and outposts, only to be left on some hidden forest runway supposedly known only to smugglers. J.B.'s men, identifiable to Kazumasa by the clips on their lapels and shirt collars, bounced Kazumasa and me around from town to town, dribbling us from hotel to hotel, passing and tossing us in a series of complicated moves to outsmart the opposition. Kazumasa was never sure himself where he was. This sort of moving around was worse than when he traveled the railways; at least, in those days, he could refer to a map and a train schedule. After a while, Kazumasa realized how, once again, he had become a solitary person alone in a busy world, with no one to talk to or trust but his ball. Everyone was after a piece of Matacão plastic, in particular, Kazumasa's own piece of plastic, me. It was soon apparent to Kazumasa that while many had good intentions, a few of the people who were running after us did not. Life-threatening notes had suggested that some people were not averse to ripping this precious satellite from its orbit, namely, Kazumasa. Greed was a horrible thing. Kazumasa could, if necessary, divest himself of his monetary fortune, but he could not rid himself of me.

Kazumasa telephoned back to São Paulo on a line that J.B. had scrambled and rerouted in several impossible directions.

Tia Carolina could barely hear Kazumasa through the entangled connection. "Seu Kazumasa? Is that you?" she yelled.

"Lourdes?" Kazumasa could barely hear. He thought he was talking to Lourdes. He repeated over and over again, *"Saudades, saudades, saudades."*

"Seu Kazumasa!" Tia Carolina screamed. "Where are you? Lourdes is looking for you! She went to the Matacão to look for you. Seu Hiroshi too. Everyone is looking for you!" It was true. Secret agents and journalists and inquisitive people had been there; they had slipped past the apartment house guards and had come up to the fourteenth floor and asked so many questions. Tia Carolina didn't know what to say. She kept Rubens and Gislaine upstairs and instructed them to talk to no one. She called Lourdes at Radio Chico, and they both agreed that Seu Kazumasa must be in some deep trouble. Tia Carolina screamed into the phone, "Seu Kazumasa, you're alive! Call Radio Chico! R-A-D-I-O C-H-I-C-O, and pray!" Suddenly, of course, the line went dead.

Radio Chico? Kazumasa wondered what this could mean.

*   *   *

In the meantime, Hiroshi had himself begun to wonder what had happened to Kazumasa. He received a repetition of happy postcards scribbled with short notes about seeing more of Brazil, but the postcard photos never matched the places from where the cards themselves were mailed. The months passed, and there were only postcards. He could trace his cousin up to the moment when Kazumasa reached GGG Enterprises, but everyone, including the president of the company who had graciously met and shook Kazumasa's hand during his VIP stockholder's tour, could only report that, to their knowledge, Kazumasa had returned home to São Paulo. Hiroshi did not want to start a panic. He had found Lourdes working at Radio Chico, but he did not want to confirm her worries. He knew that from time to time, Chico Paco asked the faithful over the radio if anyone had seen the Japanese with the ball. Despite Hiroshi's efforts to keep his suspicions to himself, newspapers and magazines began to pick up the story about the disappearance of the Japanese Santa Claus. There were newpaper articles headlined in bold letters: WHERE IS THE JAPANESE WITH THE BALL? The articles surmised that he may have been kidnapped or that he had had a nervous breakdown and returned to Japan.

After all, people had been waiting in line for months, having been told that Kazumasa was sure to return within a few days. A message telling the throng to wait just one more day nearly caused a small riot on the street. Some wept that they had traveled hundreds of miles for nothing. Others raged against the cruel fate of being only second or third in line. Finally, people dwindled reluctantly away, a few remaining vigilant and praying for Kazumasa's return.

Hiroshi began to wait for some sort of ransom note or telephone call. Not a few unscrupulous people thought that Kazumasa's very disappearance should prove lucrative in itself. These people called Hiroshi saying that they had information about the missing Japanese, which they would be able to divulge for a small price. Hiroshi hopelessly paid everyone for this useless information. He met the most preposterous kidnappers in every dark corner of his karaoke bars, but no one could produce the Japanese with the ball. At one point Hiroshi paid an unheard-of amount for the key to an airport locker where, the informant told him, he would find clear evidence of Kazumasa's whereabouts. Having obtained the key, Hiroshi rushed feverishly to the airport and tore open the appointed locker. Inside the locker was a note and a small box. The note said: "If you want to see the *rest* of the Japanese alive, leave one million dollars in cash in this locker by next Tuesday." When Hiroshi opened the small box, he jumped in horror. There inside were the lifeless remains of my purported form, having spun to a dead stop. Hiroshi cried out in anguish, his worst fears having come to life, but closer examination revealed, of course, that the ball in the box was a mere imitation, a clever but flawed replica.

Ironically, at the same moment, in another place near the Matacão, industrial spies were meeting surreptitiously, gloating over the contents of another small box. Unknown to the buyers, the contents of this box were as fake as the one Hiroshi was horrified to find. "What about the Japanese?" the buyer asked, slipping a thin feather past his ear.

"You only asked for the ball," was the answer.

"You mean—?" asked the buyer.

There was no response.

"I see," said the buyer. "But how will I know if this is really the ball?"

The spy produced a photograph of a dead Japanese.

"And if this ball does not work?" asked the buyer.

"That is no concern of mine. We made a deal."

* * *

Back on the Matacão at Radio Chico, similar false leads were called in. Lourdes contacted Hiroshi as soon as she heard anything, but "the Japanese with the ball" that someone had seen in some remote backwoods town was usually one of those persons who had become attached to one of those imitation satellite headbands or some other such visual mistake. In fact, people had seen Kazumasa and me and had truthfully reported this to Radio Chico, but J.B.'s undercover agents skillfully shoved us out of sight, stopping any and all pursuers, sending out false scents and confusion in our wake. Also, Kazumasa was made to wear a headband with a wire poking obviously from the band and pointing at me. This, for some reason, worked rather well.

In the beginning, searching for new deposits of Matacão plastic had been a kind of challenge for Kazumasa. Kazumasa had become tired of the charity business; he realized that his usefulness as a disperser of funds was limited by imagination and reality and that many people were too hungry and too poor to have much imagination or even much hold on reality. He realized further that his pleasure in granting any wish was as ephemeral as the wish itself: a woman who received a washing machine had no plumbing to run water to it; a family with a new refrigerator had no food to store in it; wheelchairs broke down without oil and repair; medical facilities had no personnel to run them.

Kazumasa was familiar with the technical challenge of scrutinizing railroad track wear; he did not miss that business, but he wondered if I did. He thought that searching for new deposits of Matacão plastic was a scientific venture, that he and I would be contributing to science and progress and the future. So he agreed to J.B.'s strictures on secrecy and went forth for the greater good of society, abandoning his family (Hiroshi) and friend (Lourdes), thinking that he would be able to explain everything to them in due time.

But lately, Kazumasa missed karaoke. He missed singing with abandon in his specially built karaoke shower at home. When he sang in hotel showers, he was asked to keep the volume down because it might arouse suspicion, all this singing of popular Japanese songs. And then, he missed Lourdes with a passion he was utterly unfamiliar with. The Brazilians called the longing for someone or something *saudades*, and Kazumasa thought that this must be what he was feeling for Lourdes. He heaved great sighs, and I shuddered sadly for him.

Lourdes, for her part, kept busy at Radio Chico, supervising calls for telephone pilgrims and always keeping an ear out for any news that Kazumasa had been found. When Tia Carolina called the toll-free Radio Chico number, Lourdes's heart lifted with joy. At least, she thought, Kazumasa was alive, he was alive somewhere.

In fact, contrary to many rumors, Kazumasa and I were quite alive. Kazumasa wondered now how he had ever gotten into this secretive business and when, like the funds in his checking account, the sources of Matacão plastic would simply dry up. He would simply tell J.B. Tweep and GGG Enterprises that this was it. Matacão plastic was a finite resource, and they would have to do with what they had. Kazumasa did not know that J.B. had plans to send us to Greenland, central Australia and Antarctica, not to mention every pocket of virgin tropical forest within 20 degrees latitude of the equator. I knew myself that Kazumasa and I would not be released from our duties so simply. J.B. had posted his undercover agents with their clipped lapels and shirt collars at every door and window, behind every tree, at the arc of every rainbow. No one could find us, nor could we escape. And so Kazumasa slept fitfully in strange beds in hotels that had all begun to look the same, dreaming the same dream night after night—dancing with goblins in plastic jungles.

CHAPTER 23: REMOTE CONTROL

DR. MANÉ PENA (recently conferred an honorary degree by the Matacão University) walked barefoot away from the podium and sat down amid a chorus of cheers and lingering applause. Mané's insistence that he owed all of his fame to his secretary, Carlos, was taken as so much false modesty. He was known throughout the world as the Father of Featherology. Thanks to Carlos, Mané Pena was the author and coauthor of numerous books and articles on featherology, none of which he himself could read, including the introduction to the famous ten-volume, leather-bound Encyclopedia of Feathers. His videotaped courses in featherology were translated into several languages and distributed to schools all over the world. He had been interviewed nationally and internationally. He was considered the foremost authority on feathers, corresponding with researchers from all over the world, heading seminars and commissions, directing the university research institute, dedicating his life to feathers. For reasons Mané Pena could not explain, his life had changed.

Mané's wife Angustia and the younger of their many children had long since moved back to the small town where Angustia had been born. One day, Dona Angustia got tired of feather talk, the buzzer on Mané's fancy watch, autograph parties for books she could not read, photographs of old Mané on the Matacão at sunset and the constant crowd of pushy interviewers and researchers. She was afraid of the telephone machine and always spoke before the beep. She was embarrassed to answer questions in interviews, pulling at the hems of her short cotton-print dresses and curling her toes into the rubber thongs to hide her rough feet. Mané Pena had stepped, barefoot, into a strange world where Angustia could not follow. She wondered where the old Mané Pena had disappeared to, longed for the old days when she could send one of their youngsters to the open cafe to fetch her husband for dinner. She took the embroidered lace towels off the tables and the TV, hauled off the sofa she had brought with her from her first marriage, packed the young ones up and left.

The older children had already slipped off one by one to a variety of jobs in distant cities in Brazil. Mané Pena rarely saw any of his family anymore. He missed the little ones, Beto and Marina, and all the grandchildren who once drifted in and out of his house. He missed talking to the youngsters. "Is this Junior's boy?" he would enjoy guessing with Angustia. Or "This one looks like Toninho did when he was a kid, eh Gustinha!" He liked his children best when they were young, their hands small, their feet bare and padding around the house, scurrying in bands to greet him in the streets. But now they were all gone. Even Chico Paco, who could understand Mané's predicament, did not come around after Angustia and the family had left. It was not the same, not the same full house of poor but generous people who shared everything they had. And, too, Chico Paco was now so busy with Radio Chico.

Mané Pena whisked a feather over his ear philosophically and pressed the buttons on the remote control for his color TV. This, he was told, was the price one paid for progress, for dedication to an ideal. He fast-forwarded to lecture no.7, in which he heard himself describe the invisible lines connecting points on the earlobe to all life. There was once a point on his lobe that attached him to Angustia and points attaching him to every member in his family. He had explained that the feather had a way of sorting these lines out, of untangling the confusion in a big family. Now there was nothing connecting him to any of them. It was as if these buttons on his remote control had suddenly been reprogrammed to bring up a whole new set of programs, as if his TV were suddenly made to pick up signals from some foreign country like the United States. All the old shows he loved so well, all the old soap operas, everything had suddenly been made to come out somehow differently. Everything was so much finer; nobody picked their teeth or squatted at the crossroads to contemplate the right way. Everything seemed to work; all time was taken up with a purpose. And yet, Mané missed the old jokes, the old characters, the simple plate piled high with rice and beans and manioc. He was sad, but he had been told that history would exonerate him in the end. By then he would be dead, but in the meantime, he consoled himself with the company of his color TV, which for the moment, still brought him the same old programs every day.

Mané Pena talked to Chico Paco on the phone. "Well, my son. How are you?"

"Gilberto and my mother are here now, you know."

"Gilberto? Your friend who was cured by the miracle?"

"The same."

"You sound tired."

"They're driving me crazy."

"Is that a fact?"

"It's not that I'm not happy they are here. I had prayed to Saint George for them to come."

"I remember. This Gilberto can walk now, can't he?"

"That's the problem. Gilberto can walk, climb, jump, run, crawl. He's like a baby—no, more like a monkey. He gets into everything. Yesterday I found him crawling up the side of our building."

Mané thought about this. "He must be like me. You won't find me in one of those metal boxes that go up and down."

"Elevators? No, Mané, he loves elevators. The second day he was here, he rode up and down all day. All day!"

"What about your mother?"

"I had to build her a clay stove."

"Gustinha used to swear by them."

"I had to build the clay stove in my apartment, Mané."

"I don't know how you can live in that beehive."

"They bring up wood every day for the stove."

"If you didn't live on top of that beehive, I'd come eat your mother's cooking," laughed Mané Pena.

"She's raising chickens, too," sighed Chico Paco. "And she plants vegetables in the bathtub."

"We old people are stuck in our ways," observed Mané Pena.

"What about you, Mané?" asked Chico Paco.

"Nothing's the same since that woman left," Mané Pena shook his head. "I always tell them that a feather can't replace a good woman."

Chico Paco heard the sadness in Mané Pena's voice. It was a sadness that he was not used to hearing from him. Mané had always been a man of balance. Chico Paco could not imagine Mané getting upset about anything. When the government handed Mané a ravaged piece of the forest, Mané signed his mark on the dotted line. One-half of his children had died at birth, but he had just sighed. When the priest came around and told him that after twenty pregnancies his wife should consider taking her temperature, he agreed. When his first wife died from meningitis and a lack of medical facilities, he bowed his head. When powdered milk mixed with an impure water source spread worms and dysentery among his grandchildren, he shook his head. When *sauva* ants devoured his crops, he threw up his hands. When the drought came and the sun seared the land and decimated his fields, he prayed for rain. When the rains finally came and washed the land away, Mané shrugged. What could poor people expect? He had heard that some poor people had gotten angry, formed unions, and they had been killed. It wasn't just that rubber tapper, Mendes, back in the old days (Mané Pena had seen the movie on TV; he noticed it was dubbed.); it had always been that way. Poor people survived, or they got killed. Mané Pena pressed the feather over his ear. As he had told Batista, a man needed tranquillity. But Chico Paco heard the sadness, the loneliness in Mané Pena's voice. It was one thing to weather hardship with others, but it was another to stand alone.

Lately, however, Mané Pena had not had much time to think about being lonely. "There's this big to-do over birds, you know," he told Chico Paco. It was true. There was a slowly escalating hubbub from a growing group of naturalists who were contesting the use of the feather. The list of petitioners was long, everyone from the membership of the Audubon Society to groups of schoolchildren in Ranger Rick Clubs, all concerned about the preservation and protection of birds, especially those nearing extinction. There were also vegetarians in leather jackets and tree lovers with digital sketch pads, who often picketed Mané's lectures, accosting him with wild threats, following him everywhere, holding candlelight vigils and making videos of performance-art pieces in front of his house.

Mané Pena, armed with his feather, was quite patient with all the protest. On the other hand, many Brazilians expressed indignation at the presence of these foreigners who came from big cities with high crime rates and serious drug problems and who arrived via Varig, sipping expensive wines and pecking at cold salmon on rye, to criticize a national figure raised from humble beginnings and a lucrative source of commerce for an impoverished country.

Mané Pena, however, was simple enough to recognize the moral dilemma raised by the use of the feather for human well-being and the human avarice related to the destruction of thousands of beautiful and often extremely rare birds. "They are right, you know," Mané said to Carlos, who read the letters signed by hundreds of petitioners. "These are the ones that really get you," he said, pointing to the packets of pencil-scrawled notes from children, accompanied by crayon drawings of birds being killed or poor featherless birds with tears dribbling to the bottom of the pages. Mané sighed.

As the Father of Featherology, Mané Pena had to take an official stand: he and his institute opposed the senseless killing of birds for their feathers for purely decorative uses, such as in costumes, headdresses or on hats, and supported efforts to create laws for stricter control of the commercial production of feathers. (The few Indians left living in the forest who continued to practice the ancient traditions were, of course, excluded from these restrictions.) However, Mané Pena, the official statement read, continued to support the use of feathers for the greater cause of science and human health.

For the moment, Mané Pena's diplomacy was supported by multinationals, top-echelon executives, single parents with full-time jobs, politicians, front-line soldiers, computer programmers, advertising art directors, supermarket checkers, high-tech designers and anyone in a position of defense, stress, wakefulness or excitement. A novel, attractive, clean, healthy and legal habit had been discovered which virtually replaced smoking, chewing gum, alcohol and coffee. With a little research or the help of a feather consultant, one could discover the correct feather for one's situation and personality. The feather, people claimed, was beneficial for every sort of situation. Couples going through divorce had given testimony to the rational and balancing effect of the feather on their emotional states. Law students claimed the feather was a tremendous aid in passing bar exams. Some people even claimed it had improved their sexual lives. Smokers were changing over to the feather in droves. Companies were sponsoring feather campaigns to encourage their employees to support a clean working environment. In some public places, one could already see signs segregating "Smokers" and "Feather Users." Feather-vending machines were becoming commonplace and could usually be found next to the coke machines. Everywhere, people were proclaiming the wonderful effects of the feather on their working, social and private lives.

At the same time, there was a growing cult of people who were not simply feather enthusiasts but feather worshipers. Unlike the feather user who dabbled in the feather, following Mané Pena's famous and usually abridged *Guide to the Feather* and subscribing to one feather magazine or another, feather worshipers applied mystical and mythical meanings and powers to the use of the feather. There were secret chapters of feather worshipers, who initiated members into their societies, taught methods of voodoo and black magic associated with certain bird feathers and moved, in general, to control the physical and social world around them. Some former members, who claimed to have been brainwashed and subsequently deprogrammed, spoke of seances to call down the spirits of birds, the unleashing of power in certain feathers to produce hallucinations, intense training in bird language and the always dangling promise of the potential power of flight. It was discovered, in a case shrouded in mystery, that two known members of a cult had thrown themselves from the roof of a twenty-five-story condo on the Matacão. Their bodies were found plastered to the shiny surface, their hands clutching bunches of feathers. Mané Pena publicly denounced the secret feather cults as weird aberrations that had abandoned the sacred and life-giving powers of the feather in favor of unscientific pursuits and evil.

No matter what Mané Pena's personal or official opinion regarding the use and commercialization of the feather was, it was evident to everyone that birds everywhere were in grave trouble. Although GGG Enterprises had the largest legal concession on the purchase of feathers around the Matacão, smaller entities, both legal and illegal, were already operating in the area and ripping the feathers off every sort of bird imaginable. GGG Enterprises, officially, dealt only with legal operations that farmed parrots in large quantities, but good deals on the black market were difficult to pass up. On the Matacão, it was a simple matter to make contact with an illegal dealer in rare feathers. Everyone was selling them. Depending on the feather, a dealer could get an enormous amount of money from an unsuspecting tourist. The consumer was often wise to buy from an authorized dealer who offered some sort of warranty; entire shipments of feathers were often found to be chicken feathers dipped in dye to resemble parrot plummage. Despite the risk of imitations, the black-market trade was heavily exploited; but far greater were the unknown quantities of precious feathers which took flight via various smuggling routes, across the Andes to Peru or the Guyana Highlands into Venezuela.

Those dealers who had held off from signing long-term contracts for their feathers found that their gamble had paid off. The price of feathers of all types inflated every month by 100 percent. For feathers, the sky seemed to be the limit. There was a story going around that a rare tanager feather of exquisite coloring had gone for $250,000 at a recent auction. The value of feathers created new difficulties for such places as zoos and gardens with aviaries. These public places now had to be guarded twenty-four hours a day by police. The zoo in Rio de Janeiro had already been robbed of several of its finest Amazonian birds on five different occasions. Individuals with birds had to install sophisticated electronic detection systems to protect against pilferage. Some bird owners caged their birds behind heavy iron grids to protect them both from robbers and from the savage dogs used to patrol the cages. Batista, for example, after an article restating Mané Pena's old preference for pigeon feathers appeared, was forced to acquire fierce dogs and hire guards to protect his Djapan champions. Even dead birds were no longer safe. The natural history museums in several cities had reported the loss of many of their stuffed parrots, storks and cockatoos.

Naturally, the success of the feather gave rise to speculation about imitations. As far as anyone could tell, dyed chicken feathers were perfectly satisfactory implements in most cases and for most purposes. It was as Mané Pena had always maintained: the feather depended on the skill of the user. Of course, there had been other discoveries about the greater energy-absorbing powers in rarer feathers, which led executives and others with high-pressure jobs to demand more expensive feathers, but most people were into feathers for appearance's sake. Those who followed the trends, who carried feathers in order to be popular, could easily be accommodated by chicken feathers. Predictably, it was exactly these people who rejected cheaper feathers. Still, research went forward in the attempt to create a successful plastic feather that would perfectly imitate that of the rare tanager and could be mass-produced for an eager populace.

Mané Pena looked at two feathers J.B. had sent to him. One was real, the other made of Matacão plastic. He could not tell the difference. Mané scratched his head. He felt confused. He did not want to think about this problem. He looked at his television, which he never turned off anymore. He missed noise, and the noise from that machine seemed to comfort him. He stared at the TV, then he stared at the two feathers. He pressed the buttons on his remote control. Lately he enjoyed watching himself give lectures in languages he could not understand. He liked to watch his own mouth moving with these strange noises coming out. He found it especially amusing to hear himself talk

Chinese or Japanese. Often he would call Carlos, putting the receiver up to the TV and ask, "Carlos! What language am I speaking now?" Today, it was Russian or German. He stared past the feathers at himself—the same toothless grin, the same grey stubble of unshaved beard, the strange language flowing from his lips—and fell asleep.

CHAPTER 24: TRIALECTICS

AS I SAID BEFORE, it was not that Michelle spoke up in public. Her very presence beside the obscure J.B. was enough to make anyone reevaluate the man at her side. To J.B.'s embarrassment, he was suddenly on the cover of *Business Week* and *Forbes,* billed as the man behind GGG, with an exclusive article following him around the Matacão, through the corridors of GGG and onto his private plane. The tabloids leaked the news that J.B. had proposed to Michelle Mabelle. Their marriage was touted with great fanfare. Soon they appeared cheek-to-cheek on the cover of *People,* were featured in an interview in *Cosmopolitan* in which he and Michelle were asked point-blank whether sex with three arms was indeed everything it was rumored to be, and followed unremittingly by Robin Leach and his camera for a spot on *Life Styles of the Rich and Famous.*

Robin Leach was forced to dump most of the footage because J.B. actually led a rather dull life, aside from his physical escapades with Michelle, which were, of course, untapeable. Footage of Michelle's exotic and extravagant bird collection and Napoleon eating slices of Camembert in J.B.'s penthouse condo was kept, but the newfangled Matacão plastic projects, the abandoned 9.99 stuff and J.B.'s clip collection really had very little stylish appeal, especially as everything was arranged in the haphazard fashion of a tropical forest.

There was a particularly romantic scene where the cameras caught J.B. giving Michelle a tiny jewel box. "Oh, Jonathan," Michelle cooed. "You shouldn't have."

J.B. glowed lovingly as Michelle removed its velveteen cover and discovered the solid-gold diamond-studded paper clip within. Leach kept the footage of the sunrise over the Matacão, aerial views of the Amazon Forest from J.B.'s personal helicopter and Michelle's habitual early-morning trek through the forest as she sighted riverside cormorants, egrets and spoonbills. Leach also shot a lot of footage of Michelle Mabelle as she worked with Paris designers on custom clothing to promote her special attributes, but it was too much trouble to go to Hong Kong to interview Huang, who had been J.B.'s tailor ever since J.B. could remember requiring a suit to go job hunting.

J.B. and Michelle were soon the target of an enormous amount of gossip, mostly regarding their sexual lives. Both were approached on numerous occasions to pose in the nude. Despite a certain perversity that their extra extensions aroused, there were some positive results. The growing curiosity about extra arms and breasts brought hundreds of closet cases with extra fingers, toes, tails, etc. into the public light. These people, suddenly liberated by J.B. and Michelle's obvious success and fame, congregated in large and small groups to proclaim their rights before a society that had relegated them to freak shows. The trialectics movement, known colloquially as the "freak movement," with its call for freak rights and so forth, turned out to be an enormous and heretofore unknown contingency for politicians to respond to. (The term *trialectics,* first coined by J.B., was immediately given a larger meaning to encompass the physical as well as philosophical basis for J.B.'s original ideas.) While Michelle Mabelle supported the freak movement with generous donations and public appearances, J.B. felt no empathy with the painful self-consciousness most of these people spoke of. He had always felt that he was one of the more privileged human beings, a more advanced specimen. It was only a matter of time, to him, before other human beings with only two arms or two breasts would begin to feel inadequate.

Public rapture over the love affair of J.B. and Michelle Mabelle seemed for the moment to raise a transparent but impenetrable barrier of Matacão plastic between the couple and what environmentalists were generally calling the rape of Mother

Nature. As with all such charismatic people, the media surrounded J.B. and Michelle like adoring handmaidens and
makeup artists, transforming warmongers into peacemakers,
criminals into saints, the inept into the apt, the empty into the
full. How, for example, could an ornithologist, a French ornithologist at that, who kept an aviary of tropical and rare birds
inside her apartment, who trekked daily into the forest to look
for new species, be anything but a lover of birds? When Michelle Mabelle tearfully told reporters of her anger over the illegal
sale of rare feathers, everyone agreed that she was concerned.
"Buyers must take the care and time," Michelle emphasized in
her melodic voice, "to discover the origin of their feathers. They
should use a respected brand like GGG, which only deals in the
legal farming of feathers and supports serious scientific research and the preservation and study of all birds. Since GGG
committed itself to generous grants to ornithologists all over
the world, hundreds of new species have been identified! To
other such illegal feathers, you must just say, 'Non!'"

Then, there was the growing concern over the mining process
of Matacão plastic. The chemical runoff from GGG's secret
technique had been collected and analyzed and found to cause
genetic mutations in rats after five generations. The mutations
were most bizarre and grotesque. Rats were found to develop
fangs and tiny horns and an eager appetite for blood. The idea
of vampire rats caused a shudder of horror and speculation
about a tropical Transylvania. However, some later generations were found to sport extra appendages—research that J.B.
followed with particular interest. Such aberrations of the general mutation process caused by Matacão mining runoff gave
J.B. reason to justify the pollutant. The GGG official write-ups
stated, "GGG Enterprises has a firm policy of environmental
concern. All runoff from Matacão mining is collected, encap-
sulated in stainless-steel containers and sealed at strategic disposal locations. GGG's disposal locations will not impact the
social or environmental structure as they are usually spaces
made vacant by the mining itself. Sophisticated collection pro-
cedures guarantee a 98.2 percent collection of runoff material.
Additionally, research and development is proceeding to find

methods to extract and employ the currently known benefits from runoff."

While Michelle Mabelle bathed warmly in the public lime-light, J.B. twitched uncomfortably. He was typically terse and uncommunicative, which somehow got translated as subtle and mysterious. He would not have accepted all this attention except for Michelle. He and his third arm owed everything to her, but he was now in constant fear of finding himself deposed from the top, lopped off the twenty-third floor of GGG. It had happened to Geoffrey and Georgia; it could happen to him. Having exposed his hand, as it were, there was no department, no obscure clerical or unnecessary managerial position in which to hide. He constantly dialogued with the American mag-pie Butch and even attempted for a time to "jus' chill out," as was the magpie's usual suggestion. "I'm trying, Butch," J.B. insisted. "I'm really trying."

To which the magpie replied, "Love is a many-splendored thing."

"Yeah, Butch, Yeah."

"Splendid. Splendid."

"Yeah."

"Love love love."

"Yeah," J.B. agreed. "Love love love." What else could he do but ride those currents from obscurity to fame? As with Mi-chelle Mabelle, everything was obscured for the moment by love. So after those initial and passionate serenades, poses, flaps and thrusts, J.B. and Michelle Mabelle nestled comfor-tably in their plexiglass high-rise overlooking the Matacão, cooing contentedly among the birds, rearranging plastic ob-jects, clips and old 9.99 oddities. J.B. wrapped all three arms around her. She was pregnant, and it looked like triplets. *Liberté. Égalité. Fraternité.*

CHAPTER 25: RADIO

IN ORDER TO CONTINUE the good works of Radio Chico and the Foundation for Votive Pilgrimages, listeners and supporters were urged to send their generous donations. Money was needed to send pilgrims out to the far reaches of Rondônia and Rio Grande do Sul, and pilgrims could not be expected to arrive at the Matacão again without food, clothing and shelter. In return for subscribing to the foundation, supporters received a newsletter and a small replica of the statue of Saint George originally sent by Dona Maria Creuza—God rest her soul—with Chico Paco to the Matacão.

Many listeners supported the foundation by housing and feeding pilgrims whose travels they followed closely through the radio's constant updates. As a pilgrim approached some town or village, Radio Chico would receive dozens of calls offering some form of assistance to the weary pilgrim. In more than one case, pilgrims were feted by entire towns, greeted by mayors, some approving priests and not a few of the so-called beatified. Pilgrims were known to have spent several weeks in welcoming towns, until a stern telephone call from Chico Paco or a confused plea by the blessed urged them on toward their destination.

Occasionally the foundation was forced to send a second pilgrim to take the place of the original. One pilgrim had a sudden heart attack on the road and died. Another was almost killed by a speeding car. One pilgrim fell in love with a lonely widow who had offered her home as shelter. A few offered no reason for quitting other than that the scenery or the company in one place was too attractive to continue on. The foundation frowned upon such irresponsibility, was forced to draw up stringent rules and standards for pilgrims and began to withhold favors until pilgrimages to the Matacão were actually completed. Despite the possibility of losing one's surrogate pilgrim before even reaching the Matacão, people continued to call upon the foundation for help. The foundation, at least, had a reputation for replacing lax or unpromising pilgrims, and people enjoyed the assurance that, eventually, their votive requests would be kept. Also, people knew and believed that Chico Paco kept his promises, and that despite human failure, foundation pilgrimages were stamped with Chico's approval.

Thus, Chico Paco and his pilgrims were deluged every day by new requests. To sift through and filter out the lesser requests from the honest and truly urgent pleas was now a massive job for which dozens of workers were required. The radio station was inundated by paperwork and swamped with telephone calls. Not only had the pilgrimages become an institution in themselves, Radio Chico was now a bustling entity with new and popular programs, eager sponsors, and thousands of new listeners every day. There were bills to be paid, accounting to oversee, meetings to attend, newsletters to edit, plans to develop. Then, too, there were religious leaders to see or placate, some of them irate, some oozing with religious unction, some looking for an eight o'clock spot. Overnight, Chico Paco was faced with an operation that was bursting at the seams, expanding in every direction without control.

Becoming an evangelical radio institution was the sort of coming of age that a cartoon character or a kid whose face appears on a cereal box must experience. Chico Paco would forever, even if he grew to be a very old and decrepit man, be the boyish young angel of everyone's dream pilgrimage. Maybe it was because his voice over the radio—the single identifiable characteristic by which thousands of people could immediately identify Chico Paco—never changed and the photographs the institution sent out of Chico Paco over the years were always the same. Meanwhile, the young fisherman from the coastal village of multicolored sands had grown to be a man. Pilgrimages and food had filled out the long, thin frame and thickened the growth of blonde hair on his face. His eyes, however, were still the same iridescent green, the same mysterious color; they did not betray the changes within the man. Chico Paco had learned to be verbal and vocal on the radio. He had learned the happy banter of the disc jockey, casting his voice into a sea of invisible waves, hooking and drawing in thousands of people in distant places. "That's true, Brother So-and-So," he would say with his now-characteristic drawl. "We must thank the Lord for miracles by keeping our promises to Him." The exhilaration and momentum of what seemed to be a great religious movement buoyed Chico Paco. People followed because he was an identifiable banner, different from the others, his bleached hair in a sea of black and brown. For one brief moment, Chico Paco was exactly the figure soon to be congealed in people's minds — a young fisherman with a simple heart and boyish honesty, the twinkle of promises in his eyes.

But Gilberto had come to the Matacão. And so had Chico Paco's mother, Dona Feliz. It was through these two people that Chico Paco could see the changes in himself — through Gilberto, the possible extremities of these changes, and through his mother, the distance of his old life. The Matacão was as strange a place to Gilberto and Dona Feliz as it was to Chico Paco, but while Gilberto grasped at every new sensation like a baby learning to walk, Dona Feliz installed herself in this new world as if it did not exist. She wandered barefoot around her son's carpeted apartment (almost as if she had never left her home on the beach), cooked the foods Chico Paco loved on a clay wood-burning stove (which he had especially installed in a modern kitchen for her) and continued to wash clothing by hand at the river. She claimed it was the only way to get clothing really clean. Every day, a taxi waited for Chico Paco's mother to descend the elevator of the apartment house and drove the woman with her basket of dirty clothing down to the river. The driver waited while she squatted at the river's edge, slipped a bar of coconut soap from her pocket and spent much of the morning pounding and slapping the wash on the smooth rocks. Chico Paco's mother kept the floors swept, but she had never known glass windows, bathtubs, toilets or sinks in her old mud shack on the beach and, consequently, never washed them. Chico Paco had a maid come in occasionally to scrub down the the bathrooms, wash the windows, dust the furniture, and run the vacuum cleaner over the rugs — the noise of which always sent Chico Paco's mother cowering into a safe closet.

Although she never quite got used to the vacuum cleaner, Chico Paco's mother did adapt to some novelties of the modern world. She agreed to empty all the toilet bowls and bathtubs of

dirt, thus giving up her bathroom flower and vegetable gardens. It had seemed like such a good idea with the added convenience of an easy water source. But she would not give up
raising chickens on the twentieth floor. Although she attempted to confine them to the kitchen and service areas, occasionally Chico Paco would wake to the sound of a rooster crowing off
the end of his bed or be surprised by an entire family of newborn
chicks bedded down in the disarray of shoes and strewn clothing in a dark closet, the frantic mother hen clucking angrily at
the closed door.

Gilberto, on the other hand, adapted easily to this new life,
probably because, having been an invalid for so many years,
taking his first steps coincided with his discovery of the world.
Like a curious and rambunctious toddler, Gilberto got into
everything. Chico Paco would find Gilberto on a ladder in the
kitchen exploring the exhaust system over the clay stove, strad-
dling the railing of the balcony that extended over the Matacão
twenty floors below, or swimming in the bathtub while the
water sloshed over the edge of the tub. Chico Paco's heart
would always leap when he saw Gilberto up to some mischief.
He scolded Gilberto like that mother hen and rebuked him with
the suggestion that he, Chico Paco, should have stayed home
on the beach instead of making that pilgrimage to the Matacão
for such a fool.

But Chico Paco could not mean this, for the exhilaration and
imagination with which Gilberto ran after life charmed Chico
Paco, and he forgave Gilberto every sort of madcap mischief
because he loved Gilberto as much as his own life. In truth, he
could not be without Gilberto. As soon as Gilberto arrived on
the Matacão, Chico Paco felt both the calming sense of the
familiar and the giddiness of an old friendship. Gilberto, like
the newborn child he was, had run to the comfort of Chico
Paco's eager arms. The two men cavorted together as in childhood, trying to make up for the lost time of Gilberto's illness.

When Gilberto had exhausted the possibilities of his apartment surroundings, he began to look elsewhere. "Paquinho, I
saw a woman driving a red car with no top. Can you imagine?
Her hair was blowing in the wind, and she was going so fast. I
want a car just like hers. Please, Paquinho!"

"Do you know how to drive? Do you?"

"If you want to turn this way, you turn the wheel this way. If you want to turn that way, you turn the wheel that way. What's the secret?"

"It's too dangerous."

"Paquinho, can you imagine all the pilgrims with little red cars? They would arrive at the Matacão in no time!"

When Chico Paco refused to get a little red sportscar for Gilberto, Gilberto discovered some way to get it himself. It was the same with a score of other whims and toys: a pair of roller skates, an iceboat, a motorcycle, a dune buggy and a skateboard. Inevitably, Gilberto would crash or tumble in his escapades, and Chico Paco would find himself running out of his radio shows to find that Gilberto had scraped his knee or bumped his head. "What are you trying to do?" he screamed at Gilberto. "You want to be paralyzed all over again?"

"Don't get so upset, Paquinho. It won't happen again, I promise you. I was almost getting it, really I was."

Chico Paco did not know whether to laugh or to cry. He could not chain Gilberto down. Chico Paco was witnessing the miracle that had brought him to the Matacão. After Gilberto could walk, he wanted to run. And then he wanted to run faster and faster and faster. Chico Paco could not deny Gilberto his new liberty. So when Gilberto began to insist on an idea to create an amusement park, Chico Paco listened with the mixed emotions of amusement, love and terror. Gilberto had seen these parks on television and thought that they were wonderful. "They have trains that go so fast that when they go upside down, the people don't fall out."

Chico Paco tried to ignore Gilberto's wild idea to build a roller coaster, hoping that some other toy might placate him. But he was mistaken and, as before, unable to circumscribe Gilberto's activities in any way. When J. B. Tweep gave him an enthusiastic response—"This amusement park idea is just the sort of project GGG would be interested in. It's the perfect way to introduce the new technology of Matacão plastic to the world"—Chico Paco realized that Gilberto would accept no limits to his love for movement and speed.

The idea had so excited J.B. that he had tipped over the magnetic clip holder on his desk. He instantly committed GGG Enterprises to 50 percent of the project. "A joint venture!" J.B. announced. GGG would provide the know-how and the Matacão plastic to accomplish this dream. After all, Matacão plastic had been molded into everything imaginable, both life-size and lifelike. An entire world could be created from it.

*　*　*

Chico Paco commiserated with Lourdes, who he felt must understand because of her experiences with her son Rubens. "I understand," she nodded sympathetically. "If Rubens could walk, it would be the same thing. As it is, poor thing, he fell out the window."

"What should I do?" he asked for her advice. "I can't lock him up."

"This is just a phase," she assured him. "He will get over it. It might take a scare, but he should settle down."

Chico Paco wondered. "How is Rubens? And Gislaine? Have you heard?" he asked.

"Tia Carolina called yesterday. Gislaine, of course, is an angel—going to school, studying hard. She will be someone someday, but imagine Rubens. He ran his wheelchair down some stairs. Why he would do such a thing, I don't know. Now one wheel is bent. What will I tell Seu Kazumasa . . . if I ever see him again?"

Chico Paco smiled. "I miss Rubens," he said.

Lourdes sighed. She missed her children, but she had made a promise to herself, however long it might take, to find Kazumasa. Ever since Tia Carolina's call, several months ago, asserting that Kazumasa had called home, Lourdes was sure that Kazumasa would, if he could, find a way to call Radio Chico. In her heart, Lourdes felt that Kazumasa was alive. This time, when he returned, she would let him know how she felt, would turn this Japanese into an honest man. I myself wondered about this. My clairvoyance was somewhat limited to fact; human emotions often escaped me.

* * *

As only J.B. could promise, Chicolándia was completed in an amazingly short period of time. This was because all of the structural forms were shipped in and quickly cast near the Matacão, much in the same manner of the great, cloned GGG skyscraper on the Matacão. Everything in Chicolándia was being made of Matacão plastic, from the roller coasters to the giant palms, the drooping orchids and the buildings, whose interiors and exteriors were designed to imitate scenes from Gilberto's favorite movies—*Cabaret; Heidi; Cleopatra; Snow White; Spartacus; Hello, Dolly; Cat Ballou; Raiders of the Lost Ark; The King and I; Star Trek IV* and so on. The animated animals, also constructed in the revolutionary plastic, were mistaken for real animals until people questioned their repetitive movements, their obviously benign nature, and the trade-off in smells: the warm stench of animal refuse for a sort of gassy vinyl scent. Elephants, lions, kangaroos, zebras, anteaters, camels, sloths, buffaloes, panda bears, vultures, penguins and crocodiles—to mention only a few in an enormous variety of thudding, crawling, creeping, hanging and flying fauna—would soon create a bizarre ecology as they tramped through a projected maze of magnificent scenes: Babylonian towers on a desert oasis, the Taj Mahal, the docks of Amsterdam, Times Square in New York City, the Miami International Airport, the French Riviera, the Las Vegas strip, Patagonia, the California gold rush, Egyptian and Peruvian pyramids, Indonesian temples, medieval castles, the *Titanic,* ancient Rome, mythical Greece, and the moon. Gilberto's imagination and memory of television were endless. The former invalid, who had never known any place other than his birthplace on the multicolored dunes, and now the Matacão, could soon be suddenly anywhere both in time and space.

Chicolándia was built next to the Matacão, as if the Matacão itself were the polished road leading to that paradise of plastic delights. As everything was being assembled in its proper place, Gilberto ran around like a child, climbing into everything, chasing the animated elks through the eternally fresh jungle foliage and the monkeys around the Parthenon. He never tired of taking a miniature train through a series of tunnels; Chico Paco waited patiently while Gilberto insisted on riding one more time. "Chiquinho!" Gilberto would yell and wave as the train disappeared under the tunnel. As for the Ferris wheel, Chico Paco insisted on going up with Gilberto, fearful that he would certainly try something daring like swinging from one car to the next while the wheel churned him skyward as high as twenty-five meters. For Gilberto, who was used to the twentieth floor, twenty-five meters was nothing at all. Chico Paco inevitably gagged upon going around the twelfth time, and Gilberto sadly but obediently accompanied his friend to the ground.

As if this were not enough, Gilberto loved to be on television. Besides the regular attractions, where people would one day be able to observe themselves (thanks to souvenir videotapes) wandering around in famous scenes from Gilberto's favorite movies, there were hundreds of hidden and planted cameras, usually focused on some possible source of danger to Gilberto. Chico Paco posted a twenty-four-hour guard to scan these monitors, making sure Gilberto was not up to some mischief. But Gilberto knew of all the monitors and purposely arranged elaborate situations in order to be seen doing something fantastic on the screen. The guards became used to seeing Gilberto disguised in elaborate costumes, often representing an odd combination of human and animal attributes rescued from discarded pieces of the ever-assembling plastic fantasy, stealing up the Eiffel Tower still in construction or the fire escape of a prop for King Kong, sliding down the back of a brontosaurus, or threatening to swing from the plastic vines of the jungle onto a subsequent scene, bouncing off the spongy bed of Marilyn Monroe. Chico Paco would hear the warning peal on his beeper and race with his heart pounding anxiously to the monitoring room, only to see Gilberto in some Arab garb trying to force a mechanical camel to fly off a steep precipice into the sparkling white sands below. Gilberto got out of most of these episodes with only bumps and bruises, but to Chico Paco's dismay, even a broken bone did not slow his friend down much at all. What had happened to the invalid quietly weaving lace in the shade of a coconut tree? thought Chico Paco, gripping his heart and wondering whether he could live through another one of Gilberto's crazy escapades.

As more and more of Chicolándia was completed, Chico Paco wondered at the wisdom of this joint venture with GGG Enterprises. No sooner had the deal been closed than that strange skyscraper on the Matacão began to churn Gilberto's mad ideas into forests of paper, high-priority meetings, pressurized schedules, jobs, egos, ulcers and the odd result that came to be Chicolándia.

* * *

The message Hiroshi received was as cryptic as all the others but more meaningful and distressful than any: "We have two pretty children, a boy and a girl. Rubens and Gislaine. The boy can't run anywhere. And the girl . . . ? We will be happy to exchange these precious children for the Japanese with the ball. Let us say, one child for each commodity. The girl for the Japanese himself, but more importantly, the boy for the ball. You will be hearing from us again."

CHAPTER 26 : PIGEON COMMUNICATIONS

WHERE WAS TANIA APARECIDA NOW, Batista asked himself. Was it Rome she had written on the pigeon express message? Zurich? Amsterdam? He could not remember. Where was she when he needed her? Who was she with? What was she up to? She sent him packages from everywhere she went, trinkets and souvenirs, things, she said, that had reminded her of him: a postcard of *Au Pigeon Voyageur* in Lille, France, monument to the 20,000 pigeons killed in action during World War I; a painted porcelain Hummell doll with a dove on his finger; a Donald

Duck hat; a photographic encyclopedia of birds; a stuffed replica from the Smithsonian of Cher Ami; the famous homer who in 1918 saved the "Lost Battalion"; and so forth. The packages came daily, but Batista had lost the desire to figure out what about the presents reminded Tania Aparecida of him. He threw the unopened packages in a pile angrily. When was that woman coming back?

Djapan Pigeon Communications International, he mumbled to himself. Thanks to Tania Aparecida, they were an international communications system, but being able to communicate for free with Tania Aparecida over thousands of miles seemed a lousy trade-off to having her right there in bed with him. How she missed her dear Batista — that message had traveled along the distant pigeon routes, but there she was, still out there somewhere in Europe, Asia, Africa or America.

Batista was alternately consumed with jealousy and depressed with his inability to treat their separation with nonchalance. He imagined Tania Aparecida in every sort of situation of infidelity. He tossed in his bed at night with visions of Tania Aparecida in the arms of another man, or even several men. He envisioned her escorted into fancy hotels and restaurants, drinking expensive wines out of stemmed crystal glasses, flaunting her hips or exposing her legs, making seductive passes, her brown eyes narrowing under their thick lashes. He imagined the men of every race, creed, religion and color running their foreign tongues up and down the curve of her neck and touching all those secret places only he was supposed to know. The blood rushed to Batista's head at the very thought. He flushed purple and spit venom, but Tania Aparecida did not return. There was always one more place to see, one more deal to close, one more client to keep at bay. "I'll be home by your birthday, darling," Tania Aparecida would promise, only to break her promise and send him a singing telegram in her stead. "That woman can go to hell!" Batista screamed at the poor baritone who choked on the word *happy* and ran off in a fright, forgetting to deliver the bouquet of flowers that went with the telegram.

Tania Aparecida's international life was a whirlwind of meetings and deals. How little did she realize that her first meeting, when she had put on her very best dress and shoes and persuaded that cute old man Carlos Rodrigues of the Pomba Soap Company that Djapan Pigeon Enterprises could put his company on the map—that meeting would be the prototype for all future encounters. Now she had a dress for every sort of client and situation.

As Batista had long known, Tania Aparecida had a phenomenal head for figures, and she never forgot a face or a name. A captivating smile, a quick mind for details, a voice full of charm and resonance—Tania Aparecida herself was a woman few could forget. "If only they'd run that country the way this woman runs her business!"

"Pigeons are very clean and quiet," Tania Aparecida would say. "You can keep them practically anywhere. Djapan Enterprises will provide you with a starting couple or a larger brood, if you like. We show you how to build your roosts, and we start you with a three-month supply of our famous feed. Once your brood is established, which doesn't take very long at all, you are ready to make them available for our communications network. Then, we provide you with messenger tubes, sample greeting messages, and a map of our network posts. The larger your brood, of course, the more messages you will be able to handle, but we believe it is best to start out small. So you begin with one network post, exchanging your birds back and forth. As you become more comfortable with our network, you can grow with us and add on more network posts." Tania Aparecida was able to convey this information with such charm that people everywhere seriously considered starting a network post in the same manner that they might consider buying Tupperware.

"Now, we have a starting fee, the amount depending on how large a brood you are willing to start with. If you have a large area and more capital, you can use our Plan B or C, but most people start with a couple and Plan A, and they can grow from there. Some clients do not want to get too big, and they simply limit their messages. Djapan is very flexible that way. We work with a lot of mothers who are busy at home with their children and who can make a little extra money on the side. I know one woman, Dona Clara in Campo Verde, who buys all her groceries from her profits in the network." People always liked Tania Aparecida's personal way of talking. They all thought of Dona Clara and her six children and how the network was feeding her family.

"Now, we have monthly membership dues for using the network and a per-message service fee, which is charged to the customer, of course. Besides putting you on the Djapan network map, membership entitles you to our special services—our pigeon wellness hotline, veterinarians and medicines at a discount, our professional advice and our network newsletter."

If Batista could hear his Tania Cidinha, he might have been impressed, but he had no idea. He got the newsletter, which was now published in several languages; it amused him to read about himself, but he wondered why Tania Aparecida insisted on putting a new squab recipe in the cooking column every week. He had seen the network map grow into a mass of posts over the globe. He knew that their operation was big, but he had no real sense of it. He was too busy breeding new pigeons to cover these distances. All he knew was that Tania Aparecida was far away. It made very little difference how far. Batista's jealous imagination could follow Tania Aparecida to the next room or to the moon.

Tania Aparecida would have laughed if she could have known Batista's imagination, which placed her in the midst of glamour and international escapades. Tania Aparecida sold network posts all over the world in basically the same manner she had sold them in Brazil: door to door. If Batista imagined Tania Aparecida hobnobbing with men in pinstripe suits, wining and dining them, he was far removed from the reality of a pigeon communication business, which had to be built in a series of steps from one neighborhood to the next. It was something like setting up hotdog stands or small post offices everywhere. Certainly Tania Aparecida was no stranger to the big cities and grand hotels, but just as setting up a coke machine in a lobby did not require speaking with the president of the company, neither did establishing a pigeon post.

That Tania Aparecida attracted attention and admiration, there was no doubt. If people wanted to look, what was it to her? If it helped sales, then all the better. Tania Aparecida was indiscriminately charming, but there was something about her, a wanderlust, which kept her from staying anywhere long enough to form attachments, no matter how friendly or attractive the admirer. Perhaps, it was part of something the Brazilians called *saudades,* the bittersweet sensation of exuberant but temporary joy. To have it all the time, you have to keep moving on and savoring memories. It was something like putting a pack of misbehaving kids to bed after a very wearing day and spending the evening poring lovingly over an album of photographs of the same naughty kids. The reality of love and life with Batista was so much sweeter at a distance; Tania Aparecida could forget Batista's insane jealousy, his volatile fits, their crazed fighting. But each time, when the memory swelled so deeply and so painfully that Tania Aparecida could only think of rushing back to Batista's arms, an angry message would come through the network, betraying Batista's jealousy and startling Tania Aparecida's sense of reality. "I will teach that man a lesson," she would say to herself.

It was possible that absence and time would make Batista forget as well. Months of absence were quickly turning into years. But people who have a propensity for jealousy are usually the sort who cannot forget, and Batista could not forget. Work was a salve, but when the evenings came, there was no work. So it was with more and more frequency that he wandered over to Hiro's to find companionship and to sing his loneliness away. As always, the women flocked around him, dropping their eyes and their hints. Every evening, Batista strode into Hiro's with a new determination to find some sort of revenge for Tania Aparecida's absence. He found the most attractive woman in the nightclub and danced and drank with her all night, but that was all. He could not follow her out. Sometimes he paid the taxi driver to take off without him. Or he made a trip to the men's room his excuse to slip out. The women talked among themselves; they badgered and laughed at him, but they could not help loving him. Later, some of them boasted having been with him;

he did not contradict this. It would seem embarrassing not to have won such a claim, so after awhile, all the women lied about their passionate rendezvous with Batista. Everything about Batista's jealousy was a wild fabrication, but he could not see this.

Michelle Mabelle, who was nearing the last months of her pregnancy, still managed to find a way to get to Hiro's with Napoleon and sing Catherine Deneuve's old hit songs. Besides her usual repertoire of French songs, Michelle liked to sing some of the new protest songs written by members of the trialectics movement. "We shall overcome the use of one more thumb," and so forth. Then there was a tropical bird-call song with the authentic songs of birds in their natural surrounding, which Michelle loved more than anything.

Batista noticed the French bird professor in her modified form. He noticed also that she now came alone to Hiro's, and he wondered about this.

"I'm communing with music, you see," she said, pointing at her large belly. "I have so much on my mind lately. It must not be good for these unborn ones to have me so pensive. Music cleanses the spirit."

Batista did not know what Michelle Mabelle could have on her mind lately, unless it was all the controversy about the conservation of birds.

Part VI:
Return

CHAPTER 27: TYPHUS

LOURDES WAS BESIDE HERSELF with worry and guilt. "Maybe it was wrong to come here, to leave the children like that. Poor Tia Carolina. It's not her fault. What will I do? What will I do? My poor babies. My poor babies," she sobbed.

Hiroshi tried to console Lourdes. "Be calm. Be calm. We will find a way."

"Do you think they are well? Do you think they are a—, a—" Lourdes gasped at her worst fears.

"Of course they are alive! Of course! Put this out of your mind!" Hiroshi paced about. "If only those scoundrels would take money. I could unload that GGG stock on them."

Lourdes shook her head. It was a terrible dilemma: her children for the man she loved, Kazumasa. But where was Kazumasa? If he only knew what had happened, he would turn himself in in exchange for Rubens and Gislaine. He would do it in a moment, without a second thought. Lourdes shuddered. It was a horrible choice. Everything was lost. If she lost her children, she would not care for anything again in this world. And if she lost Kazumasa forever, it would be the same.

"We have to find Kazumasa," said Hiroshi. "I have sent detectives out everywhere, but whoever is hiding him has managed to make him invisible. I can't understand it," Hiroshi threw up his arms. "How do you make a Japanese with a ball invisible?"

"Every other day the radio station gets calls," said Lourdes.

"Yes, but he can't be everywhere!"

"We have to keep trying," insisted Lourdes. "The people who subscribe to the foundation are loyal to Chico Paco. Let them be our eyes. Let the radio be our voice. Let the votive telephone operators be our ears!"

Hiroshi thought Lourdes was beginning to sound like Chico Paco over the radio, but he said nothing. Hiroshi knew now that Lourdes did not love him, but he looked fondly at her tear-stained face. He wished that he could be the one to kiss her fears away, and he envied Kazumasa, wherever that fool cousin of his might be. Hiroshi thought of his own choice to stay in Brazil, to become a Brazilian. He remembered the salty breeze on the beach of Ipanema and smiled to himself. In those days, he had nothing but a soft spot in his heart for this country. He thought about how so many things had changed since Kazumasa had also arrived in Brazil. He thought about his karaoke business and about Kazumasa's endless wealth. Hiroshi bowed his head. It was all his fault; he had betrayed Kazumasa's trust. If Hiroshi could not find Kazumasa to confess everything, he would never be the same, and those first beautiful days—when the warm sea had churned the white sands over and over, scrubbing away his shedding skin to reveal the new—would all come to mean nothing.

Lourdes ran to the radio station. The message was sent out everywhere. "Kazumasa! The Japanese with the ball! Call Radio Chico! Call Radio Chico! Call R-A-D-I-O C-H-I-C-O!!"

*   *   *

The death of the two feather cultists, remembered by most people via an award-winning color photo spread of their lifeless bodies, their outstretched arms clutching bunches of feathers, had sent out a wave of speculation concerning the darker side of the feather. The photograph of the dead feather worshipers had captured the gruesome tragedy in an extraordinary metaphor of flight; several filters and some fancy developing techniques had produced a representation in which the bodies seemed to be floating through a shiny mercuric matter, which was, anyway, the steel-like surface of the Matacão.

It was revealed that the feather worshipers, prior to flight, had attained a trancelike state which resembled the hallucinations of the old LSD trips, similar to those described by Tom Wolfe in *The Electric Kool-Aid Acid Test* or to those induced by peyote buttons and described by Carlos Castenada during his discipleship with the Yaqui Indian sage, Don Juan. However, in subsequent interviews with cultists, even those former cultists who claimed to have been deprogrammed, no one would admit that these so-called flights had not actually been real. Everyone who had attained this privileged nirvana were adamant in their claim of having experienced actual, physical flight. When questioned by the prosecutor why no one, neither the Air Force nor air traffic controllers scanning the Brazilian skies, had picked up any evidence of flying human beings in the atmosphere, all the witnesses asserted that flight could only be accomplished by birds whose forms they had naturally taken. What then had occurred to the two people whose bodies were found spread-eagled on the Matacão? These people, said the chiefs of feather worship, had been abandoned by the very birds that must carry them in flight. It was a clear sign of revenge, a message to the human animal that the destruction of so many beautiful birds without proper ritual and payment to their spirits would no longer be tolerated. The judge, like most people, looked askance at this testimony and sent the chiefs of feather worship to jail for their roles in these deaths.

However, some people began to wonder when new instances of human death were discovered. These bodies, different from the first two, were found a great distance from the Matacão, as far as two or three hundred miles, clutching similar bunches of feathers, their heads buried in nosedives into the muddy pasture of some poor farmer or skidding across an abandoned highway, all of them a great distance from any tall buildings or cliffs from which they could have leapt or been pushed off. One body was found impaled on the dry branches of a dead tree. Another was discovered by Indians in the deeper regions of the forest. Strangely, the cause of death was always found to be the impact of an immovable object, in this case the earth, meeting that delicate fleshy mass of falling organs, blood and bones. Some coroners simply called the cause of death "gravity."

The chiefs of feather worship spoke from prison, crying out that their followers were dying for the sake of birds. All of the bodies discovered were identified as having been members of the feather-worshiping cults. However, one of the names on the list of dead struck the attention of Mané Pena. "Camilo Santos," Mané Pena murmured in disbelief.

Camilo was a young man who did errands for J. B. Tweep in the offices of GGG. Mané Pena had gotten Camilo the job as a favor for Camilo's father, one of Mané's old-time cronies. Mané had not known that Camilo was involved in feather worship. He had always supposed Camilo to be one of those simple feather enthusiasts who used feathers occasionally. Upon further investigation, Mané Pena discovered that Camilo's body had been found, unlike the others, without the accompanying bunches of feathers, and no one could trace Camilo's activities to any secret feather worshiping. This raised the horrifying possibility in Mané Pena's mind that the simple feather user might in fact, unknowingly, be in danger of taking flight. Mané Pena spent sleepless nights pondering the possibility, reworking every piece of evidence surrounding Camilo's death. For the moment, he kept these thoughts to himself, tortured by the possibility that all his work might suddenly come crashing down. Cause of death: gravity.

For the moment, however, Mané Pena's worries regarding the feather and flight were overshadowed by another much graver malady. Government officials and the press had generally disregarded the public health reports and outcries regarding the growing number of cases of what seemed to be typhus in and around the Matacão. As is often the case, news of what public health officials were now calling a major epidemic had been relegated to information of minor interest as long as the epidemic remained with the poor and destitute. Even when middle-class families were stricken with the disease, people generally thought that those affected had not taken the proper precautions with their domestic help. But when the hospitals began filling up and, in fact, overflowing with people from the loftiest places in the social pyramid, there was an outcry against any former generalizations regarding the natural selection of the species, especially when the statistics counted more rich people with the disease than poor. This disease, like other diseases, was indiscriminate in its choices; it afflicted rich and poor, young and old, good and evil, beautiful and ugly, clean and dirty, wise and stupid, optimist and pessimist, innocent and cynic, powerful and peon, beatified and atheist, philanthropist and criminal, rational and mad, peaceful and warlike, complex and simple, activist and indifferent, ingenue and pervert, heterosexual and homosexual, and everyone else in between.

Everyone knew someone or had someone in their immediate

family with the disease. Soon, everyone on and around the Matacão could recognize the first symptoms of the disease—the
red rash that began to cover the neck and ears and the menacing
headache that soon overcame the afflicted with such intensity
that people were often seen rolling in the streets with their
hands pressed to their heads. Then, there was the high unabat-
ed fever that racked the body, sending its victims alternately
into stupor and delirium. The end was almost inevitable. Nine
out of ten people died. There was no cure. This particular strain
of typhus did not seem to succumb to any of the normal proce-
dures or recognized remedies. The typical vaccines were pro-
nounced useless. Antibiotics such as Aureomycin, Chloromy-
cetin and Terramycin and even *para*-aminobenzoic acid were
of no avail. Everything attempted was a mere placebo on a rotting wound. Epidemiologists were dumbfounded by this tide of
horror, the prospect of burying hundreds of new victims every
day, limited hospital facilities, dying people lying in cots and on
mats or on the cold floors in the corridors and on the steps of all
the hospitals, incinerators burning day and night to destroy the
old clothes and bedclothes of the dead. A cloud of doom settled
over the Matacão. People huddled fearfully within their
houses, staring at the ghostly visions of their televisions in the
dark, watching the figure of death strut and reel and carouse
across the screen.

The Matacão itself was suddenly swept clean of devotees and
tourists. Instead, it was strewn with votive candles, like an
enormous birthday cake, thousands of prayers to match the
thousands of dying. At night, the candles flickered throughout
its enormous expanse, mimicking the starry skies above. That
the Matacão could be the center of so much pain and doom
seemed to everyone an impossibility, an evil turn of events.

Even worse was the fact that the disease was not limited to the
environs of the Matacão; there was a discernibly widening circle of affliction. At Radio Chico, where the enormous maps
usually followed the routes of pilgrims approaching the Matacão, little red tacks now spotted new outbreaks of the epidemic as people telephoned in requesting votive candles for
loved ones with the disease. As the little white tacks repre-

senting pilgrims seemed to inch their way toward the Matacão, the red tacks multiplied in every direction, spreading farther and farther. Chico Paco himself read the map's demoralizing tale—the unholy war—saw the puny forces of his pilgrims amid the growing splash of typhoid death. Someone at Radio Chico calculated that the disease was spreading on the map at an average of an inch per day, which meant 50 miles per day. If things continued at this rate, the epidemic could reach as far south as Patagonia and as far north as Canada in three months!

Just as the disease would not remain with the poor, it would not be confined to the Matacão. It had become a national disaster. For the moment, most people assumed that it would confine itself to the Third World. Europeans, Asians and Americans eager to see the Matacão simply rearranged their vacation plans that year. Wait until they find a vaccine, they thought. Epidemics, plagues, drought, famine, terrorism, war—all things that happened to other people, poor people in the Third World who cavorted with communism and the like. When we travel, we don't drink the water, some said. Terrorists shouldn't be negotiated with either, others said.

Mané Pena had not seen his wife Angustia since even before he had been granted the honorary title of doctor. The old couple now clung to each other in complete pity, weeping for an irrecoverable past and for their youngest two children, Beto and Marina, now dead and buried. Cause of death: typhus. Mané Pena had rushed to the bedside of the little ones he had been so particularly fond of only to see his wife desperately rubbing a series of feathers over their ears. "To ease the pain," she held back her tears. "To help them to sleep." But the feather, always useful in any of their former family crises—the time their son Edivaldo was drawn out of a violent seizure or daughter Suely was cured of thumb-sucking—was now absolutely useless. Mané watched their feverish eyes roll up under the lids, the sweat roll off their foreheads and their small hands clutch the sheets. Mané kissed their hands and feet and moaned helplessly while Angustia continued tenaciously with the feathers. "Gustia!" Mané wailed. "It's no use! Can't you see?"

Angustia bit her lip till the blood ran, watching her husband crush the feathers in his hands, sweeping the little porcelain vases filled with feathers from the television in anger. The colorful feathers floated everywhere, deceitfully. Mané Pena had heard of new cases of fallen bodies, the descriptions of their deaths similar to Camilo's, ordinary everyday feather users with no connection to the convoluted rituals of the cults. The feather was becoming, in the eyes of its inventor, a monster. And it had not curbed the terrible disease, had not even demonstrated a ray of hope, much less eased the pain of his children's deaths. Mané Pena wept, cried out against the deception of his dubious fortune. In less than a week, he would join his buried children. Cause of death: typhus.

Dona Angustia was forced to tie Mané to the bed, and although she had closed the shutters and filled the open chinks with pieces of cloth, the neighbors could hear his continuous screams for five days and five nights. Angustia, in desperation, literally sawed at her poor husband's ears with the powerless tanager feather. It was as if all the pain, irritation and emotions so carefully absorbed by the once-indefatigable feather had suddenly released themselves in a cursed torrent. So torn were Mané Pena's ears that the morticians were forced to sew the old leathery ears back into place before displaying the body to the paltry remnants of Mané Pena's family, friends, colleagues, students and close associates. Chico Paco gazed upon his old mentor, dressed in the striped tailored suit he had worn on only two occasions—the autograph party for his autobiography and the conferring of his doctorate. Chico Paco noticed with sadness that the morticians had found a shiny pair of black shoes into which they had smashed Mané Pena's callused feet. Former admirers and ordinary feather users, who all owed their habits to the Father of Featherology, remained in their homes, cowering, watching only one of many sad processions to the graveyard. International telegrams and cards of sympathy fluttered in, but Mané Pena's secretary, Carlos, had already died several months before.

CHAPTER 28: CARNIVAL

THIS TIME, Rubens did not have his pigeon to save him. He and Gislaine sat huddled together in a small dark room. They had agreed that they would do everything possible to stay together. Gislaine wisely made it known to their captors that Rubens could do very little for himself, and she would be needed constantly as a nursemaid to feed, dress and help him get about. Rubens, for his part, made himself as helpless and dependent on Gislaine as possible. For the moment, this plan seemed to be working. Gislaine was a tough young girl approaching adolescence. She had her mother's eyes and facial expressions and the same thick brush of black hair. She put her arms around Rubens, who bounced between ideas of great courage and deep depression. "Quiet," she said. "They'll hear you, and then they'll put those gags over our mouths again."

Rubens whispered, "Maybe I could lay down in the doorway, and when the guy comes in, he trips, and you take something and bash his head."

"I have to have something to bash his head with," remarked Gislaine, looking around the empty room.

Rubens thought about this and felt depressed again. "Ginjinha, what do they want with us?"

Gislaine patted her brother's head and tried to smile. "Mama will find us. Don't worry."

Rubens sighed and soon fell asleep.

* * *

In the midst of death, Radio Chico and the Foundation for Votive Pilgrimages were busier than ever. It was not because people in times of extreme suffering turned to God and prayer; the churches and the priests were, of course, overwhelmed by these people. It was because out of so many sufferers, some people, indeed, survived. After all, Radio Chico and the foundation were in the business of praising God for the victories, the miracles, the "answered" prayers. The rest was God's will. In this typhus crisis, one out of ten people afflicted were reported to survive. If a hundred new cases of typhus were reported each day (and this rate of infection was expected to rise steadily to, some predicted, a thousand), Radio Chico and the foundation could expect an average of ten new calls per day from survivors of the epidemic, requesting votive pilgrims. Radio Chico was, amid this harsh tragedy, a singular voice of triumph and hope.

Despite Radio Chico's expression of optimism, its offering of the chance of life, some people had begun to feel that the typhus epidemic was heralding the inevitable apocalypse, that the Matacão was the center of God's storm, the very door which would soon open to release the cataclysm that would cause the ensuing devastation. These people were further convinced of the end when more and more bodies of people, who seemed to have been tossed out of airplanes in midflight, were strewn over the Brazilian countryside. Those feather worshipers must have been in cahoots with the devil, and this was part of the final judgment. In preparation for such finality, people began to reappear again on the Matacão but, now, in various acts of self-flagellation: people baring their backs under whips, fasting under the hot interminable sun, puncturing their hands and feet with nails, pulling their hair out from the roots, dipping their hands and feet in scalding water or actually burning themselves over smoldering coals, filling their mouths with hot peppers. Then there were those who began to crawl on their knees the length and width of the Matacão, holding various banners or votive pictures of saints or dead loved ones. The Matacão being a perfectly smooth surface, the first such knee-crawlers lugged bags of sand and gravel that they tossed in handfuls before them to roughen the way and eventually tear at the soft flesh of their knees. In no time at all, peddlers could be found selling everything from candles and small whips to bags of sand of varying coarseness.

Chico Paco watched these demonstrations of ardent suffering with a great deal of repugnance and personal pain. It seemed as if, daily, hundreds of people died from typhus, but those who survived or who were yet unclaimed believed that they had been saved for some greater suffering unless they could somehow purge themselves of sin. Chico Paco had gone on the radio again and again to denounce self-inflicted pain as a purgative for sinfulness. He invited these people, instead, to show their devotion by becoming votive pilgrims, telephone pilgrims, volunteers for hope. Chico Paco felt that there must be some way to pull them from this insidious dread. Fear permeated the social fabric, a cancer worse than any epidemic. It might turn into the lowest common denominator of human degradation; Chico Paco could not imagine what that might be, but it did not sound pleasant. He remembered his life on the sea on his *jangada*, that flat raft with sail, whose every rough-hewn board and characteristic he had once known. He looked out over the Matacão, at the stretch of sky and clouds, and felt confusion. Back in his home on the coast, he would have been able to wake at dawn and look out across the sky from east to west and north to south and read the day's weather in that stretch of sky. It would say, for example, cloudy morning followed by mist and drizzle, winds at noon, clear by afternoon, cloudless sunset, crescent moon, starlit night, sudden gusty winds and heavy clouds, torrential rains by dawn. But the skies over the Matacão were a mystery to Chico Paco, unpredictable and inscrutable. He could read no weather, no future there.

Chico Paco's mother, Dona Feliz, continued to wander barefoot around her son's carpeted apartment, just as if she had never left her home on the beach, oblivious to the human tragedy surrounding her. As I have said before, Dona Feliz spent most of her days on the Matacão at the riverside, washing the clothes the only way she knew—by beating and pounding the dirt out of them. "Clothes need to be beaten to learn to stay clean," she would say. The hired driver who accompanied Dona Feliz would carry her basket of dirty laundry to the river side and then sit and sun himself on the rocks or smoke languidly while staring out across the river. Daily, the driver would recognize the same two people in a small boat for hire rowing out to the distant center of the river to dump a package into the water. He guessed every day that this package was another corpse. The two people in the boat no longer waited for the furious swell which eventually occupied the waters where the body had been deposited, the piranhas snatching wildly at the flesh to expose the bones, soon to be bleached flotsam bobbing at the river's edge. The driver tossed his cigarette stub into the flotsam mixed with Dona Feliz's soapsuds, picked up the heavy basket of tightly wrung clothing and followed her to the car. Back at the apartment, Chico Paco's mother carefully spread the wet pieces out on the patio Astroturf to dry in the sun.

Chico Paco continued to be traumatized by Gilberto's inexhaustible energy and his dance with danger. Nightly, he would find himself coaxing Gilberto, who liked to straddle the railing of the balcony overlooking that gross display of torment on the Matacão twenty floors below, to come away. "Please Gilberto. Not tonight. I can't take any more accidents. I need some peace." After some amount of begging, Gilberto would be coaxed into a round of video games, pinball or some fast-paced movie like *Raiders of the Lost Ark,* which Chico Paco had now seen 100 times. At some unexpected but inevitable point, Gilberto would suddenly drift off to sleep. Chico Paco would take one long, loving glance at his wild friend and close his eyes in relief. Dona Feliz, used to waking at dawn, might find the two young men wrapped snugly in each other's arms, swinging on the balcony hammock, and cover their sleeping bodies. They were momentarily huddled together against an unknown doom, and although Chico Paco insisted that they were a part of the lucky 10 percent, his own insistence betrayed him. He clung to the former invalid and slept fitfully, always hearing the distant sound of waves.

When the construction of Chicolándia was completed and most of the contraptions and confabulations had been tested or broken by Gilberto, a date was set for the inauguration. Chico Paco chose Carnival, that devil-let-loose time of the year, which would provide the people with a genuine experience of surfeit and intense celebration, something to release — with some finality, he hoped — the dismal atmosphere of gloom which had settled everywhere. Wouldn't this be the sort of thing that would make people forget their suffering, promote that ray of hope, that they might just be one of those lucky people in the surviving 10 percent? The people, Chico Paco felt, were desperately in need of a change of spirit. By opening the doors of

Chicolándia, Chico Paco hoped to turn the ugly presentation of suffering on the Matacão into a new dance of hope. Once again, the Matacão, lately so grossly stained, must become a stage for celebration. In preparation, the government had hired a nightly cleaning crew, which consisted of a couple hundred men and women with brushes and mops followed by a tank which sprayed a roaring torrent of water, to cleanse the Matacão, that would-be polished road leading to a paradise of plastic delights.

Along with Chico Paco's preparations for the inauguration of Chicolándia, bands, samba schools, costume contest organizers, famous singers and announcers flooded onto the Matacão to add to the long list of twenty-four-hour, four-day entertainment planned. Chico Paco's proclamation of a new era had spurred thousands of survivors into a flurry of creativity, song and dance. Now there was the constant beat of the congas flowing over the Matacão while people walked and bounced to its rhythm. Occasionally, the *trio elétrico,* a truck strung with enormous speakers and a band of balancing musicians, rolled along the Matacão, everything blaring at maximum volume. The *trio elétrico* was surrounded and trailed by an enthusiastic crowd of jumping people, sweat streaming from their bodies, everyone bounding after the truck in one agitated mass. Gilberto would hear the music from the twentieth floor and scramble down all the flights of stairs to join the excitement, but Chico Paco, watching from above, would often see a funeral procession solemnly passing the *trio elétrico* in the opposite direction, and in and among the dancers, there were always people with the rash-ridden signs of the inevitable disease. Many people would dance their last dance, drink their last drink, suffer their last hangover.

Still, Chico Paco insisted on the answered prayers. As the day of the inauguration approached, Chico Paco himself walked a pilgrimage for a little boy saved from the ravages of the disease. Chico Paco and the foundation planned for his triumphant arrival on the Matacão on the inaugural opening of Chicolándia and first day of the Carnival festivities. Radio Chico purposely hailed Chico Paco's historic walk, speaking of his prayers for a new era. People clung to their radios and the message from Radio Chico as if it were their last piece of salvation. Many people claimed that if it were not for Chico Paco, more people would be dead, as if Chico Paco, himself, were more than a messenger, more than a simple angel of good news.

But many people at Radio Chico and the foundation, not to mention the personnel who now administered Chicolándia, were beginning to gossip openly about Chico Paco and the former invalid, Gilberto. Some pilgrims were secretly envious of Gilberto and the special attentions Chico Paco, they said, showered on that frivolous child. The guards were more than aware of Chico Paco's obsession with Gilberto. What if, they thought, we fail to save Gilberto from himself? What miracle, what pilgrimage could possibly save Gilberto from falling off a roller coaster or drowning inside a sea lion suit? If things continued like this, Gilberto might send everything and everyone flying off together on that roller coaster. Perhaps, Chico Paco needed to be saved from Gilberto. For the moment, the gossip was fettered by an undercurrent of guilt. Chico Paco was a sort of saint, an angel, was he not? He was the very salvation of thousands of believers. So what if he were gay. So what if he *were* gay?

But these speculations were strangely unknown to Chico Paco, who had inherited from his mother a certain obliviousness. It had never occurred to him that his affection for Gilberto might be interpreted as sinful, even though more than one of his pilgrims had walked to the Matacão for so-called reformed homosexuals. "Praise the Lord," the letters had proclaimed. "My son is normal." Normal. Chico Paco had never thought much about what was normal. Miracles. Answered prayers. The lucky 10 percent. There was more to Chico Paco's life than normality. And Chico Paco had never been happier in his life. He walked briskly toward the Matacão, thinking of Gilberto, praying that Gilberto was keeping his promise to stay out of trouble, and imagined the glow of childish surprise on Gilberto's face under the spectacle of fireworks slated for the grand opening.

* * *

Despite the intense arrangements for the opening of Chicolándia and Carnival, Lourdes had not lost hope that Kazumasa would somehow hear her call for help. Kazumasa and I saw the writing on the wall while waiting at a stoplight. Kazumasa's name was scrawled in big letters on the side of a building. So was, for that matter, my name, "The Ball." Kazumasa memorized the telephone numbers as our car sped off.

Hiroshi had inserted into the radio station's telephone system a message which would be understood by anyone speaking Japanese, most hopefully by Kazumasa, if he happened to call. The kidnappers had set a deadline for receiving the goods (Kazumasa and me) in exchange for Gislaine and Rubens, and time was running out. The exchange was to be made on the Saturday of Carnival at 9 PM on the Matacão. The reason for choosing the Matacão was that the kidnappers assumed that my attraction to the great slab would be proof of Kazumasa's authenticity. Hiroshi was himself ready to go to the Matacão on the intended Saturday evening and to press a replica of me and his own forehead into the Matacão, in hopes of saving Gislaine and Rubens. As it happened, Kazumasa made that call.

Kazumasa and I walked away from that phone with a sense of mission. We would not allow Gislaine and Rubens to come to any harm. We did not consider the danger to our own lives. We were tired of hiding and running. And all Kazumasa could think of lately was Lourdes. If he could see her again, he would embrace her, dance with her, sing with her, laugh, kiss and love her. Yes, he admitted to himself, he loved Lourdes. He promised himself, if he lived to see her again, he would tell her everything, but she must not lose her children on his account.

But there was treachery all around us, and even as we walked away from the telephone booth, an undercover bodyguard with a clip slipped into the booth and surreptitiously removed a small electronic device hidden in the mouthpiece of the receiver. Someone would be watching us every step of the way.

*   *   *

As the days approached for Chico Paco's triumphant arrival on the Matacão, Gilberto thought about a genuine surprise for Chico Paco. He had once seen in a magic show how the magician had been stuffed into a gigantic cannon and fired out to a spot behind the audience. He imagined himself being fired out of such a cannon into the clear night air above Chicolándia and miraculously wafting down to the Matacão to personally greet Chico Paco. Such a cannon was secretly arranged with the help of the guards, whom Gilberto thought had been hired to tape his escapades for Chico Paco's delight. "This will be the greatest thrill of his life," Gilberto sighed, racing around to put together a suitable costume for such an appearance. He settled on a glittering silver spacesuit with matching boots and helmet, all of which glowed in the dark. The parachute would also be a glittering phosphorescent silver. He planned his spectacular arrival, rehearsing over and over in his mind the details without ever questioning whether a trick like this was even feasible. The guards shrugged their shoulders innocently. They were only there to protect and humor Gilberto. The thing wasn't supposed to work anyway, they thought.

On Saturday, the first day of Carnival, people began milling around on the Matacão early in the morning. Batista had released thousands of Djapan pigeons into the skies to hail the opening ceremonies. The *trio elétricos* rumbled up and down the Matacão, and several samba schools had already demonstrated a certain amount of frenzy, even in those early hours. By nightfall, things were getting hot. Chico Paco supporters were pacing the Matacão with ghetto blasters, the Radio Chico deejay's voice crashing into its own voice in a myriad of stereo reports. The costumed carousers were beginning to arrive as well. There were dozens of people sporting my replica, the "Kazumasa ball," secured by transparent headbands. Some had even cut and dyed their hair jet black to imitate Kazumasa's. And there were also dozens of people with third arms or third breasts, not to mention people with third eyes or third legs and so forth. Then there were the usual crowd of masqueraders, pirates, clowns, Arabs, Indians, cartoon characters, Hawaiians, gypsies, Candomblé priestesses and gods, Carmen

Mirandas, *malandros,* transvestites and many who simply sported skimpy attire. Breasts and buttocks, in big demand as always at Carnival, were in abundance on the Matacão.

Lourdes and Hiroshi, also sporting my ridiculous replica and ready at any moment to smash his head into the great slab, marched through the revelers with determination. Behind them, following first at a distance and then more closely as the crowds grew, were two people Kazumasa might have recognized. But Kazumasa and I, too, were being watched and followed. We were used to this and had rather lost track of the number of people who surrounded but never really befriended us in a way Kazumasa would have appreciated.

We, too, were intent on keeping this appointment. Kazumasa did not consider that it might in fact be a trap. He promised himself that only when he saw Gislaine and Rubens safely in Lourdes's arms would he give himself and me up. Kazumasa did not have to ask my forgiveness for deciding my fate in this way, but he did so anyway. "Forgive me," he said, "but it is for a good cause."

Together, Kazumasa and I ran among the crowds in the streets, trying to confuse those agents J.B. had trailing us everywhere. Luckily, there were so many odd representations of us on the streets, the agents found themselves spread out everywhere chasing mirages of the Japanese with the ball.

Chico Paco was already met several miles before the Matacão by a crowd of supporters all grasping candles, marching alongside the living angel in the decisive and fervent expression of an earthly but sacred mission. People wept openly, fell to the ground and wrung their hands, as Chico Paco passed.

From his private helicopter above, J.B. could see over the dark land a river of tiny lights approaching the Matacão. As Chico Paco's feet touched the Matacão, fireworks broke into the night sky.

Under the lights of that suddenly radiant sky, Lourdes could see the outline of her two children, Gislaine and Rubens, propped ominously between two large men. Lourdes and the children all cried out together in recognition, but their cries were muffled by the thundering sky and the blaring music. Hiroshi sensed Lourdes's tension and saw the men and the children as well. He made ready to throw himself onto the Matacão, but a hand grabbed his shoulder. Lourdes looked around and exclaimed, "Seu Kazumasa!"

Kazumasa and I walked forward. Kazumasa stopped and smiled at the children. He motioned to the men, who could see immediately that this was the real and true Kazumasa, that there could be no mistake. I was always very impressive in person. Hiroshi's idea about pressing his replica ball and head into the Matacão was nonsense when confronted with the truth of my existence. I could see that the men themselves were quite astounded. They relaxed their grip on the children, who scuffled away as best they could and fell tearfully into Lourdes's awaiting arms. When Kazumasa could see that the children were safe, he and I walked toward the men who readied their weapons with a certain fear of me. They did not know what a ball might be capable of.

Kazumasa had seen J.B.'s paper-clipped agents following Lourdes and Hiroshi. We could also sense their presence, and Kazumasa knew that they would not give up their assignment just because Kazumasa and I wanted to get involved in a little heroics.

At the same time, Chico Paco was trying to move forward into the oppressive crowd. His walk was joyous and purposeful as he saw the skies lit above Chicolándia. He felt, however, a passing touch of sadness. Where was Gilberto? Why hadn't he come to meet him? Chico Paco pushed aside his sense of abandonment amid the glorious reception surrounding him. People were cheering, dancing, chanting. Confetti poured. Flowers were strewn.

Suddenly, Chico Paco sensed a vibration near his heart, the insistent buzz of his beeper in his shirt pocket, the warning signal of approaching danger. Chico Paco's stomach churned, waves crashing in his inner ear, his knees wobbling at the thought of another episode in Gilberto's continuing saga of mad escapades. The monitoring room. He must get there. What was that crazy former invalid up to now? Chico Paco pressed forward frantically.

Kazumasa and I were shoved aside by the approaching crowds. Chico Paco himself was only a few paces away. We tried to stand our ground yet another moment, hoping that Hiroshi was dragging Lourdes and the children as far away from danger as possible. The armed men approached us impatiently, but suddenly, the glint of a silver clip caught Kazumasa's eye. Just as the agent withdrew his gun, Kazumasa whirled with me to the ground, tumbling across Chico Paco's path. A shot was muffled under the sound of drums. One kidnapper fell away clutching some part of his wounded body, but the second kidnapper aimed for Kazumasa's head. Kazumasa rolled under a three-legged masquerader, avoiding the bullet that pierced the heart of the great pilgrim.

Chico Paco clutched the beeper over his heart, the iridescence of his eyes flashing unspeakable panic. Blood poured from his heart, flooding the shattered beeper, as he sank to his knees on the Matacão. The crowd caught the kidnapper and pounced relentlessly on him, smashing every part of his body into the Matacão. Confetti dripping from his golden head, Chico Paco lifted his hand as if to protest the massacre, but it was to wave at the sight of a distant glow, the silken silver wings of an angel emerging among the crack and spray of a sky lit by gunpowder.

CHAPTER 29: RAIN OF FEATHERS

AMONG THE BODIES that continued mysteriously to fall out of the sky were found the charred remains of Gilberto. The silver phosphorescent parachute, made of Matacão plastic, was nonflammable and it alone remained intact, its bulbous billowy form sailing out across the shimmering night skies with a human candle. It had risen to an incredible altitude, much higher than Gilberto himself might have imagined being shot from a cannon, fueled by the rising heat of its burning traveler. When the scarcity of oxygen at that height squelched the flame, Gilberto had become, perhaps, the very angel of Chico Paco's last vision.

It was discovered that many of the fallen bodies, whose demise could not be traced to feather worshiping, were those of people who had been experimenting with the use of a new feather made of Matacão plastic. Further investigation revealed that the natural magnetism of the Matacão plastic could in certain circumstances, feather rubbing being primary, produce hallucinations. This would, scientists said, account for the rising number of people who claimed spiritual encounters during self-flagellation on the Matacão or the inordinate number of crazed individuals who had, emergency room records insisted, overdosed on four days of frenzied dancing on the Matacão. People were calling it the "red shoes syndrome"; Carnival revelers on the Matacão had actually been unable to stop dancing. Doctors testified to treating the physically exhausted dancers—their feet still kicking and their bodies twitching under the sheets to an inaudible beat for days after.

But the music had stopped long ago. Batista Djapan's weekly pigeon messages had themselves forecast the end. "Look for the charcoal angel in the sky," one read ominously. "Escape the rain of feathers," the next warned. Batista himself did not know what the messages meant. He would only know when reality itself had deciphered the meaning. What was it he or anyone else must glean from such a message? Batista was always puzzled by the messages, but lately he had felt a growing sense of fear.

Where was Tania Aparecida when he needed her? She would know what the messages meant. She would be able to interpret his fear. "Tania Cidinha!" he would call out. "Come home. I need to talk to you!"

"I'm just a pigeon call away," she would say.

"Where are you? I'm coming to get you myself!"

"I'm right here, darling. I'll be here for the next hour. If it's urgent, you can fax it to me at the following number . . ."

Batista groaned. He did not know what he felt any longer. He did not think it was jealousy, as Tania Aparecida insisted. But then, just when he was beginning to fear that he was losing his memory of her, that he would not recognize her if he saw her, that the memory of her face was only of the photographs she had sent him, he would catch a whiff of some scent, some odd perfume in the air that could only belong to Tania Aparecida. Then the memories would flood back in rushing torrents, his heart heaving, a deep moan cupped in his throat. He often thought that it would be easier if Tania Aparecida were dead, but then he knew that it would be worse. He wanted to tell her that it was no longer jealousy, but a terrible longing, a painful necessity. He would never be jealous again if only she would stay awhile.

But Batista's emotions were left simmering with the onslaught of a more immediate threat: typhus. It was not so much that the disease had virtually decimated the workforce of his pigeon operation, causing a general stagnation in the usually prompt service the Djapans had been known for; people were so depressed by the typhus crisis that they no longer got very excited about slow service, and if it were bad news, people would rather hear it later than sooner. Neither had typhus really made a significant dent in the pigeon message business; while festive sorts of pigeon messages were practically nil these days, messages of sympathy and death filled the airways. Batista had continued to supply the Foundation for Votive Pilgrimages with pigeon pilgrims, and that service had hardly slackened with the typhus crisis. The true threat of typhus was in its cause: rickettsia.

Rickettsia were microorganisms that traveled via a minute species of lice, which in turn traveled via feathers, which, of course, traveled via birds and, of late, humans. The lice that transmitted rickettsia were practically invisible to the naked eye, but they were the nasty creatures that invaded the pores in the ears and around the neck and sucked the skin into a rash.

The first thing to go were the feathers. Plastic feathers had already been outlawed for their severe hallucinatory effects, but now the natural feathers—from the cheap chicken-feather imitations of the rare feathers to very expensive rare feathers themselves—were all dumped with extreme disgust and loathing into incinerators. Feathers burned night and day all around the Matacão. Some people gave up the feather habit with easy distaste, like some passing fad gone sour, but others found their dependency on that soft, light object had grown beyond their expectations. Many people experienced a weight gain. Others returned to smoking cigarettes. A number of stressed-out executives actually jumped out of their office buildings. Some had to be treated for shock and withdrawal.

Banning feathers, however, was not enough, authorities stated. It would be necessary to go to the source. It would be necessary to attack the rickettsia in the lice in the bird feathers. Batista was frantic. The authorities were adamant: no birds could be spared if the disease were to be completely eradicated. Batista himself had tried out DDT on a small selection of his own birds. Every bird had died. "It's not an insecticide," he ranted. "It's a birdicide!"

The authorities admitted that some birds might not survive the application of DDT, but that a particularly strong solution of it was necessary to kill the tenacious lice. Batista himself could even vouch for the ineffectiveness of the DDT solution; long after the death of his birds, he was sure he could see the lice crawling around under the barbs. Batista was furious. What was the purpose of this mandate if the birds died but the lice survived? Some officials, who did not want to be quoted, claimed that if the birds were dead, the lice would not have the advantage of that parasitic relationship.

Michelle Mabelle, the French bird professor, telephoned Batista almost every day now to voice her alarm. Batista could hear the cries of Michelle's triplets in the background. "Ah, is it Liberté?" Batista could hear Michelle asking. "Poor baby." From where he stood, Batista could observe a new clutch of Djapan champions, the parent birds regurgitating the curdled pigeon milk in their crops for the hungry squabs. And from the other end of the line, Batista could hear Liberté's sobbing shudder and its contentment as it nudged into one of Michelle's copious breasts. Michelle made herself comfortable with the nursing baby and continued her conversation with Batista. "You're the only one who understands the situation around here, Batista," she began. "Only someone like you, someone who could take such extreme care to make the best bird feed in the country, could understand. Where, I ask you, are the other bird-lovers in Brazil? I've spoken to everyone, given interviews to all the papers, sent letters and telegrams to politicians and conservationist groups all over the world. No one seems to have the time to listen! Some ask me if I didn't know there was a drug war going on. Others say that human beings and the unborn fetus are more important than birds. Others ask me if triplets are not enough for me to worry about," Michelle fumed.

"What about your husband? He must have some influence," suggested Batista.

"Ah, Batista, we argue about it continuously. He is so involved in the pressures of the market these days, I can't seem to get through to him. Of course he is concerned. This will be the end of feathers. The end!" Michelle tried to contain her sobs. "He is still trying to recoup the losses from those horrid plastic feathers. There have been lawsuits, you know."

"Dona Michelle," Batista pleaded respectfully, "Mr. Tweep has to understand about the loss of all the birds. You must talk to him."

"You don't understand. I have tried. He's still convinced that artificial plastic feathers are the answer. It's a problem of removing the magnetism, he said. With proper marketing, he believes it could work again."

"Work again?" asked Batista.

"Yes. It's a problem of technology, my husband says. Plastic feathers would not harbor lice."

"But the real birds!" cried Batista. "What about the real birds!"

Michelle Mabelle's voice trembled, "I have asked him the same thing over and over. Ever since Chicolándia, I think he is convinced that everything can be more easily reproduced in Matacão plastic. What can I say? It is like talking to the Matacão itself! I try to tell him that half—HALF—" Michelle screamed, "of the world's species of birds live in the Amazon Forest. There are many I have never even seen," she sobbed, remembering her bird lists. "I ask him about my pioneering work on the neotropic family Thraupidae. Imagine the green and gold tanager, the *Tanagara schrankii*. I finally saw it the other day. The beautiful black eyes, the soft yellow and green hues tapering into the sky blue of its wings and tail feathers. Everything shimmering softly in the sunlight. I could hardly breathe for the joy I felt. It was such a momentary happiness—" Her voice broke off in long hopeless sobs.

"Dona Michelle," Batista tried to console the woman. "Please don't cry. I will try to do everything possible to save the birds."

* * *

Batista stalked all the halls of government trying to save his pigeons from the inevitable. The old dispatcher, once fluent in the language of paperwork and former sophisticate of the easy bribe to cure any bureaucrat's thirst, saw all the doors close before him. No amount of money or hustle could supplant this now indelible code. Batista wondered at the purpose of a bureaucracy which could not be subverted. Things had certainly changed since his days in the business. "We know your situation, but the public must be attended to. Too many people have died, and thousands more will die if we do not stop the spread of the disease now. It would be impossible in such an operation to single out particular locales of noninfectious habitation. We are infinitely sorry for the loss you will have to suffer, but think of it, Batista, this is for the good of mankind."

Batista went home, exhausted and dejected by his inability to save not only his own prize Djapan pigeons, but any and all birds. In a last frantic effort, he ran about opening all his pigeon cages and shoving the frightened birds from their roosts. "Go!" he commanded. "Fly away before it is too late," he screamed. But while many flew up, sweeping the skies with their circular routes, most returned within a few hours to the home they had been trained to return to.

Batista sat in the dark and wept. He could hear the small biplanes and the camouflaged bombers flown by the Air Force, flooding the air with their drumming propellers. Hundreds of these planes flew back and forth all day and all night long, dropping their poison bombs and spraying a dense fog over everything—the town, the Matacão, the farms and plantations, and the beautiful and still-mysterious forest. For weeks the odor and the fumes lingered over everything. Not only birds died, but every sort of small animal, livestock, insects and even small children who had run out to greet the planes unknowingly. The odd mice with suction-cupped feet and the rusty butterflies of the forest parking lot died, too. Strangely, as Batista himself had predicted in his own and last pigeon message, the birds had risen from the dense forest in a panic to escape the horrid fumes. Millions of birds of every color and species, many the very last of their kind—ebony toucans with their bright orange beaks, red-headed blackbirds, paradise tanagers in clear primary colors, scarlet ibises, spike-billed jacamars clothed in metallic green, miniature darting hummingbirds—filled the skies, pressing the upward altitudes for the pure air, but the lethal cloud spread odiously with sinister invisibility. The Matacão was soon covered, knee-deep with the lifeless bodies of poisoned birds. Indeed, for countless days and nights, it rained feathers.

CHAPTER 30: BACTERIA

By the time GGG researchers and scientists discovered the true nature of the Matacão and developed a reasonable hypothesis for its existence, Kazumasa had disappeared. The Matacão, scientists asserted, had been formed for the most part within the last century, paralleling the development of the more common forms of plastic, polyurethane and styrofoam. Enormous landfills of nonbiodegradable material buried under virtually every populated part of the Earth had undergone tremendous pressure, pushed ever farther into the lower layers of the Earth's mantle. The liquid deposits of the molten mass had been squeezed through underground veins to virgin areas of the Earth. The Amazon Forest, being one of the last virgin areas on Earth, got plenty.

Kazumasa did not care how the Matacão or the plastic had gotten on Earth. None of these explanations seemed to have any connection to him or to me. The fact that the Matacão was made of nonbiodegradable garbage seemed to have very little bearing on me or my ability to detect large masses of the plastic stuff. Kazumasa felt he had had enough of Matacão plastic, intrigue and danger. He stared cross-eyed at me with a certain sinister irritation but eventually relented. It was not my fault. One did not simply separate oneself from a lifetime of close proximity. Kazumasa felt ashamed of his desire to be released from me; I was actually looking rather haggard and even, Kazumasa detected, sad these past few days. We had certainly been through some trying times.

Ironically, Kazumasa and I were rescued from all those agents and counteragents by J. B. Tweep himself. From his helicopter, J.B. had spotted Kazumasa and me running from the tragic scene of Chico Paco's murder. J.B. hid us in the confines of his penthouse apartment with the clip collection and all the 9.99 artifacts.

Michelle's exotic collection of birds and their cages and the bird caretaker were all conspicuously absent, as was Michelle and the Tweep triplets. Michelle Mabelle had remained through the typhus epidemic despite the danger to her newborns. She had remained like foreigners often remain in war zones and military dictatorships, writing home to their friends and families to tell how the situation isn't as bad as the press makes it out to be, strangely immune to the turbulence surrounding them. But allowing the birds to die had been the end, the unforgivable end, she told her husband. She did not wait to see the slaughter of the tropical birds, their thick, stinking blanket of corpses covering the Matacão. She swept up her three chubby babes and all the birds and their cages and had everything transported via private jet back to her birthplace in southern France.

J.B. had run to the airport, gesticulating with all three hands in a helpless penitent manner as the airplane lifted off and carried them away from the Matacão forever. Long after the plane had gone, J.B. wept on the tarmac, wringing two hands and wiping his tears and blowing his nose with the third. He emptied all his pockets, scattering clips everywhere. "Liberté!" he cried. "Égalité! Fraternité!"

But Michelle was gone, and there was nothing J.B. could do about it. They had had a last irreparable argument about nature vs. technology. He had said unforgivable things about French breasts and culture and she about uncouth American arms. J.B. could not convince Michelle that birds reproduced on a production line were ultimately more valuable to mankind. "Just think of the jobs we would create!" he had exclaimed. J.B. remembered the horror in Michelle's face. She would not even let him touch his own three babies. She threatened to get plastic surgery and donate her third breast to an organ bank. "You are a monster!" she had screamed. "I am not a monster. No. No!" she cried, hurling a rash of French expletives at J.B.

"At least she could have left Butch," J.B. confessed to Kazumasa and me, even though we did not understand any of J.B.'s personal traumas. We were simply relieved to be hidden at the quiet center of the mad tornado surrounding us. We cowered in this center helplessly, frightened by the horrible death of Chico Paco in Kazumasa's stead and despondent about the attempt to get Kazumasa's ball by snatching it from his dead body. "If I could remove you myself," Kazumasa grabbed me in demonstration, "there would be at least some chance of hiding you somewhere."

After several days of wandering around J. B. Tweep's apartment, among those 9.99 artifacts, Kazumasa and I were removed to a new hiding place attached to Hiro's Karaoke. Kazumasa resisted mightily his desire to rush into Hiro's and burst into song. His resistance to this urge was greatly reduced by the arrival of Lourdes. In a moment saturated with all the romance that any soap opera could possibly muster, Lourdes and Kazumasa fell passionately into one another's arms, actually forgetting that I even existed.

When Lourdes emerged from that embrace, she remembered the horror of the past few days, the terrible moment when Kazumasa and I exchanged ourselves for the lives of her children and the death of Chico Paco and of Gilberto. She shud-

dered at the thought of her own dreams, the vision of the murderers dragging Kazumasa's dead body around with the ball
which would never detach itself. She would be the same, she
thought, like the ball. She would attach herself forever to Kazumasa; those murderers would have to drag her dead body
around, too.

But it was Lourdes who first noticed something physically
different about me. Kazumasa had felt a slight light-headed-
ness, and certainly, my attraction to the Matacão was more
than noticeably weak. That Kazumasa had not been thrown by
my attraction onto the hard surface of the Matacão that fateful
Saturday night was a definite indication of my diminished abili-
ties. Kazumasa imagined that I was suffering from the stress of
our travels or the psychological trauma of our isolation and the
obvious danger involved. There was, too, the fact that so many
things were now made of Matacão plastic; anything built or
devised within the last several years might no doubt have been
created out of Matacão plastic. My energies were conceivably
dispersed. But perhaps my powers of magnetism to the Matacão were actually waning, thought Kazumasa with relief.
J.B. could arrange some sort of press conference, a public statement to impress upon everyone, those agents and counteragents, those greedy and power-hungry murderers, that I was
now only a worthless object of curiosity. But this was not necessary.

"Look, Kazumasa," Lourdes pointed at me one morning. "It
looks lopsided today." Kazumasa could not quite see the difference, but he did notice I was spinning with a sort of awkward
limp, if balls could be described as having limps. I no longer
spun with my old snappy precision but with a sort of dizzy
unpredictable turning, like a planet losing its star. On closer
inspection, Lourdes and Kazumasa discovered that I was no
longer quite spherical and that I seemed fraught with tiny
holes. At night, Kazumasa was tormented by what he thought
must be his dreaming impressions of the sound of something
chewing.

"Lourdes!" he screamed. "It's eating my ball!"

It was true. Something was eating me, carving out delicate
pinhole passages, which wound intricately throughout my

sphere. Of this, I confess, I felt nothing but my own disappearance, bit by bit, particle by particle, my world falling away. Kazumasa alone felt pain, and it was sad to see this. Every day, Kazumasa watched more and more of me disappear, my spin grow slower and more erratic. He was helpless to stop the strange decay of his beloved ball. Kazumasa was disconsolate. Lourdes would find Kazumasa alone, speaking sadly but comfortingly in Japanese to his poor dying ball, as if I would feel more comfortable with the language of our childhood. Kazumasa continued his monologue for many days, sitting with an incurably sick and dying patient, apologizing, reminiscing, and always thanking me. One day, he touched me tenderly and was shocked to find his finger pierce the now very thin veneer of my surface. Within, I had been completely hollowed out by something, by some invisible, voracious and now-gorged thing.

The next day, Kazumasa awoke and wept uncontrollably at the unobstructed view of the room before him.

CHAPTER 31: THE MARKET

WHAT WAS APPARENT to Kazumasa was slowly becoming apparent to everyone else. The tiny munching sounds that became so familiar to Kazumasa while he kept a vigil for his dying ball were now a deafening unison. Chicolándia and its plastic jungle, once void of insects and real living creatures, had been invaded by devouring bacteria. The enormous Matacão plastic palms and the giant *jatubá* trees crashed and slumped, crushing the mechanical monkeys and unhinging the plastic sloths. Employees in hard hats picked through the continuing rubble, the powdered debris of Matacão plastic flower gardens and Cleopatra's tomb, the mechanical innards and sole remains of stegosaurus and other prehistoric imitations. J.B. wandered about what once was a plastic paradise, now horribly disfigured, shot

full of tiny ominous holes, the mechanical entrails of everything
exposed beneath the once-healthy plastic flesh. He shook his
head. It was just as well that neither Chico Paco nor Gilberto
had lived to see the crumbling destruction of their fondest
dreams.

The Matacão, too, was slowly but definitely corroding, as
was everything else made of Matacão plastic. Buildings were
condemned. Entire roads and bridges were blocked off. Innocent people were caught unaware — killed or injured by falling
chunks of the stuff. People who stepped out in the most elegant
finery made of Matacão plastic were horrified to find themselves naked at cocktail parties, undressed at presidential recep-
tions. Cars crumbled at stop lights. Computer monitors sagged
into their CPUs. The credit card industry went into a panic.
Worst of all, people with facial rebuilds and those who had added additional breasts and the like were privy to grotesque scenes
thought only to be possible in horror movies. And there was no
telling what might happen to people who had, on a daily basis,
eaten Matacão plastic hamburgers and French fries.

As for the Matacão itself, so-called Matacão plastic conser-
vationists ran all over it, tearfully trying to find a solution for the
preservation of this contemporary geological and, many insisted, spiritual miracle. But every day, more and more of the
Matacão disappeared. J.B. observed the Matacão from his
apartment, watching its once-shiny surface defaced irrepara-
bly by the footprints of thousands of devotees, the famous altar
of Saint George sinking into its deteriorating base.

Everything at GGG was falling into shambles as well. The
sale of feathers had come to a sudden halt with the news that
typhus was being spread to its victims on the wing, so to speak.
Now, GGG could no longer depend on Matacão plastic. The
president of the company had made a public statement regarding the demise of their revolutionary material, and GGG was
beset with civil suits for everything from bodily injuries to
damaged reputations. The stock market plunged as the invisible bacteria gnawed away, leaving everything with a grotes-
quely denuded, decapitated, even leprous appearance.

J.B. sat alone on the twenty-third floor of GGG. All the windows and any other portion of the building made of Matacão plastic were slowly crumbling to dust. The dense tropical humidity had begun to replace the artificially fresh air-conditioned atmosphere. When the air conditioning began to fail, most GGG employees photocopied their resumés and left. Floor by floor, they descended the elevators with their coffee cups and left forever. They left J.B. alone with his three arms, scattered paper clips, and a selection of old 9.99 objects which had escaped destruction, being made of traditional metals and plastics. One of the objects was a prosthetic arm, which his third arm caressed like a lost partner. J.B. mumbled quietly, with tired confusion, to the prosthetic arm, which he had named Butch, unwilling to admit his true longing for the flippant magpie and the third breast. His third arm was once again undergoing a slow atrophy, and J.B. was aware that he would have to leave the Matacão if he wanted to save his extra appendage. He thought absently that the old plastics and metals were still viable—not as realistic but viable. People were still interested in third arms, he nodded, his mind sluggish but still moving as if in perpetual motion across the old Matacão. The Fashion and Accessories Department could be substantially revived by the introduction of third-arm fashions. He could propose the development of a new typewriter, not to mention pianos, keyboards, new games, new sports, new magazines to guide people through increased productivity and sexual activity, an entirely new way of life. That's right, J.B. thought, conquering his loneliness with one sweeping gesture of his weak third hand—he would go into the arms business. Geoffrey and Georgia Gamble would have smiled; they themselves had predicted everything. At this he laughed hysterically, walked to the gaping edge of that twenty-three-floor plexiglass corporate structure and threw himself over. The spongy nature of the Matacão below did not save him. Some people later speculated that he might have used his golden parachute, but Jonathan B. Tweep, unlike poor Gilberto, had always known the truth. All the parachutes were made of Matacão plastic.

CHAPTER 32: THE TROPICAL TILT

As THE LAST VESTIGES of the Matacão were but a fine powder drawn up in the sigh of an indecisive whirlwind, Chico Paco's body—encased in a hermetically sealed and ornately carved box of jacaranda and followed by Gilberto's similarly encased remains—arrived at its seaside birthplace of multicolored dunes.

Chico Paco arrived as he had always traveled, on foot, on the shoulders of devotees and votive pilgrims.

The long procession, which gathered mourners and momentum as it proceeded from the Matacão toward the sea, took most of an entire day before it even vacated the Matacão and was several miles in length as it snaked its solemn way through the now-muted forest. A torrent of rain snuffed out the candles and followed the mourners, rivulets flowing into the raw road, soon a river awash with slogging feet and red clay silt. Large plastic tarps draped the caskets, born deftly on the uncomplaining shoulders of a constantly changing guard. The procession marched on, day and night, sleeping briefly on the roadside and nourished by the human poverty it encroached upon, continuing for weeks through the festering gash of a highway, through a forest that had once been, for perhaps 100 million years, a precious secret.

Retracing Chico Paco's steps, the mourners passed hydroelectric plants, where large dams had flooded and displaced entire towns. They passed mining projects tirelessly exhausting the treasures of iron, manganese and bauxite. They passed a gold rush, losing a third of the procession to the greedy furor. They crossed rivers and encountered fishing fleets, nets heavy with their exotic river catch of manatee, *pirarucú, piramatuba, mapara*. They crowded to the sides of the road to allow passage for trucks and semis bearing timber, Brazil nuts and rubber. They passed burning and charred fields recently cleared and parted for frantic zebu cattle, long horns flailing and stampeding toward new pastures. They passed black-pepper-tree plantations farmed by immigrant Japanese. They passed surveyors and engineers accompanied by excavators, tractors and power saws of every description. They passed the government's five-year plans and ten-year plans, while all the forest's splendid wealth seemed to be rushing away ahead of them. They passed through the old territorial hideouts of rural guerrillas, trampling over unmarked graves and forgotten sites of strife and massacre. And when the rains stopped, they knew they had passed into northeast Brazil's drought-ridden terrain, the sun-baked earth spreading out from smoldering asphalt, weaving erosion through the landscape.

Chico Paco's weeping mother was helped along the procession. She had insisted on walking barefoot, and despite her strong constitution, had to be carried through the last weeks of that exhausting trip. As she caught sight of the dunes laced in undulating shades of orange and purple and the white tips of the waves beyond, Chico Paco's mother thought sadly that her son should never have left this place, but she said out loud, "This is the way he always wanted it. He wanted to be buried here, near the sound of the waves."

* * *

Batista Djapan walked with his guitar, the only possession that had not been touched by typhus or ravaged by bacteria, to the middle of where the Matacão was no longer and to what had once been Mané Pena's small unproductive farm. Batista knew that Tania Aparecida was coming home. He knew because he himself had written it down out of habit for the weekly pigeon message. Having lost all his pigeons, Batista stuffed the small piece of paper away in his pocket.

A band of children were chasing each other. These few children, having escaped the typhus epidemic and the DDT, had crept cautiously from their homes to find great sport in tossing pebbles at the Matacão, taking turns at biting off the brittle remains and sliding down the sides of this widening valley. Now that the Matacão had disappeared, the children remained, habitually meeting in what was now an enormous pit. Today, the children had brought a soccer ball, and Batista watched them scramble after it in an uncontrolled jumble of scrawny bodies. The children were all covered in red mud, celebrating every goal by jumping and sliding into large eroded puddles which marked the perimeters of their playing field. Beyond the excited shouts and cries of the children, Batista could see a small figure emerge on the horizon, the figure of a dark-skinned, saucy woman he knew so well. He propped the guitar into the curve of his body and strummed for his life.

* * *

Kazumasa and Lourdes had not waited to see if the Matacão would follow the ignominious course of the disintegrating ball. The day after my death, Kazumasa and Lourdes with Gislaine and Rubens, anxiously slipped away from the Matacão, filled with a mixed sense of relief and longing. The loss of the ball to Kazumasa was strange, as if he had undergone radical plastic surgery. People no longer recognized him; even Hiroshi was taken aback by the enormous change. Perhaps it was because some part of his face had always been obscured by me or that no one, not even Lourdes herself, could observe his facial characteristics without blinking or flinching. In this newfound sense of anonymity, Kazumasa's old happiness about love and life in Brazil began to return. He immediately moved Lourdes and the children onto a farm filled with acres and acres of tropical fruit trees and vines and a plantation of pineapple and sugarcane, sweet corn and coffee. Rubens wheeled happily around the guava orchards, and Gislaine sat in the branches of a *jaboticaba* tree, sucking out the sweet white flesh of its fruit from their purple-black skins. Kazumasa ran around Lourdes like another child, filling her baskets with miniature bananas, giant avocados and mangos, which seemed to him to reflect the sunset. Lourdes put her baskets down on the rich red soil of their land and embraced Kazumasa, who now stood casually with a rather newly formed posture, the sort to accompany, quite naturally, the tropical tilt of his head.

* * *

But all this happened a long time ago.

Now, you may look out across this empty field, strewn with candle wax, black chicken feathers and those eternally dead flowers, discarded jugs of cane brandy, the dirt pounded smooth by hundreds of dancing feet. Press your face into the earth where the odor of chicken fat and blood and incense still lingers and the intense staccato of the drums still quivers long after the gyrating bodies of dancers—spinning until their eyes glaze over in trance, sweat spraying forth from the tips of their hair, from the drenched outlines of swaying spines and laboring loins—are gone. The acrid stink of tobacco churned in human sweat and cane brandy still saturates the morning air.

On the distant horizon, you can see the crumbling remains of once modern high-rises and office buildings, everything covered in rust and mold, twisted and poisonous lianas winding over sinking balconies, trees arching through windows, a cloud of perpetual rain and mist and evasive color hovering over everything. The old forest has returned once again, secreting its digestive juices, slowly breaking everything into edible absorbent components, pursuing the lost perfection of an organism in which digestion and excretion were once one and the same. But it will never be the same again.

Now the memory is complete, and I bid you farewell. Whose memory you are asking? Whose indeed.